RAVEN

APRIL

I remember the day I lost my mind.

Fireside

PUBLICATIONS
www.FiresidePubs.com

by
Nelson Trout

Fireside Publications II
5144 Harbour Drive
Oxford, Florida 34484
www.firesidepubs.com

Printed in the United States of America

Copyright © 2013 by Nelson Trout

ISBN: 978-1-935517-26-9

For additional copies of this book, please visit:

www.amazon.com or
http://kadinbooks.com

Raven

Raven April is a millionaire/serial killer with a unique calling card.
Driven to madness by an unspeakable childhood horror, there is only one way for Raven to end the torture of his own existence.
He must kill the source.
Travel with Raven, and the lovely Lydia –his 'little mermaid – on this incredible, globe-crossing journey that finally sets him free.
What starts as a murder-for-revenge tale ends up as an epic battle between good and evil.

Praise for:

Raven April

"After having served in Vietnam and then as a police officer for twenty-five years, I've seen some mighty gruesome sights. "*Raven April*," however, delves deeper and more deliberately into the mind of any evil person than I've had the misfortune with which to come in contact. Raven's duel personality is a clever "mind trick" perpetrated on the reader. Which is the Raven that can be so generous with his time, and money? Which is the predator/killer Raven, which has a penchant for eating eyeballs? Thrilling to the end!"

Charles "Chick" Bennett
Police officer, Ret.

"WOW! This book blew my mind. Then put it back together again. I hated to see it end. I want more of Raven April. He is the most incredible character I have ever met in a book – or in real life, for that matter. Sequel, please!"

Kerry Silvers, inventor; singer/songwriter;
Author; and voracious reader.

"A tightly-wound thriller, compelling and vivid until the very end. Trout keeps the reader's pulse pounding throughout. I couldn't put it down."

Phillip Tomlinson, reporter.
South Jersey Media Group.
www.nj.com

"If you like *Dexter*, on Showtime, *Raven April* is right up your alley. Raven is a best-selling author (with the *nom de plume* of "B.V. West") who also happens to be a serial killer with a rather unusual calling card: he has a taste for his victims' left eyeballs. Gritty, riveting, and awash in thrills, *Raven* will take you on a journey from South Florida to L.A., ending with an epic battle between good and evil, deep in the jungles in Kenya. Author Nelson Trout breathes life into Raven, making him both frightening and enthralling. A 'must-read' for your list."

Eileen Bennett, editor; reporter.
Blogger on "Boardwalk Empire,"
For: The Press of Atlantic City.
Author of: *Amanda's Voice* and *Silver Strands*

"I was very pleased and honored to voice '*Blood on the Ceiling.*' I cried, laughed and paused for thought at the incredible insight of author Nelson Trout. The insight became incredible imagination in '*Raven April,*' also taking me deeply into the soul of the character. Well written, story well told. May be a masterpiece in hiding."

Michael Ray Davis, experienced actor; voice actor; and author.
His extensive film and acting credits can be seen on IMDB.

"Trout is a master at weaving fiction into believability. Riveting at every turn. Raven April is a smart and cunning thriller with energy and realism, but with heart, soul and humor."

"Dark, twisted, and brilliant."

Robert Benavides, Jr.
Ballistic Films;
Writer, Director, Producer

Contents

1~ Miami , Florida   *1*

   Six Years Later   1
   Lydia   5
   Beach Bar   16
   Bus Stop Bench   17
   Back at the Bench~ with Art   28

2~ Boulder, Colorado   *33*

   Next Morning   37
   Joe Lofton Arrives   40
   In Joe Lofton's room   46

3~ On the Plane~ Back to Miami   *51*

   Ft. Lauderdale Airport   54

4~ FBI Headquarters, Quantico, VA   *57*

5~ Home Sweet Home   60

   Art's Bench   62

6~ The Day I Lost My Mind   *67*

7~Life Changes   *80*

   The Appointment   80
   The Tedesco Twins   82
   Personal Stuff   92

8~ FBI Headquarters, Quantico, VA   *95*

9~ Back at the Mansion   *99*

   The Next Morning   114
   A Confession   118
   Four Days Later~ Calling Joe Lofton   119

10~ Macabi Cigar Bar~ Ft. Lauderdale, Florida 123
   The Next Day~ 1 p.m   135

11~ Miami, Florida~ Police Headquarters   141

12~ The Mansion   144
   Your Duties   147
   A Brief Note   155

13~ Macabis   156
   Wednesday, 5:30 p.m.   159

14~ Granite, Pennsylvania   161

15~ The Mansion   175
   Back on the Patio   181

16~ Police Headquarters, Miami Florida   184

17~ Back on the Patio   186
   Joe Lofton and Me~ On the Phone   191
   One Hour Later~ In the Den   193

18~ Landing in Kenya   200
   Victor's Bar   202
   The Wizard's Lair   206
   Room 2156 Sarova Panafric Hotel   224
   Noon, Victor's Bar   228

19~ Landing in Busia   233
   The Battle   246
   Jomo's Hut   251

20~ Miami Police Headquarters   252

21~ The Battlefield   253

22~ Epilogue   The Revelation   255

Dedication

This book is dedicated to the universe of imagination.
Understanding that reality trumps it every time.

Acknowledgements

There is not enough room on this page for me to name everyone I would like to thank for helping me with the creation of this unusual story. You know who you are.

Without your inspiration and encouragement throughout the writing of this book, *Raven April* would not exist. So, thank you all from the bottom of my heart!

I will, however, mention four people here who simply must be lauded publicly.

Eileen Bennett, who believed in this book from the day I sent her the first forty pages. She has been a constant well of enthusiasm and optimism. A true and talented friend!

Thanks, Eileen!

I would also like to thank my late friend, Todd Levow. Without Todd, the first word of *Raven April* would never have been written. When I first ran the idea I had for this book by Todd in Florida, he said, "I love it. Write it! ".

And so, I did. Thank you buddy – I hope you're proud, and at peace.

I cannot speak highly enough of Lois Bennett, my publisher and editor. Her well known talent and straightforward approach to the business of writing, editing and publishing are the magic which pulled this project all together in such a highly professional manner.

"Lois, you are the best!"

Last but not least, to Mr. Tom McGee, I would simply like to say, "Thanks for being there when I needed you, my friend."

Boulder Colorado

*I told Minero, whom I loved dearly,
"Hey look, I'll bite your eye out and
there's not a damn thing you can do
about…" then bang, I bit deep into his
left eye, pulling his head into mine with
my right hand schizophrenically,
quickly, with the strength of a madman,
which I am. I bit deeper and sucked
hard, finally snapping the optic nerve.
Minero's eye had just become my
breakfast…*

1

Miami, Florida

Six Years Later

The guy who sits down next to me on a bus-stop bench in Miami gives me bad vibes. The motherfucker just reeks of bad intentions. I take a good pull on my half-pint of Jacquin's Blackberry Brandy, *camouflaged* in a paper bag.

He studies me as I empty most of the bottle just as the sun is going down for the count.

Perfect timing is *one of my strengths, my gifts*. This has become kind of a semi-daily ritual with me ya know – the bench, the booze.

But you *have* to watch your back, and watch it good. Have eyes in the back of your head. Especially when you travel alone at night as I do, in the drug-and-murder-ridden twilight zone on the bad side of Miami.

Hey, it's what I like to do. Weird, I know. But don't get me wrong, I love South Florida and get along good with damn near everybody down here, from multi-millionaires to homeless street people to the doomed druggies.

My place is a sprawling five-bedroom mansion, with four bathrooms, and anything else you can think of, right on the beach. Who would have ever have thought that I would become one of those rich bastards? Not me, that's for sure. And in case you're wondering, yes, it's hurricane-proof and my secret paradise of anonymity. That's all I care about at this point in my big, little life.

I always carry, in my pocket or at my side in a leather sheath, along with my brief case a razor-sharp, strong fold-up Buck knife used for gutting deer right there in the woods after the hunter's kill. It supplies me with a confident feeling of safety.

I usually don't take the chance of carrying a pistol – not worth getting caught with. I keep a loaded Glock at the beach house, though. If somebody wants to take me down when I'm out on the streets with a kill shot from a 9mm or a sawed-off, hey, then I must have let my guard down, gotten sloppy.

I am still kind of in shock by the fact that at fifty-three years old I'd be sitting here, with more money than I ever dreamed of, drinking booze from the bottle on a dirty bench with a guy who either wants to kill me or rob me, or more likely, both. I light a Newport and the guy asks me if I can spare one.

I look at him close, studying his eyes, and shrug, trying to feel him out a little.

I'm 1,400 miles from home, a little hick town in central Pennsylvania. But I really like walking into downtown Miami after darkness falls, where the danger and the *real* night life is. It's pretty obvious that I'm seasoned for punishment and excitement in more ways than one.

"Yeah, sure pal," I say. "What's your story?"

Everybody in South Florida has a story. And they interest me. I mean, if I were a movie producer, I could shoot a blockbuster about some of these assholes. I might someday.

2

Most residents are not native to the area. Similar to the experience I had in Colorado a few years back which really surprised me. It's not like that in my little hometown. Who the hell would want to live there now? It's changed through the years, and for the worse. And even in her heyday, my little town was no tourist attraction. But the rabbit and deer hunting is without equal. In all honesty, a lot of us were always trying to get the hell out – most of us, really. Fuckin' escape; see the world, travel around the country. That type of shit.

Anyway, I notice my new friend's hands are shaking when he lights his cigarette with a wooden match he pulls out of a filthy, plastic sandwich bag he digs out of a beat-up old gray satchel. *My cigarette*, I should say.

He takes a deep drag. He exhales in smoke rings and the circles swirl around his head and then up and away. They dissolve in the sunset when he surprisingly spews out even more of what seems to be a helluva lot of smoke; from what I assume are black lungs. Loops of the poison gas go skirting past his rotting teeth.

But hell, my lungs are probably black too, at least brown, and my teeth have seen better days. But I do brush every day and take a shower. Or at least swim in the blue-green magical waters of The Gold Coast.

Finally, as I privately predicted, the guy tells me he is hard on his luck, like who isn't – right? He asks if he can have a pull on my bottle of blackberry.

"No, man." I say. "Private stock."

"Can you spare me a buck or two then?" he mumbles. Then he comes out with, "I need a drink bad enough to kill for."

That doesn't feel good in my gut. I look at him, closer now, and warn him in a near-whisper.

3

"Well, I don't advise trying to kill me over a bottle of booze – as a matter of fact, I'm thinking about biting one of your eyes out right now. I practice on pit bulls, and there's not a fuckin' thing you can do about it."

He gets it.

But I give him two bucks anyway, and another cigarette.

He offers to shake my hand, and tells me his name is Art.

I give him a scary look, shake his hand and then start laughing like hell. I can't stop.

Art is a little freaked at first, and then he starts laughing too.

You'll soon discover that I'm really out there sometimes.

One of those warm South Florida thundershowers plows through the sky as we literally dance in the rain. I think about slicing his jugular vein about now, but instead, I buy more booze and cigarettes and party with Art till about midnight.

"Hey man," I say. "I'll be here tomorrow night about the same time. Meet ya, huh? And, oh yeah, Art my man, bring a joint or something. I'll buy the booze and Newports."

"What's your name?" Art yells from his charred throat, as I start walkin' away.

I turn to face him.

"Raven," I say. "Raven April. Later, man."

I'll get his story tomorrow. But he won't get mine.

Lydia

I'm taking my good old time getting back to the house. I know Lydia, my current girlfriend, will still be curled up on the loveseat drinking white zinfandel, smoking Black & Mild cigars and hoping I come home with more than a hard-on. We are out of weed, which is not *highly* unusual, but unusual nonetheless. Lydia will feel like getting high. That is a given.

So on my purposely slow stroll home, I run into a good buddy of mine named Placido who is walking home from a cigar bar he and I hang out in once in a while on Las Olas Boulevard up in Ft. Lauderdale. He has a cabbie drop him off a few blocks from his house. Placido doesn't like to drink and drive, although he does it once in a while. He makes decent, but not great money, working from home as a web-site designer, basically keeping his own hours – real ladies' man, too. We party on the beach once or twice a week together mostly here in Miami. Nice work if you can get it, right?

Placido was born in Cuba. He and his mother floated ashore on a piece of wood and a life ring, after the boat they were in sank about ten miles from Miami's shore. They were two of thirty-one freedom-seekers on board, fleeing the Castro regime.

Placido, who was five at the time, and his mom were the only survivors. The rest either drowned or were eaten by bull sharks, which were migrating off the coast of South Florida at the time.

Do you know that bull sharks have more testosterone in their bodies, pound for pound, than any other creature on Earth? Well, it's true. They can, and do, also live in fresh-water rivers. Actually, the movie *Jaws* is based on a true story of a bull shark killing spree, in a New Jersey river. Nasty fuckers! – Devils with teeth and guile. *Not* perfect timing for Placido's getaway. Not when the bull sharks are migrating and devouring everything and everybody in their ruthless path. Thought you might be interested in some of the facts about bull sharks. Hope I didn't bore you. Class dismissed!

Placido is now thirty-four and lives with, and cares for, his mom as best he can. I call her "Mama Placido." I give Placido a hundred-dollar bill, and he hooks me – and my hard-on and Lydia – up with a joint of some ass-kick weed and four 30 mg. roxies.

Roxies are the street name for Roxycodone, a prescription pain killer. To be more medically precise, roxies are manufactured by combining oxycodone and hydrochloride. Let's just say that they kill pain, and then some.

Nice of him, wasn't it?

"Thanks, my friend."

Placido smiles, and we knuckle-knock.

"Any time, Raven."

Now that we're talking about Placido, I gotta tell how I met Lydia. It's really funny. Ya see, Placido is into these dating sites on the internet. Says he's gotten a lot of good pussy that way. I'm not into that internet dating junk and Placido knows it. But one night at his place, we got all fucked up on some Jack Daniels, pot and roxies and Placido got me to put my profile up on one of those asshole match-up deals. But instead of writing in the blocks how cool and wealthy I am, and how much I like to hold hands and walk on the beach and all that happy horseshit, I write that I am unemployed, on disability,

6

don't have a house, a car, a pot to piss in or a window to throw it out of. I smoke, I drink, have no plans for the future except for partying in my small, dingy efficiency apartment. And my only excitement in life is reading. Fifty-three years young. Ha, ha.

Placido takes a photo of me right then and there, uploads it – I look like hell – and all of a sudden, I'm technically on the internet looking for a date. Knowing damn well no self-respecting female in the world would respond. I ask Placido if he is finally fuckin' happy.

He laughs.

"Hell yeah," he says. "What'd you write, that you were a rich motherfucker livin' on the beach?"

Which I was, but Placido doesn't know that.

Placido keeps laughing.

"Yeah," I mutter, "somethin' like that."

Well, guess what? Not only do I get a bunch of responses which blows my mind, it has me belly-laughing like one of those fat Buddha figurines, thinking, what a crop of losers out there.

But I actually see one that I think is really cute and interesting looking – almost like I had dreamed of her face before. I don't know why, but I am strangely, almost magically attracted to her.

"I like all the things you like," are her only words in response to my ad, "especially reading, and we're both in the same boat." Signed, Lydia."

"Are you Raven?" she asks, the first time we meet face-to-face. That's when she shows up at my beach house at two in the morning with a suitcase in each hand.

I had been asleep. I was dreaming of that face again; I swear; when her ring of the door chimes rouses me. I was surprised, because I never really expected her to show up, even though we'd loosely planned it.

"Yeah, Lydia. I'm Raven. Let me get your suit cases. Come on in."

As soon as she walks in, she lights a Black & Mild and looks around. I can tell that her first thought is how the hell can I, the jobless, aimless Raven April from the internet, afford such a high-end pad on the beach in Miami – expensive furniture and artwork, two sunken hot tubs, ultra-modern kitchen, full ocean view, extensive library, and all the other *stuff,* on a monthly disability check. Some efficiency, huh?

Wow! I almost tell her who I really am, but decide to let it go. I don't want to have to kill her. Not yet, anyway. If she asks any questions, I'm gonna tell her that I hit a pretty big lottery in Pennsylvania a couple of years ago.

About fifteen or twenty paperback books, in one of Lydia's suit cases, accidently spill out on the living room floor. *Standing on the Edge of Forever* by B.V. West is one of them. I pick it up and ask her how she liked it.

She turns quickly and stares at me. A sly smile spreads across her face as if she thinks I am lying about reading the damn book. After all, it is a huge bestseller, and I am a voracious reader, which Lydia already knows. I mean, I did put it in my profile. And the library made that perfectly clear. So, in a way, I can understand her surprise that I hadn't read the book.

"Obviously you haven't read this one yet, or you wouldn't have asked that question," she says, looking through the large open doorway into my combination library and den.

She is mesmerized at the two giant walls of books, neatly organized in alphabetical order by author.

"Gee, can't believe you haven't read it, yet." We lock eyes, and she adds, "I'm reading it now for the second time. You can borrow it when I'm done."

Borrow? I'm thinking. Wanna hear a *big secret, Lady?* I *wrote the fuckin' book under my pen name, B.V. West!*

Yep, that's me, Raven April, best-selling author. Raven April, musician and songwriter, Raven April, sadistic murderer. B.V. West, *fuckhead.* He should be tortured to death! A lot of my fans keep wondering how I can hate B.V. West, a guy who really doesn't exist. Well, hang around, and everyone can find out together.

"Thanks!"

I am sure that Lydia will not recognize me from the photo on the inside of the back cover of the book. Back then I was thinner, had long hair and a fairly disgusting scruffy beard. My publisher hated that picture. We fought over it, and I won. Right now I'm heavier, much more muscular and clean-shaven. I go to a barber in nearby Hollywood every month or so and get a decent haircut, which in my case is shaved bald.

I usually spend the night there, just to walk the Blackheart Neighborhood. Oh yeah, the Blackheart Neighborhood - the police are even afraid to go in there after the sun says goodnight. Like the song says, "My kind'a town." I don't want to kill anybody in Hollywood, but you never know. Gonna try not to. I enjoy my monthly excursions here and don't want to fuck it up. *Comprende?*

Of course at this point only the Man Upstairs and I know that I am a murderer. And very few people even have a clue that I am the author of one of the biggest-selling novels in recent history, which will, without a doubt, hit the big screen as a movie, probably within two years. Let me explain something to you: It's not that I have a temper tantrum or anything like that, and then flip out and kill somebody. It's deeper, calmer and more psychotic than that. It goes back to my childhood. It roars like a lion inside my skull. And then I have to kill – with a unique twist.

Okay, so far Lydia is just pretty and interesting, and loves to party with me. She's not a prude. She's not a whore. She just *is*. So, she's safe, for now.

Placido however, will *never* be on my kill list. I couldn't do that to his mom. She is a living doll.

But on the other hand, Art, my new buddy on the bench – who knows? All depends on the roar of the lion. We'll see how it goes on the bench tomorrow night. I have a feeling that either his left eye goes, washed down with a nice cold beer into my gullet or his jugular is severed – probably both. Time will tell. I can be wrong. Art is in the "maybe" column right now. I keep this part of my life very private, and Lydia will have to realize that.

I like danger, and I'm on the run. I am Raven April and I am B.V West. The royalty checks from my book sales are directly deposited into four different banks.

I am under contract for a new book within the next eighteen months. So, when I go into the library to write, Lydia often jokes, "What are you doing, writing a fuckin' book for God's sake?"

"No," I tell her, without looking up from my computer, "just keeping up on that journal for my great, grandchildren… wanna be the great-grandmother?"

She just laughs.

"Hell no," she says, "no thank you. Hey, take a break, Raven. Let's catch a buzz and go down on the beach," – which we usually do at least a few times a week.

I mean, hell, it's our front yard. I usually swim for a while, then just lay there on the blanket next to Lydia looking up at the sky, and then over at the Lovely Mermaid herself. When I swim alone, I lie on the sand and try to promise myself that I will never feed Lydia to the sharks. Didn't somebody say, *"The road to hell is paved with good intentions?"*

Joe Lofton, my lawyer and publicist, is a great guy from L.A. who pretty much has my ass covered – and he should, for the money I pay him. Plus, if I go down, he goes down. Ya see, Joe illegally hides a lot of my money offshore. The only words I'll let him utter in public about B.V. West is that he is on an island in the Caribbean writing his next novel.

The new one, the book I'm working on now in my library/den, will be so awesome and successful that I won't have to appear in public, do book signings, interviews or any of that bullshit. Although, I *would* gladly accept an interview on the *Coast To Coast am* radio show with George Norey – coolest radio station on the planet. Other than that, I shall remain invisible and mysterious.

That approach will definitely, in my opinion, which is of course the only opinion that matters to me, sell more books, especially after the mind-boggling success of *Standing on the Edge of Forever.*

I can remain here forever in paradise with Lydia. But I am a madman, always trying to sabotage my own good fortunes. As all madmen do. I have to be careful at all times to make sure that doesn't happen. I truly do not want to kill Lydia. If the lion roars, maybe taking Art out will satisfy me for the last time, or at least for a while. And I'll stop killing until I'm face-to-face with my ultimate target, Sheriff Evil. But first I have to see if I admire Art in any way. To see if he's worthy to live, or should be allowed to die.

11

Lydia is worthy of both rewards. But I hate to admit it, or even think about the possibilities. How can I feed my Mermaid to the sharks and still be able to live with myself? It scares me. *And nothing scares me* – except for the lion that lives and breathes and roars inside the dark cage of my cranium. Lydia has now morphed into "Mermaid," in my mind. I've started calling her that. She can swim like a dolphin. Even keeps up with me – when I let her. I'm such a nice guy – at least, I think so. Really, I am.

I am also a singer, songwriter, performer and former session vocalist – all this in addition to being a top-notch writer.

As a session vocalist, songwriters who couldn't sing a fuckin' note, would hire me to sing the words to their lousy songs so they could make a decent demonstration "demo" tape in a recording studio in order to "pitch" their amateurish trash to record companies and music publishers. All hoping a major recording artist would record their song and make them a fortune.

There is only one session job I ever did where the songs were great. The writer, a black guy from North Jersey named RJ Phoenix was a genius. Right after our 12-song CD was completed, RJ up and died. Damn rotten shame. Why do people have to *do* that? He and I had gotten to be very close friends. R.I.P., RJ. Miss you, buddy.

I worked cheap in the session vocals game, because I liked it. Hundred bucks a song plus expenses, which usually consisted of a half-pint of blackberry brandy, which I poured into a 24-oz. cup of black coffee and drank in the vocal booth while I was *working*. After that, a few cold beers, a joint and then a cigarette ended the session. Ah, the rigors of busting your ass for a living.

I don't do gigs anymore since my lead guitar player, a guy named Jason from my hometown, died – as in, was murdered. He was poisoned by his son. The darling little child of thirty-one then buried his daddy under the back porch of his grandmother's house with a foxhole shovel where *The Riders*, our band, rehearsed. A cadaver dog found Jason a few days later after rigor mortis had pushed Jason's index finger out of the sandy, temporary grave. I really miss him. He was a great guitarist, songwriter and friend. At the time of Jason's death, I had only killed one person. Jason didn't know about it. No one did.

Merlino Cortez was another musician I'd met and admired while doing gigs in Boulder, Colorado with his band, *The Bandeedos*. They used to open for us. You see, after I'd replaced Jason and headed west, *The Riders* landed a 16-month-gig at The Unicorn, which was the biggest and most popular dance club in Boulder at the time. We were contracted to play every Thursday, Friday and Saturday night from 9:00 p.m. till closing, whenever that was. Let's just say it varied. Money talks and bullshit walks, so if a guy with a grand wanted to keep The Unicorn open for a *special* party till dawn, *The Riders* got $400 in cash to stay and play. There were a lot of fringe benefits, also – use your imagination.

But the greatest thing that happened for me, Raven April, in Boulder, was writing my first novel *Standing On the Edge Of Forever* right there in my cool little one-bedroom apartment, 36 B, Carrington Apartments. I'll never forget that place. I loved it there.

I know, I know, I'm rambling again – back to Merlino.

Okay, one night after the Unicorn had closed at its regular two a.m. time, Merlino and I took a ride up the side of some little mountain in my Jeep to catch a buzz and bullshit.

That's when the lion started roaring again. Louder than thunder; louder than silence; I had to kill.

After I took Merlino's eye, he was screaming so loud that I had to sever his wind pipe and right carotid artery with my Buck knife to shut him up. I, Raven April started to panic. It was only the second time the lion had roared for several years. But it's a sound you can never forget, a primal death-scream that Raven April must always respond and react to. *It was my second kill.*

I rule the world except for the roar of the lion. *That* rules me.

Merlino finally died and was released into the heavens, receiving his reward – and so it goes. They found his body exactly five weeks later. The local police released a statement that "Mr. Merlino Cortez, lead guitar player of the popular rock band *The Bandeedos*, was probably killed by local bandits and that the varmints had eaten most of him." The case was never even investigated.

Nobody saw us leave together. See, I like to look ahead and cover my ass; plan carefully and then leave no tracks or trail which could lead back to me. Tracks could be confining and endanger my freedom.

When *Standing on the Edge of Forever* became a surprise best-seller, my life really changed. The only gigs I do now are on the beach in Ft. Lauderdale or Miami. The ocean is an angelic backdrop and sitting under a palm tree singing to a bunch of sun, fun and life-lovin' partiers is crazy as hell. I love it! Cool strangers, beach people, more satisfying than playing in front of 10,000 people in an auditorium or a baseball stadium. I do my beach shows for free of course.

This big old black dude named Ruben likes to hear me play and sing so much that he gives me a blunt or a couple of joints every time I *perform*, for lack of a better word. He also dances and sings along with me. I love that guy. He ain't got a care in the world and wears a different hat every day. I never ask him why, but it intrigues me for some dumb-ass reason.

I use my old beat-up Bentley guitar that my first and only wife had given me about thirty years ago. I have a lot of nice guitars, but the old Bentley will always be my favorite. Over a hundred people have signed it, and I've written over a hundred songs on it. I'd kill for that guitar if I had to. Gonna leave it to my son, Dustin, who is a record producer and businessman out in Hollywood, CA. Dustin April. He is the friggin' man! I'm so damn proud of him. I also have a daughter, Melody, and a grandson named Raven, after me. *God, I love them so much* I see them a couple times a year and although they are both very successful, I still send them some money once in a while. Hey, it makes me feel good. They are in the very small circle of people who know I am B.V. West.

I have not seen their mother for more than ten years. She is not in the circle and thinks I'm still doing low-paying music gigs around the country and writing songs. She also thinks I'm poor. Actually though, I have made quite a bit of money in the music industry, and still do on three songs I wrote for a major country music star. I did not use my real name publicly for those songs, so she doesn't even know about that.

The circle must remain small. Lydia may wind up being the newest member. Time and the roar of the lion will tell. My kids and little Raven will love her and she'll love them if they ever meet.

Beach Bar

I am killing some time on the beach in Ft. Lauderdale where Las Olas Boulevard ends and the Atlantic Ocean begins. I'm gettin' really thirsty and walk across the street to the coolest little beach bar in the world called *The Hibiscus Room*. The whole place is wide open with a panoramic beach view and a great little three-piece band. So, I'm sitting at the bar and this famous pop singer strolls in with three incredibly beautiful women. Everybody recognizes him right away. Still, he will remain nameless here, though.

Anyway, two of his beauties are Asian girls; one is a drop-dead gorgeous blond. He also has a bald-headed bodyguard-type in his entourage who looks like he could rip the head off a grizzly bear with his bare hands and shit in the hole. They all sit down right across from me – except for the grizzly guard. He just stands there and keeps looking around – not smiling.

The two Asian girls start making out together, deep kissing, and rubbing each others' asses. It is really bizarre. The blond is all over the singer who is sporting a pair of sunglasses that have to be worth at least a few grand. You can just tell. He takes them off and puts them on the bar with a heavy sounding *Clunk.*

Some woman I am sitting next to from Germany says she would swear the frames were solid silver.

I'm just drinking my beer, pretending I'm not gawking, and casually taking it all in. Everybody is havin' a fuckin' blast. The whole place is moving to the music. Lydia would love it. I'm thinking about calling her and having her shoot up here in her Beamer.

But it's time for me to take a taxi to Miami. To the bench – to meet Art – and possibly to kill him and digest his bloodshot left eye.

Bus-Stop Bench

The cabbie drops me off a few blocks away from where I'm supposed to meet Art.

Along with *Bucky*, my Buck knife, I decide to bring an ice pick with me before I leave the mansion this morning; I drop it into my briefcase, almost as an afterthought. An ice pick pierces the skull more easily and is less messy than a Buck knife. I used one for my first kill. You'll see. I'll tell you about that one later.

The only problem is that ice pick-people don't die right away. Sometimes they run crazily around in circles for a while trying to figure out what the fuck just happened. So, they have to be silenced more quickly. Of course, if you are out in the middle of nowhere, who cares? Just watch the show and laugh like hell.

Six of one, half a dozen of the other, as one of my jerk-off bosses named Morgan Lange, back in the *real* world, used to constantly say. I hated that guy, yet in some sick, sympathetic way I admire him for moving up the ladder to become a boss in that hell-hole factory where we worked. I soon quit and have never had a regular job since.

Toward the end of this one particular workday, the lion starts roaring like an incarcerated monster from hell, and I instinctively know that I have to kill someone soon to silence the beast or die. So, after stealing an ice pick from the tool room, I decide to lure Morgan Lange, my jerk-off boss, out for a beer after work. I tell him I'll get him a blow job from a young slut who is waiting for us just outside of town.

"Only five bucks, boss. Man, she can suck a golf ball through a garden hose," I say.

He is getting really excited. Says his wife quit sucking his dick right after they got married twenty-two years ago. Well, he ends up being allergic to ice picks.

Bang!

We finish our first beer while sitting on the hood of my Ford F-150 pick-up truck, waiting for the girl, who I say, "should be here in a few minutes."

Morgan looks away, trying to see her first.

I pull out the ice pick and drive it right down through the top of his skull, and leave it there. I still laugh every time I think of the bastard running around in that little field. Obviously, there is no girl.

Bummer, huh, boss?

Remember, Morgan is Kill Number One. Merlino in Boulder is Kill Number Two. Just so we keep track. I remember just sitting there on the hood of my pickup truck drinkin' beer and going nuts with the hilarity of it all. He reminds me of a chicken running around after his head is just lopped off. I wait till he stops rolling and running around, and then pull out the ice pick so I can wipe it down clean and return it to the tool shed the next morning at work. I then suck his left eye down into my aching guts. Don't ask me why I ate his eye.

Patience, Man. Patience.

I am laughing so hard, my stomach muscles actually hurt. It's worth it, though. The lion is quiet. But that was in the middle of nowhere. This is Miami. Two different worlds, especially when it comes to an ice-pick kill.

Oh yeah, get this. A couple hours after I had left Lange's body for the vultures, coyotes and worms in that little killing field, a couple of local teenagers who had come out there to smoke a joint and split a six pack of Coors Light came across his body. Just as they were going through his pockets two deer hunters came up on them. The hunters held the teenagers at gunpoint until they got the cops out there. The boys were both arrested and charged with murder – and convicted. One of the boys hanged himself to death and the other was committed to an institution for the criminally insane for life.

Once again, as has always seemed to be the case, Raven lands on his feet. But I truly do feel bad about those teenagers getting fucked like that. I block it out.

Confession: I also carry a garrote in my brief case in the melodic form of the "B" string from one of my electric Fender guitars. It's a very deadly and silent weapon, perfect for a fast, efficient strangulation. Hey, we have to be honest about it. Agreed? I carry a lot of stuff in that brief case. More than anyone else knows.

I truly do, as you know, love walking alone through the cancerous bowels of the bad side of Miami at night, mostly in the notorious Overtown section. I am drawn to investigating the toxic underbelly of any big city, really. I blend in well. But I gotta tell you, you can't beat South Florida when it comes to the finer things in life. That's the other side of the coin, if you will; the other side of Raven April's life – and B.V. West's worthless existence, no-good *cocksucker* that he is.

I stand about 6" 2' and weigh around 225 pounds and am obviously in good shape. *Ocean swimming works every muscle in your body.* I still have to carry myself as if I own the streets, which is easy for me, because in my madman mind, I do. People feel that vibe. And they should. Any given dickhead out here can either wind up as a character in my next book, a notch on my knife, or both.

B.V. West would never understand. But I never really expected him to. Don't get me wrong, I'm glad I wrote *'Standing'* under a pen name. It helps me stay underground and pursue my other interests, instincts and *obligations* without fanfare, and hopefully, without prison, which in my case would mean the executioner's needle or the electric chair eventually.

The doomed, in Florida, actually have their choice. Not many people know that.

It also gives me the freedom to work on my new book in privacy.

Oh, Lydia? Don't worry about her. She's under control. That sweet little thing has brains enough not to look a gift horse in the mouth. I really and truly do not want to kill her. Please believe me on that. Say a prayer for her, will you?

I turn the corner to where I can see the bench. There is Art. I really wasn't sure he would show up – as if he has something better to do, which I strongly doubt. On my way, I stop in a liquor store which has black bars on the windows and doors – creepy, but cool place in my off-beat opinion. I buy three packs of Newports and a 12-pack of Budweiser for Art and me. I also pick up a pack of Black & Milds for Lydia and a scratch-off lottery ticket for Art. Thoughtful of me, I know. I'm such a sweetheart.

When Art notices me and my goody-bag, he smiles like a crescent moon, craters and all.

"Yo, Raven. Glad you could make it. Run into any pit bulls today?"

I grin at him.

"Only one, and he, *that means you,* damn well better have somethin' good for the head on him."

I hand Art a beer and toss him a pack of smokes to test his reflexes. He catches them with one hand, which means he may be more dangerous than he appears. You just never know. He cracks open the beer and downs at least half the can in one swig. Then his shaking hands light a Newport with a wooden match he pulls out of that same filthy plastic bag.

Note to Self: *Remind me never to shake hands with Art again.*

"Thanks again."

I crack a beer, light a cigarette, take a big relaxing drag and look out at the Miami sky line silhouetted by the sinking western sun. The view is quite spectacular.

You know, I keep asking myself how the fuck I got here, to this place in my life. Paul McCartney, one of my two heroes, would say it was a *"long and winding road,"* and Sir Paul would be correct to say the least. The long and *'crooked'* road would also have worked in the song, especially if the song were about me, Raven April, which it obviously wasn't.

My other hero is Tom Norris, the greatest Navy Seal of all time. Some of the things he did in Viet Nam are no less than miraculous. I go on.

"So Art, how was your day, buddy? What'cha got good?"

Deftly, he reaches down into his stinking, gray-white left sock and pulls out two blunts and a 30 mg. roxie. He hands me the roxie but only one of the two blunts. My man Art sticks the other one between his crusted lips. And I get the feeling he was momentarily imagining himself as some sort of king or something. He lights the blunt – guess what with? Yep, one of his wooden matches.

21

"This one's for us, Raven," he then proclaims, "just you and me. And thanks for the beer and smokes. You're a real sweetheart of a guy."

Sweetheart? Inside I'm thinking, *not me bro, I ain't no sweetheart. I'm a killer and a slave to the roar of my own private demon-lion. I'm on a mission over which I have no control. One you'd never understand. Neither would B.V. Coward West.* I take another pull on my beer.

"No problem Art. You know as well as I do that street people like you and me have to look out for each other and have one another's back – lots of nasty bastards out here. Cut your throat for a fuckin' five-dollar bill. There's a shitload of Glocks and pee-shooters out here too."

Ya know, it's kind of strange that Art has never asked me, nor has anyone else for that matter, why I always carry a black leather brief case with me, even on the beach. Someone will ask, eventually, I suppose.

I have an answer, just in case they ever do, like I have an answer for Lydia if she ever gets curious about my incredible wealth – the lottery. *Remember?* When it comes to the briefcase it is much more simplistic.

"None of your fuckin' business. Ask again and you'll find out the hard way," I'll say. *That's me talking tough.* Go ahead, laugh. I am. But that's my answer.

Art finishes his second beer.

"Hey Raven," he says, with a weird, dying sound in his voice, "you said you want to know my story when we were sittin' here last night. Do you wanna hear it now, or was that just a bunch of bullshit?"

I knew this was coming, and I *do* want to hear Art's story. I live for this kinda stuff.

"Hell yeah, I wanna hear your story. Mine ain't much to tell, that's for sure, but I've got a feeling yours might be. I'm all ears Art, if you wanna talk."

22

He looks up and over at the vanishing sunset through a ring of smoke, a far-off look attacks then shrouds his eyes.

"Well, Raven, mine ain't much of a story either, unless you think getting your cock and balls blown off is a story, especially if you're unlucky enough to be the main character. I was twenty years old. Viet Nam. We're a lot alike Raven. Nothing scares us. Not anymore. Ain't I right?"

I nod. He is right about that, almost. But, don't forget, I still have my lion.

"I mean it," Art continues. "I'm free now, Raven – after nine surgeries, and rehabs out the ass, because I'm not afraid of anything, not even dyin'. Fuck, one rehab was just to teach me how to piss again. Not to mention the fire fights, killing people you have nothing against, buddies getting their heads blown off for no reason. What's left to be afraid of?

"Anyway, for giving my cock and balls away in the pursuit of world peace and America's dream of a communist-free planet, I was awarded two medals for honor and valor and all that horseshit for saving two guys' lives in that fire fight. They were both dead eleven days later.

"My brother in Utah has the medals, if he hasn't pawned them by now. Oh yeah, I also got a Purple Heart. *I* pawned that one. I know you've got it hard too, Raven, but at least you've still got your 'junk'. So, if you wanna bite my eye out, go ahead and do it. Please, *do* it!"

Art smiles again, not like a crescent moon this time. More like a crazed, caged animal at the zoo, a luring come-and-get-it grin.

"But could you wait until we knock back the rest of our beers and finish smokin' this blunt? It's dynamite weed. What do you say, Raven? Deal?"

"Sure. I'm a sweetheart, right? You said so."

Art gets a little emotional on me and shoves his paw out and wanted to shake hands with me, but I ... oh hell ... I shake it. I'm a sensitive guy, don't forget that. Art is a good man who surely has endured more than any human being's share of bad breaks and misfortunes in his battered and tortured and fucked-up life.

I decide that I have to kill him. He is such a damn good dude that I really have no choice. And fuck you, B.V. West, this is *my* call. Besides, the lion is purring, and I am praying he doesn't roar. Not yet. Art and I would have to finish our beer and the blunt first. Priorities, you know, like he said. Come hell or high water, I will fight the lion as hard as I can tonight. At least until the beer and blunt are gone.

Art sits to my right on the bench.

Perfect. I wouldn't have to manipulate anything if the time came when I have no choice but to kill Art and tear out his left eyeball with my teeth.

The lion is roaring inside me again.

No! Not now, *please*!

I am so impressed with Art's story and courage that I decide to kill him as painlessly as possible if my lion demands it of me. I will bring the ice pick down lightning quick and herculean hard through the top of his skull and then instantly sever his jugular and trachea – good old razor-sharp Bucky – while eating his left eye. Ninety seconds, tops. Then he'd be free.

Maybe I will be too, but I doubt it.

Oh God, not Lydia. *Please*? I've got to push that thought out of my mind. Push, April, *push*!

24

The lion begins to quiet.

Whew, that was close. Not to mention the fact that my brain is on fire. Is it true that just above our mortal sight lays heaven? Hope so.

Art seems excited about the lottery ticket. By the light of my Bic lighter, he scratches it off with a penny. It takes his shaky hands at least five tenuous minutes. Loser. What else is new? The more fucked up we get, the more Art talks.

I decide to split the roxie with him instead of taking it back to the house. What Lydia doesn't know won't hurt her. I have to chuckle inside at that one.

There is irony in that one. That thought just strikes me as funny for some damn reason.

I laugh at my own jokes all the time. Always have. Even as a little kid. Couldn't care less if anybody else laughed or not. Though, just being human, I'd prefer they did. Henny Youngman is my favorite comedian. Maybe that explains it, maybe not. Maybe I'm just crazy.

Okay, back to my favorite Miami Mermaid not getting any of that roxie. Lydia will be more than happy with the blunt. Damn good weed. It ought to go down nicely with her wine and cigars. Gotta love that Lydia! Maybe we'll go skinny dipping in our front yard later. Or just get into one of the hot tubs. Or just do nothing at all.

I don't keep drugs of any kind at the house, except pot. It could be dangerous if the shit ever hits the fan. As you know, I'm basically on the run – a fugitive; a sadistic killer; and besides, it's too much fun hunting the dope down on the streets. You meet the coolest – and deadliest –people out there. And I love that kinda shit. Don't ask me why, because I have no idea.

I have Lydia's zinfandel brought in by the case, as well as my Heineken and burgundy wine. I pay cash, and the guy I call the 'beer-man' thinks my name is Joe Smith. Plus, I tip him well to stay on his good side and to keep his mouth shut about *Joe Smith*.

We had a little talk about all of that, and the 'beer-man' got the message and five hundred bucks. He steals the booze from the distributorship he works for. Once again, if I go down he goes down.

Oh yeah, get this, I also give the lovely Lydia $800 a week to do with as she pleases. Good gal that she is, she buys groceries out of her little allowance, and even cooks! A Cuban maid, one of Placido's cousins, comes in once a week to clean, but Lydia does the shopping. She likes pulling in to the Publix grocery store perched inside a new BMW. She looks good in it too – very hot. And she knows it. Why shouldn't she? I seldom if ever drive the Beamer, so it's basically hers.

Not only could driving be dangerous for Raven April, bestselling author and killer. It could ruin my whole world, this *fantasy* world-come-true that I worked my ass off for. Any slip-up can also destroy the plans I have for my ultimate victim – not pretty plans, either. No one could guess in a hundred years what I have planned for Sheriff Evil. Everyone will just have to wait and see. People love surprises.

Lydia still hasn't asked me about the money and lavish living. I'm supposed to be a bum, that loser on the internet dating site that Placido suckered me into.

"Thanks, Placido. Really!"

But I know she's very curious. And when she does ask, which she may, well, remember, I hit that lottery in Pennsylvania. Then again, maybe she'll never ask for fear of opening up a can of worms that could crawl all over the new-found silver platter she's been eating off of here in paradise. Smart girl that Lydia. Fuck, if you think about it, *she* is the one who hit the lottery.

I worked day and night for fourteen months writing *Standing on the Edge of Forever*. I even wrote a song by the same title for the movie, if there is one. Hey, Raven's ready. I'm always looking ahead – one of my attributes. Fingers crossed on that. The couple more million bucks a movie could make me would be nice. But what I'm trying to say is that I worked for this utopia, and Lydia just stepped in golden shit. But, I'm glad she did. I'm really starting to fall for her. That wasn't in my plans. Uh, oh, oh shit, I almost forgot to mention this. She handed me her copy of *Standing...* last night.

"Raven, she exclaimed, while pouring a glass of that cheap-ass zinfandel she likes to drink, "you've got to read this book. It's incredible. It reminded me of you on my second read – after I got to know you. You'll love it! I need it back, though. But listen, I'm going to write to the publishing company and see how much it will cost me to get the writer, B.V. West, to sign a copy and have them mail it to me. If they'll do it, you can keep that copy. Okay, Raven?"

I just looked at her and rolled my eyes.

"Hey Raven, we haven't been skinny dipping and had sex on the beach in almost two weeks."

What the hell is she doing, keeping count?

The water temperature is eighty-four degrees. She starts rubbing my dick. We hit the beach with Lydia carrying her favorite furry *love blanket* as she likes to call it. *Two hundred bucks on sale, whoopee! All I need is the sand. Oh well.* That's Lydia for you.

I swim with my Mermaid, and we have sex on the beach. I look up at the stars, as I always do on the love blanket, and say a silent, "Thanks, Lord."

Lydia is 5-feet, 4-inches tall, and weighs 119 pounds. Not an ounce of fat on her. Like I say, ocean swimming works every part of the body. She has medium-length, jet-black hair, big brown eyes and of course the perfect tan. But it's her face that holds me as the hopeless hostage of her entire being. Maybe it's because she reminds me so much of my first girlfriend. But, I am beginning to fall in love with her. I probably already have. I might have to let her in on my secrets, but not just yet.

Back At the Bench with Art

As the roxie that Art and I split kicks in along with the beer and blunt, it feels good, and I really want to talk, but instead I just listen to my man Art. Basically how all his hopes and dreams were blown away that day in Nam, along with his manhood, but he's still a man, heart and soul, and a damn good one, too.

He tells me about the life-changing fire-fight with tears cutting a path through the dirt on his cheeks glistening by the street light, like the paths Art had to cut through the jungles of Viet Nam, dripping with Agent Orange and then, his crippled life.

"You know Raven, he mutters, with all the bullshit that has happened to me in this fucked-up world of mine, my biggest regret is that those two kids I took the shrapnel in the balls for died anyway. One, nineteen years old, the other was twenty-two. They were the best!

We were as close as brothers. Just trying to kill as many gooks as we could and stay alive; and doing it without shooting or blowing up kids and mothers. Well, let me tell you, those two boys, excuse me, *men*, were the

28

lucky ones. I'm the one that got fucked. You know what I mean, Raven?" Art wipes his tears away with a paper bag.

"War is hell," he says, and looks up at the stars. And so is groping through life without even a glimmer of hope. But the worst part is that it was all for nothing, all in vain. And still is."

Time flies when you're riding on the roxie express like Art and I have been for over four hours. It is past midnight, and I fondle the ice pick a few times.

Art thinks I am reaching into my black briefcase for a cigarette. But I am deciding Art's fate. Each time I touch it I can feel the roar of the lion, *my* lion. But in the end, I decide to let Art live for at least another day. Another day in hell for Art, it isn't fair. Yeah, I know. Hell, *life* ain't fair. Who doesn't know that? Am I right, or what?

The sharp blade of fate-gone-wild misses no one; we all bare scars. I tell Art I have to get going and he can keep the rest of the blunt. I hand him a $100 dollar bill. Not counterfeit, either. Very funny!

Well, his eyes light up again, like when he saw my goody-bag over four hours ago. A questionable look invaded his pupils as if to ask, "Where the hell did *you* get a hundred bucks?"

I give him a hug. Gee I *must* be fucked up! *Very* fucked up for ingesting only half a roxie and a few beers; is it a full moon or something?

"Hey Art, don't ask me what you're thinking about askin' me, I mean about the money. Okay? If I told you, I'd have to kill you, really. I'll be here tomorrow night; maybe I'll see you. Thanks for the buzz."

Art silently says goodbye with his shrouded, hound dog eyes. I look back after taking a few steps. Art is sitting there on our bench, like an apparition, still crying a little and rocking back and forth, just slightly. He is reading a book by match-light – *damn, he must have a million of those wooden matches* – and a magnifying glass. The book and looking glass must have been in that grimy satchel he carries around. I call back to him.

"Hey Art, chin-up, what'cha readin'?"

He looks up, still sobbing a bit.

"It's called, *Standing on the Edge of Forever*, he says. A nurse at the clinic gave it to me and said I should read it. Night, Raven."

I instantly freeze in mid-step, and think about B.V. West. His time will come. Perhaps he will even commit suicide if I continue to bad-mouth him – which I will.

When I get home, I walk in through the inside garage door, down a cold Heineken, kiss Lydia, who is sipping her wine and watching *Dancing With The Stars* on our huge fuckin' television. I got it for Lydia on our first-week anniversary. Don't laugh, but what a waste. Anything for Lydia, though. I seldom watch TV.

I set my empty Heineken bottle down on the coffee table, step out the already-open sliding glass doors, walk down to the beach, and dive into the black ocean. Calm as a sheet of glass. No moon tonight. I swim about a hundred yards straight out, breathing evenly. I start thinking about taking a short trip. I make a lot of decisions while swimming. I finally turn around and calmly swim back toward shore. No bull sharks or tiger sharks tonight – although they do feed nocturnally, sometimes close to shore.

By the time I feel the sandy bottom and stand on the beach, looking up at the stars, I have decided. I will be heading to Boulder for about a week to see Joe Lofton. I'll have him fly in from L.A.

I also decide to take Lydia, which was not something I would normally do. We'll fly first-class out of Fort

Lauderdale. I figure I might as well treat Lydia to some *more* of the finer things in life. I'm telling you, I really dig Lydia. I've tried hard since my divorce ten years ago, and succeeded, up till now, to not get into a deep relationship. I'm hoping that the more I grow to depend upon my Mermaid emotionally and fall deeper in love with her, the more I *need* her, the better chance Lydia has of staying alive.

I change into my evening lounge attire, which is naked. I grab another beer then go into my den and email Joe Lofton, my lawyer, publicist and partner in crime. He's the one who arranges it so that one-third of my royalties for the book and my music go to off-shore safe havens, remember? Secure, safe, secret and illegal. Makes life edgy to be a criminal, and I like that. I always try to look ahead, while having fun in the meantime. What's wrong with that?

I tell Joe to meet me at the Ramada Inn at the base of Sundance Mountain near downtown Boulder. I book him into the room next to mine, under the name, "James Wallace."

No ocean, but the Ramada has a nice pool and the mountains are gorgeous. I hope Lydia likes it. Joe doesn't know much about Lydia and has no idea I'm bringing her. He'll be spellbound by her beauty, but nervous. Joe is a very cautious and careful guy. I like that. I'm his boss, but I always give his opinions and advice deep thought before making any kind of decisions which carry importance.

Out in Boulder, I'll give him the first five chapters of the new book to look over. I'm also gonna have a new contract drawn up which will give Joe an extra 3.5 percent of my royalties. Joe has a family, and it feels good to help the guy and his family out. See, I *really am* a sweetheart!

Oh yeah, Lydia and I will use the alias, "William L. Johnson and his wife, Emma," while in Colorado. I'll pick up a wedding band for Lydia at my favorite pawn shop in Fort Lauderdale. Not taking any chances. I might be a sweetheart, but I'm also a heartless executioner among other nefarious things, and I don't want to get caught.

Anyway, I'll call ahead and make reservations and pay everything in cash when we get there, probably a day or two before Joe flies in. A little private time in the Boulder area with Lydia would be fun. Maybe we'll climb a mountain. I'm thinking about planning it for about ten days from now so that Joe has time to prepare for his little working vacation. We have a lot to talk about, a whole lot.

2

Boulder, Colorado

Lydia and I check into The Ramada without a hitch. When we get into our room, I see Lydia admiring her pawn shop wedding ring. The smile on her face tells me she likes it a bit *too* much. Damn! I go into the bathroom to check it out for cleanliness while I take a piss. Killing two birds with one stone is but another shining example of my perverse abilities. Just kidding – but, I guess it is true.

Well, when I come out of the pisser and walk into the bedroom area – motels are basically all the same, as you probably know – Lydia is lying on the bed with her Kitty-Cat see-through night shirt on. By the way, have I told you that Lydia never wears panties, at least not most of the time, and can achieve an orgasm just by having her nipples kissed and sucked on – especially her right one. Amazing gal. I tease her for a while then go for a *hot quickie*. Lydia loves *hot quickies*, as we now call them. Hell, are we really becoming a couple? I never wanted that again. Really.

But I'm actually starting to feel like she's my soulmate, *whatever that is.* I thought I had one once before, but it turned out to be a stalemate instead. Real jokester, ain't I? Big deal, so I'm laughing at my own jokes again. I'm literally laughing out loud.

Lydia is in the bathroom taking a shower. I leave her a note on the bed that I am going out to get wine and beer, but what I really want to do is walk the streets of Boulder and see if I can buy a knife before the stores close. It is getting dark. I find a gun shop open with a nice collection of Buck knives. I pick up a beauty with a belt sheath for sixty bucks. Pay cash and leave. Very sharp and strong, damn nice knife. Too bad I'll have to leave it in Colorado when we – or I – depart. I have the feeling that I might leave it with, or more likely, *in* somebody who is worthy of having it. Probably be just some poor slob who happens to be in the wrong place at the wrong time with the wrong guy – *me*. If there is anybody I can find and kill within the next couple of hours, *great*, because the fuckin' lion is starting to purr. If not, I know there is one back at the Ramada.

Push it away, Raven.

Push that thought away, *now*! And I do. But I'm still glad there are no sharks in the motel pool.

Not Lydia. Please!

I walk down to the Unicorn where my band, *The Riders,* did that 16-month gig almost seven years ago. That's where I had met Merlino, sucked his left eye down into my digestive system and set his good soul free. Nice guy, huh? *Sweetheart my ass!*

I take a seat at the far end of the bar so I can see the door as well as everyone in the place. I am a stranger in a bar full of *regulars*. That can always – well, not always – mean danger. Nobody recognizes me from my band days. As I say, I look entirely different now than I did back then. I need to kill. I will kill tonight, but who and where and when?

As my first Heineken went down, I get an idea, a plan. I will have one more beer then go find a bus-stop bench with a guy like Miami Art sitting there. Then *bang*, a quick merciless kill.

I will have to be careful about how bloody I get. I don't have my briefcase with me. I always keep a bath towel, a pair of shorts and a clean shirt in there. As well as other tools of the trade, so to speak. And yes, as briefcases go, it's a big one. Tonight all I have is my new knife. I'll stay as clean as I can, then take a dip in the motel pool before I saunter back to our room to be with my lovely Lydia. Then we'll have a late snack and a few drinks. Sex too, if I know Lydia and myself.

I have a long red Philadelphia Phillies T-shirt on that covers my new knife which hangs at my right hip in its sheath. I leave the bartender a five-dollar-tip and walk out on to the peaceful streets of Boulder. I head for the seedy side of town. Every city has at least one. I turn the corner onto Dirk Street, the darkest, deadliest street in Boulder. I had only gone down Dirk about two-and-a-half blocks and, bingo! There he is. My experience and instincts instantly tell me that he is homeless and an alcoholic, when he can afford to be. And that he plans to spend the night sleeping on that bench – *The death bench.*

I walk up on the guy, slow and quiet.

He is curled up in the far left corner of the bench and is wearing a Denver Broncos hat. An old one, dirty, too. And sure enough, he has a pint bottle of some real cheap whiskey in his hand. I think its Hennessy. He spots me in mid-sip.

"Hey, buddy, sup?" I say, as I light a Newport, and he screws the cap back on the bottle.

"Not much man. You're lookin' at it," he says as he sits up. "Have a seat. You from around here – never seen you before."

I sit down heaving a deep breath.

"No, I reply, I'm here from Pennsylvania to visit my sister. She lives downtown. Felt like takin' a walk."

He laughs. No rotten teeth – just no teeth.

"Well, you picked one fucked-up neighborhood to take an evening stroll through."

"I've seen worse," I say, looking away from him. And I still have to get beer and wine for Lydia and me." As the note I left on the bed states – the time is *now*.

The lion is roaring so loudly that I'm certain my head will soon explode. I take a quick look around. The street is momentarily empty. I glance to the guy's right, and as planned, his eyes follow. With flashing quickness, and the freakish power of a madman, I plunge my new Buck knife through bench-man's sternum and into his heart then dive to the ground. Not a drop of blood on me!

He is dead in less than a minute. Well, maybe two.

I wipe the knife's handle clean of fingerprints and leave the blade in his chest.

I mean, it's not like I can take it home on the plane with me, no matter how much I like it. And I do. Like I say, it's a damn good knife.

He is slumped over, so I pull him up and suck his left eye out with a wet popping sound.

Kill Number Three.

The eyeball goes down easy. It is a nearly bloodless event, since his heart had already stopped pumping the 80-proof blood through his veins. I will still take that swim in the pool with my red Phillies shirt on just to be on the safe side before I go back to the motel room with Lydia.

I'll drape my shirt over the little wrought iron railing which is shaped like the letter "L" just outside of our room. It should be dry and clean of any blood-spatter there *might* have been from the initial stabbing. Guess I may as well admit that I know there is *some* blood, because I wiped my mouth with the shirt after I spit out the Bronco fan's left eye-lid. I don't care for the lids – or the Broncos for that matter. I'm an Eagles fan.

This kill I'd just made helps keep Lydia safe from the lion, at least for tonight. I am falling in love with her. I *am* in love with her. Fuck!

This is not in my plan. But Lydia's inner and outer beauty, at least in my eyes, is becoming more obvious every day. She is special. She had no problem seamlessly shifting her life from the down and outs, to the *have-it-all's*. She turns heads, but she seldom looks back. She is happy. And that fact makes old *sweetheart* here, happy too. And she still hasn't asked any questions about my super-rich lifestyle. We are both letting that sleeping dog lie – smart for now.

But I believe I may fill her in when Joe Loften and I have our meeting tomorrow afternoon. I'll swim a few laps in the morning and make my decision. I may even decide to have her at the meeting, not the entire meeting, not the illegal shit, but maybe the part where we talk about my plan for Sherriff Dead Man in Pennsylvania. My ultimate and hopefully, last kill. I'll have to think about that though. It's a major decision.

Next Morning

I had another *lucid dream* last night.

"What is a *lucid* dream?" you may be asking.

A lucid dream, just in case you don't know, is when you are aware that you are dreaming, during an actual dream. You usually realize you are having a lucid dream when something happens in that dream, which would be impossible in a real life situation. Sometimes, there may even be communications with people who are already dead. That has only happened to me three times. Damn it!

So, no, Lydia will not be present when Joe Lofton and I discuss the sheriff. But Lydia will live, in all her heavenly glory.

My lucid dream convinces me that Lydia cannot die, because that cannot be possible in Raven April's life. Does that make sense? I am relieved and happy. No need for that swim in the pool.

During the dream, I make two major decisions within those *sleepy arms of cosmic luxury* which is how I describe my lucid dreams. I love them, and can bring them on myself at times. Last night's dream came naturally, however.

First, I decide that, *Lydia will not hear about my ultimate, and final, target* when Joe Lofton and I discuss Sheriff Evil. My second decision, most important is that, *Lydia will live*.

We have sex at the crack of dawn. It is more, let's say, tender than usual. Lydia doesn't ask any questions, but I know she likes it. We are making love, not just fucking. She doesn't know why. But I do. My Mermaid will be spared and cared for. I am in love. Damn it, again! Lydia has now been placed on Placido's list of the un-killable.

Do you know that the name *Placido* means "calm and quiet"? Maybe that's why Placido and his sweet mother were not eaten alive in the middle of a bull shark migration when Placido was just five years old. His mother risked everything for freedom. Was it because they were calm and quiet that they survived? An interesting thought to ponder. I often wonder why *they* survived and not the rest. Fate is a splendid savage. So are bull sharks.

By the way, the name Lydia means "noble and kind." That description fits my Mermaid to a T.

Joe will arrive at the motel about two this afternoon. The three of us will have drinks around the pool, after Joe, aka, "James Wallace," gets settled into his room. I had instructed Joe to bring along a top-of-the-line facial disguise kit, complete with wigs and beards, etc. I had directed him to a place on Melrose Street in West Hollywood, CA, that sells that kind of stuff. I also have him pick up a replica of the shirt I wore in the picture on the back jacket of *Standing...*, and a couple of new copies of the book itself.

Remember when Lydia said that she wanted B.V. West to sign a copy of the book for her? Well, what Lydia wants, Lydia will get as long as Raven is around. Best-selling author, killer and all around nice guy. Yep, that's me. Ah, and don't forget lover of Mermaids. Fate had blindsided me again, and now, with the love in my heart for Lydia, the Raven has touched yet *another* realm of reality and blissfully landed on his feet once more, like a cat with nine unique, multicolored lives.

But the biggest cat of all, the lion, is asleep now. I have no idea when he will lift his huge head and roar again. That is the one thing I have no control over – the roar of my lion. I guess nothing and no one is perfect. As it is written, *he who is without sin or faults, cast the first stone*. I will conquer the lion's roar. My plan is already in motion; hold on!

Joe Lofton Arrives

My prediction comes true. Joe walks out to the pool after unpacking in his room, as I had told him – no, sorry – *requested* him to do. Good married man that he is, his eyes almost pop out of his head when his gaze falls upon my lovely Lydia, who is stretched out in her bright-white thong bathing suit in the powder-blue cushioned lounge chair next to me.

Ya see, Joe is not just my employee and go-to guy, he is my friend. His wife, Eileen, and their three kids mean everything to Joe. I admire that, and it remains the number-one reason I hope Joe and I never get nabbed. I am glad to see him. We hug; and I hand him a Heineken. Joe's eyes are still on Lydia when she sits up.

"Hi Joe." she says, as she takes her sunglasses off and lights up a Black & Mild. "You are even more handsome than Raven said you were. It is a real pleasure to meet you. How is your family? Raven swears they are all gorgeous!"

They shake hands and kiss each other on the cheek. I had thought about killing Joey Boy several times at the command of the lion's great roar, but B.V. West is totally against it. For once in his miserable cockroach life, he is right. And, by the way, I never told Lydia that Joe is handsome. She was just fuckin' with him – and me too, I suppose.

Like I say, you gotta love that Lydia, aka, Mermaid. And oh yeah, Mrs. Emma Johnson, while in Boulder. Remember that?

She even has a cool sense of humor. Am I nuts or what? Sometimes I really think I am. Well, I'm nuts over my Lydia, that's for sure. And it sucks in a way. So, we all sit around in the northeast corner of the fenced-in pool area. There is a little table with an umbrella, two chairs and Lydia's powder-blue cushioned lounge chair. Talk about a lovely sight! After about a half hour of small talk I stand up. I lean over to kiss Lydia, who is still sitting up in the lounge with her ultra-white Miami thong bathing suit glistening like a diamond in a display case, catching all eyes. Boulder has never seen anything as beautiful as Lydia.

"Joe and I have a little business to talk about," I say, after I kiss her. "We'll be in Joe's room if you need me. Okay, Mermaid?"

She just smiles.

"Go, boys," she says. "I'm fine right here; nice to meet you, Joe."

"Nice to meet you too, Lydia," Joe replies.

I pick up the two empty Heineken bottles and drop them in the trash container; then Joe and I disappear into his room.

Listen in; there's a little something I need to explain before we can move on with this gory story of my somewhat divergent life. Please understand, I am not writing a normal *book* here. I am really just telling you an unusual tale that I think you should hear. I just hope no one has nightmares when I finish spinning it. From Raven to you, one-on-one, okay? So, shall we move on?

Now, one of Joe Lofton's biggest and most important responsibilities to me is to keep tabs on a certain small-time county sheriff in Pennsylvania, where I grew up, who thought his shit didn't stink. That's right: Sheriff Evil, the guy I mentioned earlier.

The sheriff is seventy-four years old, now. He is still working, sitting behind that big old wooden desk like an emperor with his double-barreled shotgun lying in front of him. He is a huge ugly fish in a small green scum pond. He has been skimming money off the top of local property tax payers for years with the help of State Senator Rex Barber.

Thanks to Joe, we have enough dirt on the sheriff and the senator to burn their asses to the bone with branding irons and send them off to prison 'till hell freezes over.

Sheriff Evil should have drowned in that small, green-scum pond decades ago – but only the good die young, especially in his case. Plus, God is keeping him alive for me.

I didn't want Sheriff Evil killed, or in prison. I need him alive, for only his death by my hands can silence the roar of my lion. But he must suffer first. Before he dies he will be begging for death. My skin crawls spooky whenever I think about the sheriff's black and torturous fate.

And I smile.

Okay, back to the business of what I have planned for Lydia. Her BIG surprise! Joe and I have to work fast, just in case Lydia comes knocking on Joe's door. I always assume the worst case scenario in any situation; it's safer like that.

I didn't used to be a man of that nature, but I, Raven April, learned who I am the hard way. At first I thought it was a curse. Now I can see how being beat down into the ground then getting back up is a blessing, and if you're looking, watching with your eyes wide open, it's not even in disguise. It's all *right there in front of you.* Keeping that always in mind, it seems the harder I fall, the softer I land.

Makes sense to me, but never forget that I am a madman, and you will soon find out how and why. Just remain patient.

42

Joe Lofton could always read my mind, as he seems to be doing again this afternoon. As soon as we leave the pool area and step into his room, he begins to move quickly. After cracking open two cold Heinekens, he empties the facial disguise kit, the replica shirt and two pristine copies of *Standing on the Edge of Forever* on the queen-sized bed.

"Okay, asshole," Joe says, "go sit at the desk, take your shirt off, and close your Charles-Manson eyes. This glue will fuck your eyes up, even blind you. This is something only *you* would do, Raven – you know that, right?"

I laugh between swigs of beer.

"Or Charlie Manson?" I say.

Still laughing, I look at Joe, who grabs himself another beer and smiles at me back through the mirror above the desk.

"Just get to work, will ya?" I say. "Lydia's gonna love this!"

Joe takes an extra long drink of his beer, and swallows.

"You think so, huh?" he says, in a tone of solemnity with a hint of doubt.

Our eyes meet in the mirror again.

Joe isn't smiling anymore.

Anyway, he proceeds to go to work on me using the photo from the book's back cover as a guide. He reads the directions that come with the disguise kit, and begins to transform me into B.V. West.

When I open my eyes and put the shirt on, I look in the mirror. I can't believe what's staring back at me.

I go into a silent, internal rage, hiding it, I think, from Joe. I want to kill him – me, B.V. West!

But I remain calm.

"Grab us another beer, Joe," I say. "Good job. No, *great* job! You should quit working for me and become a Hollywood make-up artist."

Joe can read my mind, as I told you. He can feel something emanating from me. He is shaken by the sight of me. So am I. But it is time for Lydia not only to get her favorite book signed, but to meet the famous author himself.

"Okay, Joey Boy, time to go get Lydia. Hell, I hope this doesn't blow her mind, because it sure is blowing mine!"

Joe washes his hands in the bathroom and tells me to sit on the edge of the bed, facing away from the door so that Lydia will only see my back when she walks in the door.

"Hey, you're the boss, Joe," I say, as cheerfully as I can. "Very melodramatic. I like it."

He gives me a concerned look before he wanders out to the corner of the pool area where Lydia is now lying, eyes closed, on her stomach.

Her white bikini-thong is accentuating her tan and lovely ass. All eyes are still upon her. As I said, she's too much for Boulder, *way* too much.

She is asleep when "lucky Joe" gently awakens her, *after* a few seconds of a close-up inspection of my Mermaids backside. Oh well, Joe is only human.

"So, how was your little nap, Lydia? Beautiful day, huh?"

Lydia flashes her million-dollar smile to the ground then looks up at Joe.

"Sure is," she says. "What's up with Raven? Is he Okay?

She stretches her angelic body, and gently yawns.

"Joe, you've known Raven a lot longer than I have, so I don't have to tell you that he is no – how can I say this – *normal* man."

You don't know the half of it, Joe is thinking.

"That's why I worry about him," Lydia continues, "I love him, and he loves me. That surprises me right there. Hell, Raven is not the kind of man to fall in love for more than a day. I sensed that about him the first night we met in Miami. I feel so damn lucky!"

Joe clears his throat.

"No, Raven is no normal man, Lydia. You must be a very special woman. Raven gave up on the ladies years ago. All he really did was write songs, stories and poetry. Oh yes, and partied heartily – as far as I know, that is.

"You seem to have picked up on that rather quickly, and you're right. To my knowledge he's never stayed with a chick for more than a day or two. His true love has always been his children, music, books and the ocean. Now I can see that it's *you,* and I must say, I'm happy for both of you.

"By the way, Raven just ran to the store, but there is a buddy of his he wants you to meet. He's waiting for us in my room. He's one of Raven's best friends, and now lives here in Boulder. Raven wants to surprise you. They've known each other since childhood in Pennsylvania. Raven said he'd only be a minute."

Lydia laughs.

"Cool Joe, any friend of Raven's is a friend of mine," she says. "Are we friends, Joe?"

He chuckles.

"Any friend of Raven's is a friend of mine."

They smile at each other and head for Joe's room.

45

In Joe Lofton's Room

Joe opens the door to his room and ushers Lydia in.

I am sitting on the edge of the bed directly across from her, silhouetted by the sun coming in through the open window shade from the other side of Joe Lofton's neatly-made bed, as he had instructed me to do. My back is to Lydia. After a few seconds, while I finish another beer, I stand up and walk around the bed toward her.

A nightmarish squeal erupts from down deep inside Lydia's diaphragm. She slaps her right hand across her mouth, and leaves it there. Her eyes are big and scary, probably much like the eyes of the bull shark victims on Placido's sinking boat, fearing they were about to be eaten alive.

Joe sees that Lydia is turning pale, and looks suddenly weak. He gently guides her to the edge of the bed, her confused eyes riveted on B.V. West, her "favorite author of all time."

I stick to my plan, and pick up a copy of *Standing...* from the center of the bed, sign the inside-cover with a red pen, pulled from the pocket of my book-jacket shirt, and hand it to Lydia, who is still in a mild state of shock. I am scared as hell for my Mermaid but she is coming together now.

Thank God! I'd hate to kill her *this* way. But she is un-killable. Keep reminding me of that will you, please? Thank you. *And oh yeah, Fuck B.V. West!*

Lydia finally, and graciously, accepts the book.

I shake her hand, disguising my voice:

"I'm B.V. West, a close friend of Raven's," I say.

"He wanted me to surprise you with a signed copy of my book, *Standing On The Edge Of Forever*. And as you probably know by now, what Raven wants, he usually gets. I hope I didn't startle you *too* much, Lydia. Raven speaks very, shall we say, *highly* of you. I can see why."

"Thank you Mr. West," Lydia, who is still nearly speechless, mumbles. I love your book. It changed my life."

I'm thinking, *damn right it did,* but kept my mouth shut.

"Well, thanks. I'm glad you enjoyed and obviously understood my work. That makes me truly happy."

I give Joe a nod and he slips into the bathroom as we had contrived. The makeup kit from Melrose Streeet in Tinsel Town really fuckin' worked. Lydia actually thinks I'm B.V. West.

Am I?

Speaking of L.A., I love it there. Skid Row rocks my wacko world at night. Like Heaven to a freak like me. Nuts, huh? Well, I like to call it "interesting" and "culturally enlightening." Hold on, I'm laughing at myself again. Sorry about that. Now, did you know that the original Skid Row was *only* in L.A.? Born there? It's recently become a near-generic term. Every town has a skid-row now – thieving bastards – but they stole the name from the City of Angels.

Just a little useless trivia I thought might interest someone. Rambling again, am I? Okay, here we go.

Lydia is still on the edge of the bed staring up at me. I'm standing over her like a ghoulish, weird ghost man; and our eyes intertwine for an intense, morbid minute or two.

Then, as if in a horror movie, I ever so slowly remove my book-jacket shirt.

She freezes.

47

I remove my wig, peeling it off from my forehead back, tossing it on the bed on top of another copy of *Standing*.... Next is the mustache.

Lydia remains mannequin-still. Her disbelieving eyes are open wide.

I start at the bottom of my right ear and slowly, dramatically, begin to peel away the fake beard – and voila! I am Raven again. I feel relieved and happy to be free of Mr. B.V. West.

Oh shit! I watch as Lydia faints on the bed.

"Joe, quick," I yell. "Cold towel – it's Lydia!"

Joe, in a panic, flies out of the bathroom with a bath towel, which he had drenched with cold water in the bathtub and quickly wrung out. I center Lydia on the bed, and we place the cold towel across her body for a couple of minutes, while Joe hurries to get a cold washcloth for her forehead and face.

"Lydia, Mermaid," I nearly scream in her ear, "it's okay. It's me, Raven."

Or should I be saying, "Lydia, it's me, B.V. West?" Just a thought.

"Wake up Mermaid, wake up! Come back to me, baby. I'll explain everything. Everything!" *Including the insanity that has just taken place in Joe Lofton's room at the base of Sundance Mountain.*

"I promise."

It was a wild idea, like most of my ideas, which this time almost cost Lydia her life; and me, my already questionable lucidity. A rare Raven mistake for certain. I admit it.

Lydia begins to regain consciousness, and I've never felt so relieved in my entire life. She flutters her eyes and reaches out to me.

"Raven, is that you? What just happened?"

48

I try to assure her that everything is alright by rubbing her hand and kissing her nose.

"Everything is fine, Lydia. You just fainted. I'm sorry to have upset you, *so*, so sorry."

I say a silent *'thank you'* prayer to the Man upstairs. My Mermaid is back among the living. Wow, that was too close for comfort, never gonna do *that* again! But you've got to admit, it was a pretty damn cool, if not cruel and outlandish, little skit. All's well that ends well. Isn't that what they say?

Lydia is now fully awake, and recovering. Joe pours her a glass of wine while we tell her the whole story of Raven April and B.V. West.

But I've gotta tell you, once again, Lydia is a champ. My lovely Mermaid sat for over an hour, without saying a word, not even asking a question, while Joe and I exposed everything, except for Sheriff Evil – the soon to be dead, Sheriff Evil, which even Joe doesn't know about.

Then, Lydia calmly placed her third glass of white zinfandel down next to the lamp on the nightstand, and slowly walked over to me.

I am standing at the foot of the bed, shirtless and still sweating, shaking with fear and wondering how Lydia will react to this horrible, *but damn funny* joke we had just played on her.

Uh oh, she's staring at me. Here she comes!

Slap! Slap! A right and a left across each one of my deserving cheeks,

Ouch! They sting, but I just stand there in obedient silence, waiting for a knee to the balls.

But instead, Lydia suddenly throws her arms around me and begins sobbing.

"I Love you Raven," she says, "but please…" Then she looks over my shoulder at Joe,"

"And this goes for you too, Joe." she says. "Don't *ever* pull anything this heavy on me again! You could have killed me you asshole, Raven. Now kiss me."

So I do – softly.

"No, kiss me hard. Harder!" Lydia falls on the bed, pulling me down with her.

Joe grabs three Heinekens and exits.

Wow, a threesome. Raven, Lydia and B.V. "fuck-head" West all in the same bed together.

I know. Sick joke.

Joe locks the door behind him. Later that night I give Joe the first five chapters of my new book and his up-dated contract. He is very grateful for the raise. We bear hug as always before saying good-bye. Then I grab him by the shoulders look him in the eyes, smile and wink.

"See you soon, buddy. Say hi to Eileen and the kids for me. And thanks."

After placing five crisp one-hundred-dollar bills in the navy-blue pocket of his denim button-down shirt, I turn and walk away before he can say anything. Love that guy!

Then I hear his voice.

"Raven, you are an asshole, but you're a sweetheart, too. Thanks, man."

I keep walking without turning around.

3

On The Plane Back To Miami

I'll tell you, I am so damn glad that my Mermaid has such a great sense of humor to go along with all of her other exquisite qualities. Damn, I got lucky again. Maybe it's my collection of Pyramids that always helps pull my ass out of the fire.

I probably haven't mentioned that I collect pretend Pyramids, have I? Well, now you know. I've got over a dozen of them in all sizes in the den, where I'm *supposed* to be finishing my new book. The smallest one is less than an inch tall. The largest one is over three feet.

Babbling again, sorry…

It's like, Lydia is everything I thought never existed in a woman. She is lovable, not killable. You can bet your balls on that – no pun intended, Art.

Speaking of Art, as I'm looking down from 34,000 feet at some cumulus clouds from my window seat two rows behind the cockpit, I begin to think about Art. What an astonishing man, a *true to the word*-survivor. By the way, I just put him on the un-killable list with Lydia, Placido and Joe Lofton.

I know this sounds a little wacky, but Lydia hates window seats. Always thinks she's gonna fall out. Well, maybe she *ain't* perfect, but who is? We all have far-out fears that live in our primitive, sometimes nonsensical minds. Lydia is reading a book by Jeffrey Archer titled

Kane and Abel. One of the best books I ever read. Surprised she's never read it before. Maybe she has, after all, she read *Standing on the Edge of Forever* twice. Bet she never reads it again, though, not after what happened in Boulder. Can't help but laugh a little to myself about that whole horror movie episode in Joe's room.

Maybe I should be a screenwriter!

Here I go again, laughing at my own private jokes and pranks.

Lydia never looks up.

Oh Good Christ, help me. We aren't even half way to Ft. Lauderdale, and the fuckin' lion is starting to purr. Louder by the god damn second! I gotta try and stop him – deep breaths, slow and deep. Maybe a few drinks will help.

"Excuse me. I'd like to order two bottles of Heineken and two jiggers of Tanqueray gin, please."

"Sure dear," the first-class flight attendant replies sweetly, "would you like a mixer, tonic perhaps, for your gin?"

I smile.

"Yes, please," I say, just to make it look good, "with ice."

Lydia peeks up from her book and looks a little puzzled because it is only nine o'clock in the morning.

"Just celebrating, baby," I say. Then I kiss her. I'm toasting to my love for you, Mermaid."

She squeezes my hand and goes back to *Kane and Abel.*

My drinks arrive, and as soon as the thirtyish looking flight attendant, a, cute blonde named Tammy, disappears back toward the cockpit, I down one of the plastic bottles of Tanqueray in one gulp. Screw the tonic water.

Still, my lion roars. I can see his tongue when he growls this time with his mouth as far and wide open as it can go. Sharp white teeth shimmering, and that deafening roar.

My head is pounding as if my brain is trying to escape; its own gray dungeon of mini-demons kicking and punching the inside of my skull with their tiny little iron fists, hundreds of them.

Another gin down the hatch – now a beer. Now what? I will *have* to kill soon.

It's less than two hours until we land. I need to kill *now* to stop the lion's hideous roar. *Why can't anybody else hear that heartless, murderous roar?* But how can I kill anyone on the plane without getting caught? If that happens all my plans for B.V. West and Sheriff Evil could not be fulfilled, and they must be. I have to try and hold out against the thunderous mantra of the lion until we land. I will kill then, at the airport. First I must devise a plan and hold on to my sanity at the same time. Is that *possible*?

Less than fifty minutes to go.

Be strong, you pussy !!!!!!!!!! I'll need every one of my skills and instincts to make a clean, quick kill at Ft. Lauderdale Airport. As calmly as I can, I motion to Tammy.

"Another Heineken and Tanqueray, please." I am pumping way too much adrenaline to get drunk.

"Coming right up." she replies, with a cordial smile.

I must have pulled the *calm thing* off. Calm and quiet, like Placido. My plan is coming together as I stare into the stratosphere. I scribble a suicide note on a paper towel from the plane's bathroom. No, not mine, I'm not to *that* point yet. I don't have my black briefcase, but I have a handkerchief. I had a teacher tell me once, when I was about nine years old, that a man should always carry a

53

comb, a pocketknife and a handkerchief. Well, I've got my hankie. One out of three ain't bad. And it's all I'll need at the airport.

Ft. Lauderdale Airport

We land, debark, walk through the airport and gather our bags off the merry-go-round. I don't say a word to Lydia or anybody else, and Lydia knows that's not like me. She doesn't say much either. We take everything out front to the sidewalk where I'm gonna flag a taxi down and have him drop us off at home in Miami.

Motherfucker, the lion is truly showing me no mercy now. That roar!

Lydia left her Beamer at home. Since I've been a killer, I've always felt safer traveling by cab, paying in cash and leaving the cabbie a nice tip. I will not even carry - nor do I own - a cell phone. I kiss Lydia on the cheek and tell her I have to run back inside to take a leak, and I'll be right back.

She kisses me back.

"Well, try and make it quick," she says, it's really fuckin' hot out here." She lights a Black & Mild.

"Will do, Mermaid." I whisper in her ear. "How about a swim when we get home?"

Stay cool, Raven.

I start looking for the closest men's room which is about fifty feet down on the left. Putting on my sunglasses, I walk in and straight over to a urinal. I stand there like I'm takin' a piss. But my dick never leaves my pants. I scour the place with my eyes, waiting for the next guy to enter a shit stall. There are two other guys taking a piss at urinals. When they leave, I just wait.

Perfect timing again, I'm hoping, when this dude strolls in and heads right for the next-to-last stall. Like a stealthy leopard, I move quickly and quietly. Before he knows it, he has company in the stall. Me.

I instantly push his forehead back with the palm of my left hand and punch him hard in the throat with my right fist, silencing him, and then lock the door. Using my handkerchief as a garrote, I choke him to death in less than a minute; and that's hard to do.

He's fighting like a bitch for his life – squirming and kicking the whole time.

I get lucky again, and no one else enters the men's room in those final and frantic sixty seconds. I remove his belt, wrap it tightly around his neck and tie the other end to the clothes hook on the inside of the shit stall door. I pull his legs up and drop his feet into the toilet. I stick the suicide note in his pocket, which reads simply:

"Sorry. Love you all."

I look under the stall. The place is empty except for one guy taking a piss. While he empties his bladder, I gouge my fourth victim's left eye out with my house key and swallow it. This guy's eyeball tastes oddly salty, a little different than the others, and slides over my tongue and down my throat as cleanly as a raw oyster. I clean the blood off my face, hands and keys with my trusty hankie and flush it down the toilet. I slide under the stall as agile as a child and calmly walk out of the airport bathroom to meet Lydia.

"Gee, that didn't take long," Lydia says. "Now let's get a cab and get the hell home."

"Sounds like a plan to me," I reply nonchalantly after lighting a Newport, and then tossing it on the ground after a couple of strong drags. "I need to take a swim." I pinch Lydia's ass as we climb into the back of the cab. On the ride home I'm thinking, *what idiot would gouge his own eye out before he killed himself?* And then I laugh out loud.

The cabbie must think I'm nuts.

So might the police.

4

FBI Headquarters, Quantico, Va.

FBI Agent Debbie Errickson enters her office promptly at 7 a.m. – Room 36 on the third floor of the FBI building in Quantico, Virginia.

Debbie, a short, petite blonde, has pale skin and a pixie face. She always wears white slacks and a buttoned-down, light-colored blouse with long sleeves. Her shoes remind everyone of nurses' footwear. She is single, and lives in a white-glove-clean apartment with her cat Rea-Rea. The cat, in keeping with the décor, is also pale white.

Creepy.

Agent Rick Sansom, her partner, is late as usual, so Debbie, still not fully awake, starts a pot of coffee in the crowded little room. The coffee maker sits on a tiny white table in the northeast corner of the office.

She glances around when she hears the squeak of the door opening. *Gotta get that blasted thing fixed. Giving me a headache!*

"Mornin', Debbie; late again, but I'm finally here." Rick grabs his coffee mug and heads for the half-filled pot. "Thanks for getting things going."

"Whoa, partner; give it a couple more minutes." Debbie smiles as she looks at the frazzled man joining her. "Have another rough morning, did we now?" she asks.

Standing over six-feet tall, Rick is boyishly good-looking with a handsome face featuring a manly chiseled chin, and a thick head of neatly-groomed blond hair. He appears capable of handling any situation – and he can – usually.

"Yeah," he says, grinning sheepishly. "Danged kids; what one doesn't lose in the morning, the other one does. Same shit every day."

"You could have stayed single and got a cat instead of rug-rats," Debbie teased. "But it wouldn't be nearly as much fun."

Rick is married with two toddlers at home, making it hectic in the mornings at the Sansom residence to get off to work, so Debbie forgives him for his almost daily tardiness.

"Tell that to my wife," Rick counters.

In the cramped office, there's an *ancient*, seldom-used fax machine and two computers plus a telephone at each of their desks. Hardly room to move about, but cozy.

Agents Errickson and Sansom work for a branch of the FBI's Behavioral Analysis Unit called The Violent Criminal Apprehension Program, (ViCAP). Without going into much needless detail, they basically try to catch the bad guys when nobody else can, and keep us good folks safe.

Don't laugh. They do try.

Just as Rick's hands encircle the cup of fresh brew and he draws his first sip, the emails start pouring in. He silently thanks her with his smiling blue eyes for the coffee.

"Not already," Debbie moaned.

Rick walks over to his desk to read them, while Debbie sits opposite him, enjoying her first cup of what promises to be another busy day.

The first email Rick reads, which was sent nearly an hour ago is less than one page long, but it captures Rick's attention.

"Hey Deb," he says, "check this baby out." He shoots it to her, but it's already on her screen, too. The email is from their boss, Frank Harding, who runs a tight ship from his huge office one floor under them. It reads:

There may be a guy roaming around the country killing people. Which is nothing new or unusual, I know, but this nut job always leaves the same clue. He, or she, either gouges out or apparently, bites and sucks out the victim's left eyeball according to the medical examiner. We think the last killing was in a men's room at the Ft. Lauderdale airport just two days ago. Although this one may be a suicide, assume it's the eye-eater. Who the fuck gouges out their own left eye before they hang themselves? Still haven't found the eye, haven't found any of them. As soon as the forensic team is completely done, I'll let you know more. But assume it's the eye-eater. Get on it!

There is more in the email, but that is the gist of it. Debbie and Rick look at each other in silence for a few seconds.

"The eye-eater?" Debbie says, sounding confused.

5

Home Sweet Home

As soon as Lydia and I get home from the airport, I strip naked, pour Lydia a glass of wine and open a Heineken for myself. Lydia then predictably rolls a joint and takes off all her clothes except for her black thong.

The little mermaid knows what that does to me.

We sit on the deck and smoke most of the joint. Beautiful evening. We hold hands and kiss – which ain't usually my style, but, Lydia does something special to me – as the half moon dances like a ballerina on the slightly rippling ocean.

I stand up.

"Hey, doll face, wanna take a swim with me?"

Lydia leans back and yawns, her nipples hard and yearning.

"No thanks Raven, but I'll be on the 'love blanket' when you get back."

It is only about eight o'clock, and I want to grab my briefcase out of the safe in my office after my swim. I need to take a walk down to the bus-stop bench to see if I can find Art or run into Placido. For some reason, I miss those guys – they are now both on my un-killable list, as I've said before. I feel good about that.

Lydia and I have a hot-quickie on the "love blanket" then I dive into the ocean, feeling the pristine water wash my sins away – for the time being, anyway.

The water is about 85 degrees, and I swim at least an eighth of a mile out and then back to the 'love blanket' in kind of a circle. I always have it in the back of my mind that most sharks feed at night. But that never keeps me out of the water. A shark would be crazy to fuck with me, and I think they sense that – really. I ask myself again, am I nuts, or what?

Answer, NO!

Lydia and I are finally back home here on the beach, and the "love blanket" lives up to its name. Life is good. I lay there looking up at the half moon for about a half hour. Lydia falls asleep, and I watch her for a while. Gorgeous. I don't know who got luckier, her or me. I still feel like walking downtown, so I gently awaken Lydia and tell her that I am going to look for Placido.

I spilled some of my guts to Lydia while we were in Boulder, including the fact that my two best friends are a young Cuban guy named Placido and a war vet named Art. She is cool with that. The only thing she doesn't know is about the murders and my plans for Sheriff Evil Walking. She'd think I am crazy if I tell her what I have in mind for him.

We hold hands and walk inside, Lydia with her thong in her right hand, and her left hand in mine. I carry the blanket. Fuck, I really am what I never wanted to be again. In love. *Shit!* We finish the joint in the bedroom. I have a beer, and Lydia has her glass of zinfandel. I'm gonna have to get her to step up a grade or two when it comes to wine. But she had gotten used to white zinfandel when she was living on the streets.

Man, she *did* hit the lottery, didn't she? Luxury was always in the cards for her. I truly believe that. She is awesome! And she's got my back, so I really can't complain about being in love. It's kind of cool. I get dressed in shorts, sneakers, no socks and a tank top. I grab my briefcase and start off into the slimy guts of Miami's sub-culture of drugs, mayhem and murder.

My comfort zone.

Art's Bench

I don't see Placido on my way to the bus-stop bench that Art called home each night. During the day Art usually walks around bumming money and cigarettes. Nice way for society to treat a veteran – a war hero. I'll catch up with Placido later, see how *Mama* Placido is doing. I'm gonna give her a hundred bucks for groceries and her medicine. I hit a lottery in Pennsylvania, remember? No skin off my ass.

As I turn the corner, I see Art. It looks like he's sleeping, but I had picked up a 12-pack of beer for us at the place with the bars on the windows and doors. I also bring a joint and a pack of Newports for him. That'll wake him up. On top of that, I grab a slightly better bottle of wine for Lydia. Damn it, I *am* a sweetheart! As I get closer, about twenty feet away from the bench, I yell loud enough to wake him.

"Art my man, got a surprise for ya, buddy."

I am also gonna give him twenty bucks.

He doesn't move.

The half moon shines black and wet on Art's shirt as I get a little closer. Oh fuck!

Blood is pouring down on his forehead from under his hat covering his face. It's a fuckin' wonder he didn't drown in his own plasma.

I feel for a neck pulse.

Still alive.

I yell pretty loud in his right ear to see if I get a reaction from the poor bastard.

Nothing. His *left* ear had been sliced off and laid on the sidewalk about four feet away, near the curb.

I pick it up, and put it in my briefcase.

Art's precious dirty satchel is gone, too.

Somebody is gonna pay for this, but first I have to try and save Art. I decide to take him home.

Lydia honey, I'm home. Surprise!

I remember seeing a shopping cart about a block away. I sprint down to get it. When I return, less than two minutes have passed. I feel for a pulse again – still fairly strong. But time could still be a deadly enemy. I pick Art up and put him in the grocery cart, and break my own speed records getting him to the mansion. I push him the ten blocks to the house.

If and when he awakens, Art will see a world he had never envisioned before, and didn't think I had either. When we reach the mansion, I am totally out of breath.

Lydia screams at the bloody mess in the cart, which now is situated in the middle of our kitchen, with Art bleeding all over the place.

"Lydia, meet Art," I say glibly. *"Art, meet Lydia."*

Sorry about the tasteless joke, but I just can't help it.

"We've gotta save him, Mermaid!"

Lydia, quickly takes charge.

"Put him in our bed," she orders me, "and strip him down. We've got to find out if he's injured anywhere else but his head, nose and ear. Then bring as much water in here as you can and a lot of towels. Now, Raven!"

I carry him carefully to the master bedroom, blood dripping all over, and strip him down. I can see that the top of his head is split open and his nose is rearranged, with blood gushing out of both nostrils. Where his left ear used to be isn't bleeding that much anymore. There is a very clean and precise cut along the side of Arts head. That and maybe poor circulation is why it's not bleeding that much. But it's still really fucked up looking.

Lydia is gathering up all the stuff we have handy, which ain't much for a make-shift emergency room, like peroxide, bandages, Band-Aids and isopropyl alcohol. While I'm getting water, I take Art's ear out of my briefcase and put it in a glass of crushed ice. Just in case it could be sewn back on someday. Hell, he's lost enough body parts, don't you think?

We have a problem. We can't take a chance and draw attention to this for two very obvious reasons, the first one being my anonymity – I'm a killer, don't forget. And the second reason is that I'm going to destroy whoever did this to Art.

So I decide to wrap Art's ear in one of the towels I keep in my briefcase, and place the towel back inside my black leather tool bag.

Forget the reattachment idea. The why will appear sooner rather than later, I hope. Notice how fast I can change my mind, my plans?

Art is still unconscious.

Here comes Lydia.

She screams again, not at the sight of Art's beaten head and face, but at the sight of his mangled crotch area. *Butchery* was the only word I could think of when I first saw it five minutes ago.

It almost blows Lydia's mind, but she cries instead and looks me in the eyes, dumbfounded.

"Let's get to work and save your buddy, Art," she says. "I know we can't call a doctor or the cops. And put a *fucking* towel over his, his, whatever *that* is!"

64

I carefully place a towel over his, his, whatever that is. Yuck!

We go to work.

The crack he took on top of the head is probably why he is still unresponsive, along with the shock. But I'm no doctor and neither is Lydia. We are doing our best. Lydia cleans his scalp while I try to shave his hair away from the head gash.

"Sit him up, Raven," she commands. "It may lessen the bleeding, and I can see what I'm doing better. Sit him the hell up!"

There is a deep gash directly on the top of Art's skull, probably a pipe or aluminum baseball bat, but only about four inches long. I wind up shaving almost his whole head because we need bare skin so that the Band-Aids and duct tape, *yes, duct tape,* have something to stick to as she pulls the wound together, and I tape it. The Band-Aids are too small so the surgery consists of duct tape only.

We lay him back down on the bed with two pillows under his head. Lydia attempts to clean Art's face and tries to stop his nasal bleeding by tilting his head back and squeezing the bridge of his broken nose.

Ouch.

I go to work on his left ear-hole. The bleeding had almost stopped, so after the area was clean I duct tape a new white handkerchief over it. My scoutmaster would be proud. Things are looking up for Art. His pulse is stronger, but he is still knocked out.

The lion is beginning to roar.

Wake up, Art, and tell me who to kill.

I have an idea.

"Lydia, hurry and grab me a bottle of Heineken. Open it, too." She runs back from the beer-fridge and hands me the beer. I squeeze Art's swollen lips open and pour the cold brew into his mouth.

Lydia yells, and grabs for the beer.

"Are you out of your mind, Raven? You'll kill him! He could drown from that beer. I thought it was for *you!"* She takes the bottle and what's left in it and throws it at our big bedroom mirror, smashing it into a thousand pieces.

Smash, bang, crack! What the hell?

This whole fucked-up night is getting to her.

And damn, talk about timing, Art starts coughing and he opens his eyes for a second.

I knew the beer would bring him around.

I start talking into his good ear again. I need to know who did this, and soon. *The lion is demanding it!*

Lydia is talking to Art now, too. She has a feeling, as I do, that Art is waking up. Lydia slowly feeds him some bottled water. But I know Art. He wants beer.

I add about ten long, heavy duty plastic cable ties, and my Glock which was already set up with a silencer, to my briefcase. I'm going back into the bedroom and dump a bottle of beer down Art's throat again and get a name or names of the soon-to-be-dead. While Lydia is grabbing fresh, clean blankets, I pour a half bottle of Heineken into Art's mouth, and scream into his right ear: "Who kicked your ass, buddy? Give me a name!"

Art whispers, "Tedescos – the Tedesco Twins."

I smile.

Art blacks out again, and Lydia returns a moment later, never knowing about the beer or the Tedesco twins.

See what I mean? *Perfect timing.*

6

The Day I Lost My Mind

Let's take a break, my friends. We'll get back to the Tedesco twins later.

It's time for me to let the cat out of the bag, so to speak – time to tell everyone why I kill. Why the lion roars. You knew there had to be a reason, didn't you? To not confide this aspect of my life would be like a teacher giving the test first, and the lesson later.

I grew up in central Pennsylvania, a boon-dock town in the middle of nowhere named *Granite*. I loved it there in my early childhood with all the woods and fields and streams. I spent most of my time in the woods with my little beagle hound, Queenie. Me and that little dog were inseparable. She even slept with me and lay on the front porch all day long waiting for me to come home from school. Great dog. Queenie was the love of my little, big life.

But I was starting to notice females more and remember having a crush on a cute little blond haired girl named *Wanda*. Rambling again.

Back to the story. Actually, I believe I'm stalling and don't really *want to* write this. But I have to. I must. No one will know it, but I'll be crying. Here goes:

One Saturday morning in October when I was eleven, Queenie and I took a walk down to our favorite stream, which was a little less than a mile from the house.

I had been deer hunting – everybody hunted deer in central Pennsylvania – since I was nine years old, and I wanted to scout out a good tree to build a new tree-stand in for the upcoming deer season.

My dad and I hunted either on our own property or close to it, as those woods were loaded with deer. We usually hunted in trees from little wooden stands we built on a good strong branch right where it met the main part of the tree, ideally about fifteen feet off the ground. It could be a little higher or lower. The height of the stand really depended on the tree.

We stocked our freezer for the whole year, every year, with venison. Deer meat is the best meat in the world if it's cooked right, and my mom was a great cook. I remember my dad, a religious man, telling me that we only kill what we eat, and to *never let an animal suffer*.

"If you wound a deer, get out of your tree-stand and go shoot it in the head."

I never forgot that. Anyway, if I found a good new tree for a stand, I'd bring my dad back later and show him. Queenie was already drinking out of the stream, which she had reached a little ahead of me. I was thirsty too and got down next to her, cupped my hands and drank like I was dying of thirst. That water was so clean, clear, cold and pure I could never get enough of it. I sat down to take a rest and watch the stream for a while and Queenie, as usual, wanted to curl up on my lap. She was a little tired too.

Most beagles have a tendency to run off and chase rabbits or deer while you are in the woods with them, but not my Queenie. She always stayed right with me or very close by, no matter where we were. After about fifteen minutes, I scratched her head and petted her.

"Let's go Queenie," I say. "Help me find a good tree, girl."

Queenie took another drink as we crossed the stream on some rocks. There was a clump of trees about a hundred yards through the woods of mostly pine and oak trees to the west that I wanted to check out. I'd seen a pretty decent-looking sturdy old oak tree there about a month earlier. I wanted to look at the tree and surrounding area one more time, now that some of the leaves had dropped, before I brought my dad back to see it. I had to use the Buck knife he gave me to cut through some brush before we reached and crossed a small meadow, which leaned up against the piece of woods I wanted to inspect.

We walked into the woods about fifty feet and there was the tree. It was close to a deer-run, which is a path through the woods used by deer on a regular basis. I studied it for a while and saw the perfect branch for a stand to be built. I estimated it to be about twelve or thirteen feet up. Dad would like this.

I was always trying to please my father.

I sat down at the base of the tree and started whittling a little chunk of wood I'd just picked up. Queenie lay down next to me with her chin across my ankles and her eyes closed. After a few peaceful moments, I could feel her body stiffen. She stood up and got in front of me, staring into the woods.

For an instant, she reminded me of a proper English guard dog on a manicured castle lawn. I'd seen that in a movie once. Not like her at all. Queenie was always happy and easy going. Now she was growling. Something was wrong. I could taste it on the back of my tongue. I suddenly felt dizzyingly queasy. Queenie saw them first, then I heard them crashing through the brush.

At first I thought, or was hoping, it was a couple of deer coming through, and how good a spot for the new tree-stand I must have chosen.

Deer already, yeah!

But they weren't deer. The four coyotes looked like mangy cruise missiles flying low to the ground through the scrub pine and brush, their guidance systems locked in on Queenie and I like a laser beam.

Queenie showed her teeth, growling deeper now. A life-and-death growl I'd never heard before. My Buck knife was already out of its leather sheath, since I'd been whittling.

Within seconds the lead coyote was about ten feet away, and I was beyond scared. I couldn't even scream. No time to climb a tree, and I couldn't leave Queenie on the ground alone even if there was a quickly climbable tree nearby. I froze, ready to do battle, crying, a warrior's cry, I was petrified, but had no other choice.

Something changed inside of me. Innocence lost forever. Damn sad, really. We could never out run them. Impossible. They were on us! If they were human, they would have been heathens. Just when I thought the first coyote was gonna pounce on me, and probably go for my neck, I realized it was Queenie he was after. Seldom, if ever, do coyotes attack humans, but a small dog like Queenie they saw as a feast to be torn apart and eaten alive.

The first one grabbed her around the throat, and started shaking her. I stabbed him in the back near the spinal cord, and he let go, whipped his head around and bit me on the left forearm. As he went back to Queenie, like a savage, I stabbed him again, this time a direct hit on the spine. He staggered and fell over, still alive, still snarling, but paralyzed on the ground only a few feet away. Queenie was hurt but still alive when the next three reached her. She yelped and cried and tried to fight, but they were tearing her to pieces. One of the son-of-a-bitches ripped her right ear off and chewed it a few times before swallowing it. I flew into a rage born out of pure hatred. I just started stabbing, and stabbing and stabbing. I got one in the eye, but he still wouldn't stop ripping the meat off of Queenie. I sheathed my knife and picked up a stick about the size of my little league baseball bat and started bashing them in the head. One took a split second to snap his head back and bite me on the right leg; then straight back to Queenie, who was dying right in front of my eyes in the most horrible way. Her yelp was a death scream.

Was this a nightmare?

My stick broke so I pulled my knife out again. I had stabbed the demons for what seemed like a hundred times, over and over, but it didn't faze them at all. Their adrenaline must have been pumping as hard as mine. I learned later that it might have explained their high tolerance for pain. They were basically in a feeding frenzy. I finally fell to the ground, too exhausted to move. I lay face-to-face with Queenie in the battlefield of dirt and newly-fallen oak leaves and pine needles, only inches away from each other, eye-to-eye, as we often laid in happier times, yet now, barely able to see her through the blood, sweat, tears and sand in my eyes and in hers.

To this day, I don't know why the beasts retreated. Maybe because they'd eaten enough of my Queenie's body to satisfy their appetite. Maybe they heard something in the woods that spooked them or were finally getting tired of being stabbed and clubbed. The three coyotes took off through the underbrush as swiftly as they had descended upon Queenie and me.

71

Before they left, as Queenie and I lay there frozen in shock, looking into each other's eyes, the last coyote took a brief, evil moment as he left the macabre scene to rip Queenie's left eye out of her head and eat it.

God, no! I had no more tears to cry and no energy to shed them. Queenie was breathing heavy and was uttering a gurgling sound with each breath. She couldn't move. At first, I refused to believe my Queenie would die. Not now, not today, not this way. I reached over to touch her and my hand sunk into a mushy hole and I could feel her intestines.

Never let an animal suffer.

She lay still, and I could hear a faint whine behind the gurgles of breath.

Never let an animal suffer.

I started crawling, knife still in my hand, reached and stabbed the paralyzed coyote in the heart and then slit his throat. I found the strength to stand up and staggered back over to Queenie.

"Goodbye girl." I said. "I... I love you. See you in heaven."

Breathless.

"I know I will, because we've already been to, to... hell, girl. Today. Together."

Crying again, now.

I then dropped down on my knees behind her, held my bloody Buck knife high over my head with both hands and my deafening, animalistic scream, a primal scream, echoed through the woods like a werewolf's deadly howl as I plunged the blade through Queenie's heart. After a minute or two or an *eternity*, she was still breathing, so then I stabbed her through the brain.

Dead.

Finally – dead. My body and soul shook, my heart was pounding against my sternum, trying to explode. A volcano was erupting in my soul. The world blurred and a thunderous lion's roar could be heard across the universe.

My universe.

From inside *my* head – the roar of the lion. I had never heard it before. I never wanted to hear it again. Yet I was destined to. I passed out in the dirt next to Queenie. That was the day I lost my mind.

I woke up at least an hour later, because the sand, blood and tears had dried on my face. At first I didn't know where I was. Then I realized I was holding Queenie, watching the flies buzzing in and out of the holes where her stomach, ear and left eye used to be. *Then Bam!* Reality struck. I rolled over onto my back and saw a turkey vulture, which is a large scavenger with a red head that feeds on carrion, staring down at Queenie and me from the branch of an oak tree directly above us. For an instant he reminded me of a gargoyle perched on the ledge of a crumbling, vile, ancient ruin. Something I'd seen in a book or a movie or a nightmare.

I got to my feet and took my long sleeve flannel shirt off, and used it to swat the flies away from Queenie. I threw stones at the turkey vulture, almost hitting it before it flew away. I shouted at the winging demon bird.

"I ain't dead yet, fucker, and you ain't gettin' none of Queenie!"

Weeping once more, this time, tears of fury and hatred. My shirt was still dripping a little with blood though most had already dried. I stopped swatting the flies and decided to wrap Queenie up inside my now blood-red shirt that had just witnessed so much evil, and carry Queenie's body home in it. I already knew where I was gonna bury her – right under my bedroom window.

I remembered reading about how the Indians were forced to walk from the southeastern United States to Oklahoma – *The Trail Of Tears*. I wondered if they felt as bad as I did right then on my own trail of tears.

My dad was on the front porch when he saw Queenie and me come out of the woods and into our field, which was really our front yard. He called to my mom who was in the kitchen, and they both ran out just in time to catch me as I collapsed from physical and emotional debilitation. My dad carried me to my bed, while my mom called the doctor and the sheriff.

When I finally opened my eyes, I was cleaned up with bandages on my left arm and right leg, where the coyotes had bitten me. I could hear voices coming from the kitchen, and it sounded like serious talk. I called out for my dad who came in with a heavy look on his face.

Up until now, I hadn't even had a chance to tell him what went on out there in the woods. When he sat down on the edge of the bed and I told him everything that happened, for the first time in my life, I had the feeling he didn't believe me – another crushing blow on this brutal day of unspeakable terror and despair.

He looked down at the floor.

"Now, tell me again," he said, "why you killed Queenie."

So, I did. I told my dad everything – the God's honest truth.

He slapped his hands down on his knees and stood up.

"The doctor says you'll be fine," he said. "You've got a total of thirteen stitches, and he gave you a tetanus and rabies shot just in case Queenie was rabid."

What?

"The sheriff is here to talk to you. He'll be right in, Raven. Tell him the truth."

Oh my God, I hated the sheriff! Even at the age of eleven, I knew he was a bully and just plain mean and nasty. He ruled our county like a fuckin' king. King pig slop. I could hear his heavy footsteps. The fat bastard was trudging down the hallway to my bedroom. What the hell could he want?

Sheriff Brian Vaughn West scared me, but here he was. He came in without even knocking.

Cocky prick. I tried to pretend that I had drifted off to sleep again, but he kicked my bed.

"So Raven," he said, "what's this little bullshit story about coyotes in my county? You know we killed or chased off every damn one of those deer-killin' bastards. Now son, you know there ain't no coyotes left in this county, don't you?"

I ignored him, and kept silent.

He rattled on.

"Raven, did you know it was against the law to lie to a sheriff? Now, tell me, why did your little mutt bite you? Sounds a little satanic to me. The way I see it, you took Queenie out there to kill her in some sort of ritual. That's why she bit you – a cult thing. That's against the law too, ya know, boy. Raven, are you in a cult?"

If I had my knife I would have stabbed him in the neck. But I just lay there, still not saying a word.

Then Sheriff B.V. West said, "My deputies are digging up your dog right now and having her tested for rabies and inspecting the body to see if the way you killed her jibes with what we know about animal sacrifices that some of these satanic cults are carrying out in other parts of the state. Then she'll be cremated."

A knock came at my bedroom door and one of the sheriff's deputies came in, dirt caked on his feet and hands.

"The dog is loaded up, sheriff. The vet knows we're on our way."

I couldn't scream, I couldn't move. There was so much hate inside me for the sheriff and deputy, so much pain for Queenie that I passed out again. I think my body shut down to save itself. My last thoughts before blackness were fuzzy, but intense.

Where did my dad bury Queenie? I will kill the sheriff someday. Queenie would be cremated! You motherfucker. How can this be...? Then sleep thankfully overtook me.

I had a dream, a nightmare, that my dad had dug dozens of holes all around our yard for Queenie's grave, and the sheriff had went around and covered them all up; so I started digging the holes up again, looking for Queenie. Finally there was only one hole left – right outside my bedroom window. When I had dug down about a foot the sheriff exploded out of the hole and started laughing at me. I then cut his head off with the blade of my shovel; and a coyote came out of the same grave, and just like Queenie, bit the sheriff's left eye out of his lifeless head and then ran off into the woods. Then I put the sheriff's head in the sandy tomb and covered it up with dirt and then pissed on it. I woke up and in that brief cosmic moment when we realize that whatever, only a moment ago, we had just assumed to be true, was but a merciless dream.

Queenie *was* dead. I cried. Staring at the black ceiling for a few minutes, I decided to grab my flashlight and sneak outside to see just where Queenie was *really* buried by my dad before the deputy dug her up. I walked down the hall and through the kitchen, where I noticed on the lighted kitchen clock that it was 3 a.m. I must have slept about ten hours. Wow, it didn't seem that long.

Once out the back door, I walked to my right and turned at the corner of the house heading for my bedroom window. The grave was not there. I remembered. I never got the chance to ask my dad to bury her there. I was going to, but I collapsed unconscious in the yard before I could talk to him.

I walked around some more, and eventually found Queenie's empty tomb about forty feet behind the swing set, which was located about twenty-five feet outside the kitchen door. I knelt down and picked up two handfuls of dirt from the bottom of the hole and looked up at the stars. I prayed for Queenie, and vowed once again that I would eventually kill Sheriff B.V. West.

I went back to bed not the same nice, well-mannered and - as many people used to describe me - timid eleven-year-old country boy. I had changed. My warm heart was now stone cold. My soul became quietly vicious and depraved. I had heard the lion and knew he would return.

It was this enigmatic, unbearable truth that would forever change my life. Basically, I had been transformed from a happy-go-lucky boy and his dog, to a hateful recluse. After this day, I kept to myself and did nothing but play my guitar, which I hadn't touched since I got it as a present last Christmas, and worry about the lion. He was always there, just sleeping. The sheriff was supposed to come back this afternoon – exactly two weeks after Queenie died.

Come on cocksucker, I'm ready for you!

I could see the Sheriff's car, followed by the deputy's, coming up the driveway from my bedroom window. I locked my door and went back to playing my guitar, shutting the two cars and the bastards inside of them out of my mind. But I knew they would want to see me. I had a bad feeling. My dad tried the door then knocked loudly.

77

"Raven, let me in. The sheriff is here. He wants to talk to you."

"Tell him I'll be right out," I shouted. "See you in the kitchen. I don't want that asshole in my bedroom."

My dad was silent, no doubt shocked at my attitude and language. I heard him walk back to the kitchen.

Indeed, *I had changed.*

When I got out to the kitchen, the big bad Sheriff wore a devilish grin, and his blubbery belly was hanging over his belt. I wanted to shove his badge and his hat up his ass. He was standing in the doorway reading over a piece of paper with my dad. My mom was sitting at the table crying into a tissue.

Oh fuck, I'm thinking, *what the hell is this all about?*

I didn't even talk to my mom. My eyes were fixed on the sheriff, and when he looked at me, I thought I saw a flicker of fear, just for moment in those evil, shit-brown, beady eyes.

Then the sheriff tossed the paper that he and my dad had been discussing on the table.

"Well, Raven," he said, "seems the vet determined that you killed that mangy, no huntin' dog of yours. 'Cause of death' appears to be knife wounds and mutilation. Seeing here that you also disemboweled the animal leads me to believe my first hunch was right, boy. You killed the bitch as a sacrifice, some sort of satanic thing.

Since my county don't have any cults, *or* coyotes, we figure you probably found out how to *properly* kill your dog, and all this other cult crap, out of a magazine or something. So, your dad and I here have come up with two options. You can be admitted to the county mental health facility for observation, and they may decide to keep you there, or your dad can pay a fine to the county, plus cover expenses for the man-hours wasted by my deputy in this case."

All eyes were upon me.

Mine were seared into the sheriff's. I broke the silence.

"I can prove what happened. I told you from the very beginning I can take you to the dead coyote. But there's nothing left of it now and you damn well know it, you fat fuckin' crook!" He didn't like what I said and took a step toward me.

Once again, I wanted so badly to stab him in the neck and chew his beady eyes out. I was hoping that my new companion, the lion, would not roar. If he did, the sheriff would die right here in the kitchen, in front of my parents. I had a butcher knife hidden in the back of my pants, the blade cold against the small of my back and crack of my ass. He didn't come any closer.

Sixth sense?

But he warned me.

"Boy, not another word about coyotes or you'll be sittin' your ass in a padded cell."

He shook my dad's hand and started to leave. The deal was done. The bastard had just shaken my dad down for a few hundred bucks.

"Where's Queenie?" I asked as he was leaving.

He turned his ugly head and laughed.

"Smoke and dust, boy," he mocked. "Smoke and dust."

I didn't say a word, but inside I knew that the sheriff had just signed his own death warrant. I would kill him some day.

7

Life Changes

Although my outlook on life as well as my personality had changed forever, it would be another thirty years or so before the lion roared in my skull again. It came without warning the day I ice-picked my factory boss, Morgan Lange – my first kill.

Once I had made enough money on my book *Standing on the Edge of Forever*, as well as a substantial amount on some of the songs I had written, I had Joe Lofton arrange a secret session with a famous head shrinker out in L.A. I needed some answers.

The Appointment

I tell the shrink, Dr. Rothstein, the entire truth, except for my true identity, from Queenie and the first roar of the lion up to the present, murders and all.

The guy is understanding and friendly. We like each other right off the bat. That's cool. The little bald guy in the white jacket explains to me that I am suffering from a delayed case of post traumatic stress disorder, which manifests itself into the roar of a lion inside my brain. That, in turn, then tells me that I must kill to avenge Queenie.

The doc suggests medication, which I refuse. I prefer to medicate myself, as you know – just *our little secret.*

I also ask him about my hatred for B.V. West, my pen-name and invisible hated enemy. Hell, he doesn't even exist.

He explains that I am jealous of B.V. West and have transformed him in my mind into a real person who takes all the credit for "your work, your success."

"Sir," he continues, "I recognize from our discussion that you are no doubt a brilliant man, and there is no doubt you are suffering from delayed PTSD.

"Now, PTSD is an all too common disorder, but rarely manifests itself in this way. May I add that I am fascinated by all of this? Since we've been comfortably honest with each other so far, may I add that I am also frightened of you?"

I grin, and glare into his intelligent blue eyes.

"You should be," I say.

Perhaps I can handle things like the lion's roar better now. But down deep inside, I know this will never end until "Sheriff Shake Down" is tortured and killed. At the end of our nearly two-hour meeting, I hand him $10,000 in cash, with a warning.

"Yo, Doc, thanks for everything. At least now I understand why the lion roars and why I hate B.V. West. And by the way, if you ever utter a word about this friendly little get-together, you will be dead, and I will eat your left eye."

He nods, and says nothing.

We shake hands.

I have my hand on the doorknob, when I remember that I have one more question for the good doctor.

"Hey doc," I ask, looking into his nervous eyes, "how come when the lion roars, I seem to acquire the strength, quickness and night vision of a *real* lion?"

He instantly replies, but in an ominous tone.

"Because the mind is more powerful than the flesh, my friend. Also, you were probably frightened by a lion at some point in your childhood."

I stop in mid-step. Damn, what is he - a mind-reader as well as a psychiatrist? It is true I became petrified and hysterical at The Philadelphia Zoo with my parents when I was about five or six years old when I, always curious, inadvertently got too close to the lion's den. A huge male lion suddenly leaped toward me and roared, and I just lost it. That episode scared the hell out of my parents. They thought I was mentally unbalanced for a while after that, because I had nightmares about the lion and would wake up screaming in the middle of the night. I thought I'd outgrown that. I'm starting to realize that there are few things in life that we ever really outgrow. I leave the good doctor's office. That is enough for me.

I catch a cab to the airport, and fly back to Miami. Appointment over.

The Tedesco Twins (Miami)

By the time I hit the street I am devising a plan for the two slimy bastards who had moved down here from New York City about four years ago. The Tedesco twins, known on the street as T1 and T2 are identical twins, impossible to tell apart except for the long, painful-looking scar which was burned into T1's cheek up in New York City. He deserved it, from what I find out later from Joe Lofton, and it looks like the number "1." Hence, T1.

Damn, a fuckin' hooker, probably one of the twins' whores, just offers me a blow job for $25, right in the middle of articulating my kill plan. I give her a hundred bucks and tell her to go fuck herself. I think about killing her, but don't have time. I am on a mission. She looks so street-dirty I wouldn't touch her with *Art's* dick. Get it? Hey, ya gotta keep a sense of humor.

All right, all right. Back in the day, the Tedesco twins had made a pile of money as models in New York and later, out in L.A. They were in every magazine you could imagine, a bunch of commercials, TV shows and a few movies. I got sick of seeing them. In the advertising and entertainment business there has always been a huge demand for identical twins, especially if they were so pretty that they looked like a couple of chicks with no tits. Their straight black hair was always combed perfectly back. They stood about six feet tall and weighed roughly one hundred sixty pounds.

Now, they are still in model shape, except for T1's nasty scar, and soon to be dead. Hey, maybe somebody will turn them into mannequins and make some more money on them. Nah, not after I get finished with these two scum bags. They'll probably look more like something you would find hanging in a meat locker. For the first time in my life, the roar of the lion feels good, and the sight of his teeth are an inspiration. We are comrades tonight. I am deep into Tedesco territory now.

The twins control the drug and prostitution business in a roughly five-square-block area and occasionally would pull shit like they did with Art tonight, just to remind their competition and customers who is in charge. They had run the same sort of operation in New York before realizing that Miami is fertile ground, and the weather is warm year-round. Oh yeah, and T1's encounter with a small, but red-hot branding iron, which was made from heating up a butter knife on an electric stove top, also helped in their decision to head south. Besides, the scar on T1's cheek put the fire out on their acting and modeling careers.

What a shame.

So, here they are. After investing most of their money in the stock market and real estate, the rest went into the lucrative, but dangerous world of drugs, prostitution, mutilation and murder. The Tedesco twins find their excitement and their profits there.

Anyway, my plan is coming together. Good thing, too because I am only a block away from their condo. I have been there many times before to cop weed and roxies. They know nothing about me except that I am homeless, a good-paying customer and go by the name "Fish." They trust me and know I keep my paltry belongings as well as my wallet in my ever-present black briefcase. They also think I'm a little crazy in the head and nobody to piss off, so we always make our transactions quick, and they get me the hell out of their place. Very nice place, I might add. In other words, I had them perfectly bull-shitted.

Okay, I'm there now – on their front steps. I push the intercom button.

"Yeah, talk to me." one of them says. I think it is T1, because when his face got sizzled in New York, it destroyed his maxillary nerve, which runs inside the cheek, so he talks a little funny.

"Fish." I say.

"Okay," T1 says, "make it quick, Fish."

On the other side of the door, a big black dude named "Monster," who I have grown to like, opens the door as always. Monster is part bodyguard and part doorman for the twins. I assume he is packing something, probably a Glock. As he opens the door, I smoothly grab mine out of my briefcase in those two seconds when he couldn't see me through the peephole.

The door opens.

"Sup, Fish," Monster says, "how ya been? The streets treatin' you okay?"

Without a word, I quickly put a bullet through Monster's left eye.

Thank God for silencers.

It blows the back right side of his brains out.

Kill Number five.

I break his fall so the boys upstairs won't hear his 330-pound thud when the big boy falls.

Step one. Complete, quick and successful – wrong place, wrong time and wrong guy for poor Monster.

Some people call me a sweetheart. Some will never have the chance to say I'm not; because they'll be dead.

Don't forget Sheriff Evil.

I haven't. Stick with me on this. And oh yeah, you too, Mr. B.V. West, *both of you*, go fuck yourselves. These boys are mine. Wish I had more time.

I'm walking up the carpeted steps toward the heavy wooden door with the fancy brass knocker at the top of the stairs. The lighting is subtle and comforting on the stairway, I guess preparing guests for the gaudy, in my opinion, but rich decoration of their expensive condo.

Lydia doesn't even know I have left, and she sure as hell isn't gonna find out why. I will tell Art, though, when the time is right. This has to be *fast* – *a*nd once again as bloodless on my part, but not theirs – as possible.

Knock-knock. Who's there? Fish. Fish who? The fish that's gonna kill you. My apologies – just another impromptu joke. As usual, Henny would get it, especially because it was spur-of-the-moment with some deadly drama just seconds away. Oh My God, I really wish you could hear the lion now! He is roaring so loud I can't think. *Concentrate, Raven. We (my lion and I) are ready.*

T2 opens the door, annoyed, because I never spend a lot of money at one time. But I'm regular. T1 walks in from the kitchen and says, "Sup, fish, the usual?"

"Yeah," I say, "thanks, guys."

The "usual" was five 30 mg. roxies for $155. I reach into my briefcase, as I always did, but instead of pulling out my wallet, with my left hand I toss Art's ear on the floor between them. With my right hand, I point my Glock in both their faces. Standing about four feet away, I move it slowly, from one to the other. Seeing the silencer makes them realize that I ain't fuckin' around.

They freeze.

I smile.

"Make one goddamn sound," I say, "and you die right here like Monster just did down there."

My eyes move to the door.

"He's already in Heaven, but you cocksuckers just met your messenger from Hell. Me. Ya know guys, you really should invest in a video camera in that stairway. Damn, always a slip-up somewhere along the line, isn't there?"

I reach down into my briefcase and pull out my filet knife. The blade is ten inches long and sharp as a fuckin' razor. I take good care of my tools.

T1 freaks, so I shoot him in the face. I didn't like looking at that burn scar anyway. Don't like seeing his brains on the coffee table, leather sofa, walls and ceiling either. But that was the lesser of two evils.

Kill number six.

A wet spot starts to spread on the front of T2's pants. Damn, he's pissing himself! He falls down on his knees and whispers a prayer for his life. Looks like a little cringing cowardly, sleaze ball – which he is.

Told ya they were pussies without tits.

I laugh, look at my watch and hand him the filet knife. Then I point my Glock at his left temple.

"Slice your dago ears off." I say.

He looks up.

"Please, *please,* Fish," he ekes out. "I'll pay you... *anything!*" Tears start pouring out.

I ignore him.

"*Now, SLICE* if you wanna live. Now, you fuckin' piece of New York City shit! I'm on a time-line here and I'd rather kill you anyway."

I shoot him down through the top of his right bended thigh. I count on the bullet not penetrating the floor to the ceiling below, because it had to travel through his thigh bone as well as his calf muscle and shin bone. I'm right. The bullet doesn't disturb the neighbors downstairs. Lucky for them, because the lion is tearing my brains apart with blood-curdling roars of death and hatred, and they could be next. Good night to stay the hell out of Raven's path.

T2 is yelping out in pain and pleading for his pathetic life.

I can't waste much more time, so I stand behind him and tell him to close his eyes and stop fuckin' sobbing.

"You make me sick, you cockroach."

He is shaking like a freezing man in the wilderness.

"Dude," I say. "Do it now, slice them off or you are D-E-A-D." I spell it out. "Just like T1. Only worse than dead. I'm gonna *torture* you first, now grow some balls – sorry Art – and slice. *NOW.*"

Damn if he doesn't do it! He slices off his left ear, so I take the knife to help speed things along and cut off the other one for him. Then I slice T1's ears off and lay all five ears in a row in front of the handmade mahogany china closet. Remember, the fifth ear is Art's.

T2 is a bloody mess and in total paralyzing shock, so I ice-pick him three times in the brain. The same way Joseph Stalin had Leon Trotsky assassinated after ousting him from power in Russia. Trotsky was killed in Mexico where he had been exiled by Stalin.

Number seven.

Earlier, I had plans of binding the twins together face-to-face in a death embrace with the wire ties or cables ties, or whatever they're called, which I had placed in my brief case. Then I would force one to kill the other with their mouths and teeth, while bashing their heads together. That is, after lying to them that the winner would live. There is no honor among thieves – even brothers. But I don't have time for that much fun. Not tonight, anyway. The whole ordeal took only about twenty minutes.

I victoriously gobble down both their left eyes. I am soaked with blood. Damn! I grab a Corona out of their kitchen and take a quick shower in their master bathroom.

Their corpses aren't far from the door.

I am prepared, as always, with fresh clothes and towels, and a hot shower will speed up my cleaning process. Lydia will probably be a little flustered and pissed that I left the house without a word. As we speak I am concocting a viable story for my Mermaid. Any ideas? Even Raven April can use some help sometimes. Never mind. *Got it!*

I grab a few roxies, about ten, that are in the open little safe that is next to T1's favorite chair. At least that's where he always is whenever I'm up here. Usually, he promptly opens the little safe and grabs me my dope, and I leave. But it doesn't turn out like that tonight for those two little alley rats. They're already starting to stink. I've gotta get the hell out of here.

Okay, here's my plan. I'll tell Lydia that I went out to cop roxies for Art, who would be in pain when he finally wakes up and no doubt will be needing them. I'd also give her a couple. She'll like that.

Finally the lion stops roaring, satisfied for now and justified. For the first time, as perhaps we always were, we have become "one." A strange transmutation has taken place. I am the lion and the lion is me. At the bottom of the stairs as I step over Monster, I notice the tough bastard is still breathing. Unreal. I respect that. So I put a bullet through his right eye and walk out. *Never let an animal suffer. Or a Monster.* I felt bad about Monster. I will send his family an anonymous check. The least I can do. A sweetheart all the way – yeah, that's me. So was Monster.

I get the hell out in the street quickly and start walking fast. I just wreaked hell on three people, and my heart is still pounding hard against my breast bone. Uh oh, here comes that pain-in-the-ass whore again.

This will be the second time she's seen me tonight. I've got to kill her. She is under a street lamp that I am approaching.

"Hey Miss Dream-Come-True" I say casually, "offer still stand? I was in a hurry earlier, but I've got some free time now." It is obvious that she is high on heroin and booze, but I still can't take any chances on her remembering my face if she is ever questioned about the murders by the police.

"Sure baby," she slurs, "my place is two minutes away. Blow job or the whole deal?"

I smile and grab my crotch.

"I'm dyin' for a blow job," I say. "There's another hundred in it for ya, Angel Face. I've had a good night."

Grinning, she says, "Gee, you're a real sweetheart."

There goes that sweetheart thing again. If she only knew.

She grabs my hand.

"Let's go," she says simply. "My name is Ginger, what's yours?"

I ignore the question.

Ginger is right; in less than two minutes we are in her small, first-floor apartment, which, amazingly, looks quite clean and tidy.

I take a quick look around, and decide to garrote her with the B-string of my favorite electric guitar.

"A Musical Kill." Hey, cool title for a movie or maybe my next book, although I've already named it. It's called *Alien Island*. I'll start on that book once the one I'm working on now is complete – haven't titled that one yet.

Anyway, I ask her if she has a beer; and when she turns toward the fridge, all smiles and perky, bingo! The thin metal B-string instantly cuts through her windpipe, and she is dead in a few minutes – struggling only for a moment, her eyes bulging in surprise and terror.

I am careful not to sever either of her jugular veins, which would have bloodied me, and I'm not about to take a shower at two strange places in one night. I must say, however, she is stronger than I thought, and ferociously but briefly fights hard to live, legs kicking and all that.

I whisper a prayer: "Lord, take her home."

What little blood I do get on me, I easily take care of with some of the supplies I keep in my briefcase and Ginger's paper towels.

I do not eat her eye. She's a female, like Queenie. As most people know, I am a sadistic, sick killer as well as a very sensitive and caring human being, *a true to life sweetheart*. Hey, is there anything you don't know about me yet? You actually know very little. I take her up on that beer, another Corona, and leave. Nothing quite like drinking with a corpse. I toast to her body.

"Cheers, Ginger."

Kill Number eight, in case you're keeping count.

One of the questions I'll bet you are asking yourself is why I don't kill my ultimate target, Sheriff Dead-Man-Walking *now*, and just get it over with. You know I can. Torture included. Kill him, and make the lion stop roaring, right?

Well, since we've gotten to know each other "fairly" well, I'll tell you. I will expose my soul, but only to you. I have not killed Sheriff Brian Vaughn West yet because I am petrified that when I do, the lion will continue to roar. And then what? See my dilemma? The timing has got to be perfect, the journey, precise. I'm trying to work those details out now. But how? I'm open to ideas. A wise man is always open to suggestions.

I have always felt that I would *know* when the time was right. Like an epiphany. I am still waiting for that moment. But for now, Raven April, writer, killer, musician (and don't forget, *sweetheart*) must survive with the lion's roar as my master. How many more kills will he demand of me?

I didn't mind killing The Tedesco twins, but I really feel bad about Monster and the prostitute with the well-kept little apartment. Oh well. Spilled milk, water under the bridge of blood. I'm home now, just walking into the house through the door in the garage which opens into the kitchen and grabbing a cold beer. *Heineken, finally.* Corona sucks. Just give me a minute – hold on, okay? Then we'll check on Art and Lydia.

Personal Stuff

If it seems like I say my own name a lot, it's because I do. I like it, but as a kid I kind of hated having such a weird first name. I just wanted to be a "Billy" or a "Nick" – a common name like everybody else.

But the day before I was born my mother was looking out the living room window onto the front yard and saw a Raven land in her favorite tree, a leafless, huge Norway maple. It was February second. So she calls my dad in from the kitchen to show him the bird.

"We are going to have a boy," she says confidently, "and his name will be Raven." In those days you had to wait until your baby was born to find out the sex.

My dad looked out the window at the big black bird until it flew off; then he kissed my mom.

"Raven it is," he said.

As I mentioned earlier, my parents were quite religious, and I think they took the bird as some kind of sign from above. I know my mom did.

"Oh yes," she then added," he will be born tomorrow."

Which I was.

I really miss my mom and dad. I hope they made it to heaven. I'm pretty sure they did. They had a helluva lot better chance than I do of getting there.

"Hey Henny, hey Monster, if you guys are in heaven, please say hi to my parents? Thanks."

My next book, *Alien Island* will probably end up being about 300 pages long, each one gripping the throat of the reader with fear and surprise. Unable to put down. Believe me on that. Ya know, I'm really grateful that the man upstairs gave me so much talent, and I say that with great humility. I also appreciate my obsession with danger and dark, treacherous streets – my desire for peril and the escape from it. Don't ask me to explain it, because I can't interpret what I do not understand. I can tell you however, that I, Raven April, writer and murderer have learned that for every gift or stroke of luck, there is a price. Mine is the roar of the lion. What is yours? If you don't mind, I'd like to show you a short poem I wrote about a year after Queenie died and was cremated instead of being buried under my bedroom window. My sixth grade teacher asked me and my parents if she could show the poem around.

"Sure, why not?" we said. Well, the poem got published and won an award. I got a few bucks and a wooden plaque. Oh boy! Here it is:

The Dive

Some men are forever
Some men are for never
Existing somewhere
Near the middle
Between everything and nothing,

Trudging through life
Weary plow mules
Under the whip
Oblivious to ecstasy
Strangers to emaciation,

Never to glow
Never to scar
No thread of adventure, never
Diving into the stars…

Not bad for a kid, I suppose. Hope everyone likes it. My mom and dad sure did. They were proud as hell.

When the plaque was delivered to the house, my parents had my Aunt Sarah, the photographer of the family, come over and take pictures of it, a couple of shots with me and my plaque and a couple with my parents and me with the plaque. Then Aunt Sarah asked my dad to take one of her and me with the damn plaque.

I was gettin' sick of that fuckin' plaque, man. I was really getting into photography myself at that time, as well as music and writing songs. It was more fun than poetry for me at that nutty point of my life.

But just a few years ago, right after I got the first big check for my book, *Standing...*, I took off on vacation for three months in Tahiti, which Joe Lofton had set up for me, and wrote a book of poetry there called, *Scalpel*. I'll let you read it sometime. There are about fifty or sixty rather short poems in it. Blow your friggin' mind, *really*. Ya know, sometimes the man makes the moment, and sometimes the moment makes the man. And being in Tahiti sure helped make this man *and* the moments. I swear, you've never read a book of poetry like, *Scalpel*.

8

FBI Head Quarters. Quantico, Va.

Agent Rick Sansom walks into the small ViCap office and finds his boss, Frank Harding, sitting there. Harding is a big man with dark wavy hair and bushy eyebrows. Neither handsome nor repulsive, he is imposing, however, both in size and power.

He is sitting at Rick's desk looking down at the black face of his new Movado wristwatch made in Italy. His mother was Italian. He isn't smiling. It is 7:06 am.

Rick thought, *oh shit*, as Agent Debbie Errickson, with whom he shares the office, watches silently.

She is dressed all in pink today except for her white nurses' shoes. She hands him a cup of coffee.

"It's okay," she whispers, so that Harding can't hear her. "I covered your ass."

"Good morning sir," Rick says, in a confident, business-like voice. "Good to see you. What's up?"

The momentary silence is deafening to Rick, once again late for work. This time caught red-handed by the big guy. But Frank Harding says nothing of his tardiness. After that long minute of silence as Harding reads over an email on Rick's computer, he gets right to the point. He peers over his reading glasses at Rick and Debbie and finally, after taking a deep breath and setting his glasses on Rick's desk, begins.

"Okay. Well it looks like the eye-eater has struck again." He pauses. "I call him the 'eye-eater' because forensics has determined that other than his kill at the Ft. Lauderdale Airport, he sucks his victim's left eye out and presumably eats it. At the airport, the victim's eye was gouged out and never found. Last night he hit hard, this time in Miami. And I don't know whether to try and arrest him or shake his hand. He took out the Tedesco twins, one of their bodyguards as well as a prostitute just a couple of blocks from the blood-bath scene in the Tedescos' condo. We think she was also employed by the Twins. And make a note that he did *not* remove either of *her* eyes."

Harding sighs deeply before continuing.

"The Miami Police department has been after these two bastards for over three years. The Tedescos have been implicated in over a dozen murders and mutilations, mostly within a five-to-seven block area near the infamous Overtown section of Miami, but the D.A. could never get enough hard evidence on them to make an arrest and have it stick in court. The eye-eater-killer solved that problem sometime last night. Seems the folks in the condo under the Tedescos called the police around four this morning when the guy got up to take a piss and noticed the ceiling in the hallway was dripping blood on his new carpet. The Miami Police chief is a guy named, Mannie Bastardo. He's an old friend of mine. He informed me about an hour ago that it's the most gruesome crime scene he's ever had the displeasure of investigating, and he's been a cop for twenty-seven years."

Harding stands up and hands Agent Sansom a plane ticket.

"Rick, I want you to go down to Miami. I've informed our two best agents there to pick you up at the airport. You will then head over to city hall and meet with Chief

Bastardo and two of his sharpest detectives. We've got to stop this guy before he kills again.

On top of that, it looks like the cocksucker has thrown us a curveball by not taking the left eye of the prostitute, so keep that in mind – could mean something later. Try and get inside this guy's head. And listen Rick, I've put you in charge of this entire affair while you're down there.

Bastardo is fine with that. Mannie's a good man and an even better cop who just wants to nail this freak-show killer and doesn't care who gets the credit.

Your plane leaves at 11:11 a.m. Go home and pack for at least two days, maybe longer. You'll be briefed on your way from the airport to Mannie's office by the two agents picking you up at Ft. Lauderdale Airport. You're flying in there instead of Miami because I want you to look around the bathroom where the eye-eater hung the guy last week. Start getting a feel for this animal, okay?"

Rick interrupts.

"Sir, how much does the press know about this? We all know how they can fuck up an investigation."

"Nothing yet" Harding replies, "and I want to keep it that way for as long as possible. The only answer to any questions the press asks is 'no comment.' Mannie already knows that and agrees, of course. Now get going Rick, there will be a car at your house at 9:00 sharp."

Harding shakes Rick's hand and wishes him luck, before adding, "And don't be late." He winks a knowing wink at Agent Errickson as he leaves the tiny office for his big office downstairs.

Debbie looks at Rick who can finally settle into his own chair.

Rick looks up, wipes his brow and exhales deeply.

"Whew. Glad he's gone. Did he say anything to you about me being late, Deb?"

She looks at Rick and smiles.

"No, not a word. Besides, I told you I covered your ass. Be careful down there Rick. This guy's a sicko."

Rick finishes his coffee, says thanks to Errickson and leaves hurriedly. He doesn't want to be late for his ride to the airport. If he misses his flight, Harding really *would* be pissed, and rightfully so, Sansom concludes. He whistles softly to himself as he opens the door to his car.

"Miami, here I come."

9

Back At the Mansion

Sometimes I feel like my skull has been split in two with a heavy sharp axe. One half of my brain hates B.V. West, the pretend glory-hound writer, while the other half admires him, *needs* him. Maybe when I torture and perhaps dismember Sheriff Cocksucker they will *both* die, and with them take the roar of my lion to the burning lakes of fire, where Satan will be waiting. I'm praying that sending the Tedesco twins head-first into that red, sizzling body of unholy water will keep the lion at bay, at least for a little while. I'm almost ready to take another magical swim in the ocean and put the final touches on my plan for B.V. West and Sheriff Walking-Dead-Man.

Don't worry Queenie, the time is near.

I will need Joe Lofton as well as Placido to carry out the lion's requested justice. But for right now, I have to go in and help Lydia with Art. Glad I grabbed those roxies from the Tedescos' *palace of gore* before I took my blood-cleansing shower there. I felt like cutting their hearts out before I left. But then I'd have to take another shower so I said "fuck it."

Damn, I'm still feelin' bad about Monster. I think I'm gonna give his wife fifty grand, no, seventy-five. She'll never know where it came from – or why. Time to eat one of those roxies. Only God and Lucifer know what I might find when I get in there. At least I know I won't find Art fucking Lydia.

Sick joke, I know. But like I've been telling you, if you can't laugh in the face of danger or disruption, you're either dead, will be shortly or might as well be already. I find Lydia curled up on the sofa asleep. Damn, she looks exhausted. Well, think about it, she had a big day, wouldn't you say? It's not easy to get a nursing degree in a matter of hours and actually save your first patient's life. On-the-job-training is always the best. Seriously though, isn't she awesome? Glad she's on the un-killable list.

So are you. I know you are. Now to look for my man Art. Lydia probably just left him in the master bedroom. I mean, how could she move him? I peek into the bedroom, and yep, there he is. He's either sleeping like a baby or he's dead. I feel his neck pulse and can tell that he's breathing. I don't know if he's still unconscious or just asleep, really. Well, fuck it for now, I'm grabbin' a Heineken. He ain't dead, but Art's gonna *think* he died and went to heaven when he wakes up. Hell, he's got a king-size bed, a huge private bathroom complete with Jacuzzi, an ocean view, a 52-inch flat screen TV and a great stereo among other expensive amenities. Of course he'd give all that up for a set of balls and a dick. Poor fuckin' guy.

Sorry Art, but this is all I can do for you, buddy.

For some reason I saluted his corpse-still body. When he comes to, I'm gonna give him a roxie, a beer and a pack of cigarettes. We'll smoke a blunt too, and celebrate the Tedescos' slaughter. Lydia can't know about the killings, none of them. Not yet. Maybe never. The house has a silent air-purifying system to take out the cigarette and pot smoke. See, I try to think of everything.

After my second beer, the exhaustion and stress of the day, in addition to a little help from Mr. Roxie, I walk out on the beach, lay down in the sand with my hands behind my head and fall into a rather deep sleep. I can seldom recall my dreams unless they are lucid, but this one I remember well. Perhaps because it was not a dream, but a ghoulish, soulless nightmare sent to me by spirits of the damned themselves. There is no other explanation. It was demonic and every zombie-looking bastard in this 'dream' bore the red glaring eyes of Satan in the flesh. It goes like this. Now listen closely, alright? Thank you...

I am standing in a dark living room, kind of like my great grandmother's living room when I was a kid with musty-smelling furniture, and I feel like I am being smothered. People have died in this room. I am staring at a fragile-looking young man standing about five feet away from me, with a few more children, boys and girls, standing like ghosts behind him against a gray brick fireplace. Hands folded behind their backs. Their blazing red eyes are like charcoal cinders. I am also young, about thirteen, in this all-encompassing hell-world-nightmare. The slender boy with wispy dirty blonde hair and I are both very still and staring at each other when he speaks these scary, uncanny words to me:

"Ever since I was very, very young, every time I saw like maybe two, three, four or five people standing together in a little group, people I knew mostly, like you Raven, I would try to decide – or should I say guess, or figure out –which one would die first, and sometimes in what manner. I would either write it down and date it, right then and there, pretending I was jotting down a poem or song lyric, which everyone knew I often did, or make a mental note and inscribe it into my "Book Of Death" upon the dark, maddening return to my lair. Yes, my lair. Yet I am human.

"Raven, sadly you were in one of those little groups. Yes, you. So therefore, and I am truly, TRULY sorry for

101

this. I do NOT want to tell you this, but I must, you are – and I am never, ever wrong – Doomed! I haven't the heart to tell you how your end will come, Raven. Goodbye."

After the young man speaks, behind him in what seems like a slow-motion cartoon, one-by-one the ghost children shape shift into roaring, full-grown male lions. The young man with the wispy hair smiles just before they pounce on him, tearing him into little shreds while eating him alive…

Thinking back on this dream now, I know I should be petrified with fear. But I am in a dream state and just accept his words in total frigid silence. I never move.

I awaken with a start. Now I am scared…

I try to shake off my nightmare by diving into the ocean. But all I can see are the red eyes of doom. I swim straight out, but not very far, and quickly get caught in a riptide. Fighting it and swimming back through the invisible undercurrent to shore would have been suicide, even for me, Raven April, writer, killer, swimmer, sweetheart.

So, I let the strong, invisible current carry me about 200 yards south, around forty to fifty yards out at sea. At that point I can swim back to shore easily and then walk up the beach to the house.

I need a beer and maybe another roxie. I'll give one to Lydia, one to Art and keep the others for myself. I'm *not* sneaky, hell, I can keep them *all* for myself if I want to, but the roxies are part of the story I'm gonna lay on Lydia as to why I slithered out silently a couple of hours ago. No need to mention the Tedescos now, is there? Yeah, I guess I am sneaky when I have to be. So are you. Admit it.

I jog the last thirty yards or so up the beach and enter the house as quietly as I had left through the open sliding glass door. The lights are dim, but I can make out the silhouette of a large man – obviously NOT Art – moving around. He is hovering over Lydia now. He flops down on top of her. Lydia screams. I say nothing as I pounce on him like, *you guessed it,* a lion! *Lions Lions, I Declare...Lions, Lions everywhere!* I feel like eating him alive.

Without thinking, I bite the intruder deep in that area between the neck and shoulder and rip some meat from his bone. He yelps, his head snapping back like a wolf howling at the moon. I have my hands around his throat as Lydia, very close to being in shock, struggles out from beneath the bastard who was trying to rape her. She crawls out of the bedroom. I yell as loudly as I could so Lydia, who is barely holding on to her sanity, would let the words sink in:

"Shut the fuckin' door, and DO NOT call the cops! Lydia my baby, DO *NOT* call the cops!"

I am gonna strangle the would-be rapist, but he deserved worse. I choke him into unconsciousness, but not death. Not yet. He will suffer. I look at this situation as a practice session for Sheriff Burn In Hell.

Hey, there's a pure platinum lining in every cloud. I flip him over. *Damn,* I can't believe it. Can you guess who it is? Okay, I wouldn't have either. Well, lo and behold, it's the guy who delivers Lydia's zinfandel and my Heineken and wine, yep, the *beer-man.* And to think, I was his biggest tipper. Some people have no gratitude at all.

This kind of behavior calls for punishment. I tie him up to a strong, straight back oak chair in the den with clothesline rope and duct tape his mouth and eyes shut. Then I run to check on Lydia. The beer-man is already coming to from his near-death experience. Wonder if he saw the white light? Oh, great – Lydia is on the sofa crying, but not the cry of terror or sadness. She is crying with pure rage.

"Raven, get me a bottle of wine and a goddamn cigar! Where the FUCK did you go? You'd better have a damn good reason for just fuckin' vanishing like a vampire bat off into the night! Before that rat bastard came up behind me, Art went into a seizure. I screamed for you, you cocksucker! I SCREAMED for you!"

I want to hold her and tell her I'm sorry, but she isn't in the mood for forgiveness. Duh.

"Lydia, I am truly sorry, but I went over to Placido's place and copped us each a roxie – one for you, one for Art and one for me. *(I know, I lied, so sue me.)* Here's yours... let me go get you your bottle and a Black & Mild, my heroine, my Mermaid."

Man, was I was layin' it on heavy or what? Not like me at all.

"I went out for the roxies because I know how off-the-wall-crazy this thing is getting, with Art and all. I just thought you would need one, that's all. I wasn't gone that long."

She is glaring right through me. Like the eyes of those shape-shifting children in my nightmare.

"I'll be right back," I say, and grab a bottle of Lydia's wine, a pack of her cigars, and a cold ass beer for me. I am starting to feel the roxie kick in. I can hear the beer-man squirming in the oak chair. It sounds like he fell over. Lydia swallows her roxie with a long swig from her bottle and lights a cigar. She tilts her head back and blows out the smoke calmly, which I think is weird.

"Where is he?" she asks. "And why the hell haven't you asked me about Art yet? Well, he's fine, by the way. I panicked and thought he fuckin' died, so I poured a half bottle of your burgundy down his throat. The old bastard came around. He drank the rest of the bottle and passed out. He's still alive. Now, where is he? Where's the dude I'm gonna kill?" Lydia is eerily calm.

"He's in the den. I'll take care of him."

"No, *I* will."

"No Lydia, I'll do it. I'll kill him for you." I've already tied 50-pound test monofilament fishing line around the base of his dick. He's gonna suffer like hell and then die a few minutes after his bladder and maybe even his kidneys explode. Pure evil torture, very simply put.

"No, no, no Raven, my dear. You don't understand, I *need* to kill him!"

Shit, the lion is starting to roar in my scrambled brain and little ghost children are hammering their fists on the inside of my skull bone. It drowns out everything else. Even this shit with Lydia, Art and the beer-man.

"Okay, Lydia, let me go check on the bastard first, but I'll let *you* kill him, honest. Wait here. And don't fuckin' move till I call you. But yes, I promise, I'll let you kill him. Trust me."

I lied again.

Exhaling the dark gray smoke of her Black & Mild, looking through me once more, she leans forward from her seat on the sofa where she watches "Dancing with the Stars."

Yuck, that show sucks!

"OK Raven, you've got two minutes," she says tersely.

"Hey Mermaid, I'll call you in less than two minutes. How's that? And I'll even have a surprise for you." She takes a long slug of wine and blows me a kiss, Betty Davis-like. Man, she is acting weirder and weirder and it's kind of shaking me up. I finish my beer, light a Newport and walk into the den. Just as I thought, there he is, sideways on the floor, twisting and turning in the chair, but there is no escape for the agony of a bladder near explosion. I sit him up-right, put my left hand behind his twisting head. As I tear the duct tape off of his eyes, I see they are wide open with fear and I almost pity the beer-man.

Almost.

I grab his sweating head in both hands like a vice to steady it then proceed to bite his left eyelid off and then suck out his left eye-ball and eat it, swallowing unusually hard. Nasty habit, isn't it? This little song is going through my head... Listen: *Beer-man, Beer-Man, go away, don't come again some other day.* I re-tape his eyes, go to my brief case and pull out a pair of brass knuckles.

If Lydia is serious about wanting to personally kill this guy - and it sure seems like she is - these will do the trick and she could vent a lot of rage at the same time. It won't be quick. Maybe fifty punches or so, or when she gets totally exhausted from bashing his brains in. Not like just shooting his head off or slicing his throat. I think about the ice pick, but settle on the knuckles for my gal Lydia. She needs the exercise. We hadn't been swimming for more than two weeks. I will be swimming later today, though.

Raven April, writer, killer, torturer, lover, already has a plan on how to get rid of the beer-man's body. You see, the bull sharks are migrating up the coast. Yep, same time of year that Placido and his Mama escaped from Cuba.

I know I told all of you this before, but, *always think ahead, always!*

I could have come up with any number of ways to dispose of beer-man. But luck is on my side again, so I decide to swim beer-man out into the ocean, tied to one of the canvas rafts we have in the garage. Don't ask me why Lydia bought matching canvas rafts. *We've never even used them.*

Okay, here's the plan: I'll swim him out about a half mile, slice him up real good and hack his head off, so he bleeds a lot.

That's why this has to be done *immediately* after Lydia finishes him off with a few brass knuckle shots to the temple and throat. If it takes longer than a half hour or so, he won't bleed out as well. I'm giving her a couple of minutes with him, tops. He'll be dead already from uric acid poisoning, but she doesn't have to know any more about the dick-tying thing than she already does, which is nothing.

Kill Number nine, once again, if you're keeping count.

Gee, I bet that was awful for beer-man. Glad I taped his mouth shut. I hate to hear people scream – makes the hair stand up on the back of my neck. You too?

The lion is getting sleepy now. God, I hope he stays that way. I wash the blood off my face. It's damn hard to eat a human's eye out of their head without getting at least a *little* messy. Raven can't even do *that*, and I'm pretty damn good at it. Now I'm ready.

"Lydia," I yell, "come on in."

She waltzes into my den, my haven, where I do my writing. It is exactly ninety-five seconds after I'd left her on the sofa.

Nice efficient work on my part, if I do say so myself.

She has the look of a seasoned executioner as she calmly walks through the killing door. I show her the shiny brass knuckles. She likes them, smiling like they are a beautiful piece of jewelry, which they were, in my contorted, madman mind. B.V. West likes them too. About the only damn thing we have in common. His day is coming soon. So is Sheriff Evil's.

Like a magician, as she crosses the threshold into the den, Lydia pulls our favorite butcher knife from behind her back and sticks it through the beer-man's throat!

Damn, I almost can't believe my eyes! What did she do, pick up some of my deviance through osmosis or something? She tries to pull it out and do it again, but the point is embedded too deeply into the back of the oak chair. The beer-man's face rests on the ivory handle of the kitchen cutlery. Well, so much for the brass knuckles. I drop them on the hard-wood floor, making a sharp sounding thud. They weigh a lot for brass knuckles, believe me. Still quite astonished at what I'd just witnessed. Lydia is scary here in the *den of the dead.* I'm thinking, *damn, should I take her pawn shop wedding ring back? Just kidding*, I think.

She is satisfied. He is dead. She killed him. *With a little help from his insides blowing up.*

I knew he'd imploded because there is bloody urine running out of every hole in his body and it stinks like hell. I have to get him to the bull sharks and quick.

I grab the raft from the garage and throw it outside the sliding glass doors. I go back into the den, open my briefcase and pull out what I call my Danger-Dagger. Solid steel, all one piece, the handle was custom-fit for yours truly and the blade is double edged, scalpel-sharp and nine inches long. I also have a special leather belt equipped with a slip-proof sheath for the Danger-Dagger.

The dagger is very special, all custom-made by a Seminole Indian up in Pompano Beach a couple of years ago. Best damn knife man I've yet to meet. I hurriedly cut the overweight, soggy beer-man bastard, and might I add, *dumb,* out of the chair and carry his pissy, bloody body out to the shoreline. *Like I really need this!*

I'm gonna run in and get the raft, but when I turn around, Lydia is already standing there with it. Smart girl that she is, she also has cut two pieces of rope. *Yes, I keep rope in the garage for occasions such as this.* One piece long enough for me to tie his stupid ass to the raft and a shorter piece to use as a tow rope for me. She's learning, right? I'm guessing she used the butcher knife to cut the two lengths of rope, because there is blood on one of the pieces. That was so anticipatory of her, and thoughtful, don't you agree? It's very spooky, too, though, because Lydia still has that look of a zombie-on-crack glaze in her eyes.

"Good luck, Raven," she says, gazing out at the ocean. Have a nice swim."

I have to get this done *fast* for two reasons. One, I don't want to be there when the bull sharks go into their feeding frenzy and devour beer-man, and two, Lydia has to be gently, but quickly, brought back from her obvious state of shock!

I remind myself of a child working in a Chinese sneaker factory as I tie beer-man to the raft and then *off I go.* The tow rope under my neck and above my shoulder blades tied to the front of the raft.

Fun day at the beach, too bad the kids and grandkids aren't here.

I swim the no-good-son-of-a-bitch out of what I estimate to be closer to a third of a mile instead of the half-mile I had intended.

"Fuck this," I say to myself, "let's get it done. Raven my man you've had a long day. Get it done and get the hell out of here!"

Yeah, I talk to myself sometimes. So what? Better than talking to B.V. West. That pussy wouldn't even have put his big toe into the water. I stop swimming and look around for fins, especially behind me, toward the beach, where lay a virtual chum line. For you non-fishers, a chum line is a long trail of blood that fisherman pour into the water to attract fish to their baited hooks. It usually consists of blood and chunks of dead fish. Chum lines are especially effective when it comes to shark fishing.

Well, my chum line had been set up by all the mixed-up liquids trailing out of beer-man's white, puffy, poisoned carcass. I have to make this happen *now*. I start by easily cutting through his neck to the spinal cord. Then I decapitate him where the brain stem says hello to the spinal cord.

For Chrissaske, his fuckin' skull is floating face up with his eye, (singular), apparently admiring the cloud formations. Just another sick joke. But his eye *is* open and his ugly gray head wouldn't sink. Who cares? Bull sharks are both top- and bottom-feeders.

After I cut him free from the rope, and he is balanced on the raft, I perform the ugly surgery of disemboweling him and stabbing his heart directly up from the empty rib cage a few times. Then I put about fifty good, deep slices into his stinking, rotten flesh, starting at his feet and working my way up to what was left of his neck, being careful not to puncture the raft.

A school of small bait-fish are already starting to gather around the raft and me. You do realize that I've been treading water this whole time, with the help of the raft, of course.

But it's still no picnic, my friends. I have to get the hell out of there like fuckin' *lickety split*. I'm really not in the mood to wrestle with a bull shark, but I am filled with adrenaline and would have the strength of a lion if that happened and Raven April, sweetheart of the seas, would be victorious with a little help from the Danger Dagger. No doubt about that.

Listen to me, it's all about *confidence*. You can accomplish nothing in life without cold, hard confidence in yourself and your abilities.

Write that down in your mind!

I have to admit that I am totally exhausted after successfully operating on beer-man, (no wonder surgeons make so much money) so I climb on the raft and start paddling back to shore straight through that putrid chum line. With my legs spread I probably look like a sea turtle from below the surface, where not only a bull shark, but any number of species of shark could be lurking. A large tiger shark for instance, could easily crush me with one bite and have me for lunch. And there are many different types of sharks off the South Florida coast that just love to chomp through turtle shells and eat whatever is inside, the shell too, for that matter. So far, so good. I am only about 100 feet from shore when... *crash, splash! oh shit!*

Something huge bites the back end of the raft, right between my legs, missing my ass and balls by about an inch. I know the man-eater wouldn't like the taste of the canvas raft and probably will come back for the real deal. *Me*. Damn you, beer-man!

I pull the Danger Dagger out of its sheath, slide off what is left of the raft and start swimming like hell for the beach. I can see Lydia put her right hand over her mouth, waving her left hand in the air, jumping up and down now, waving both arms and screaming.

"Hurry Raven, hurry, he's right behind you, he's after you! Swim, Raven, swim like you've never done before. *Look out!*"

111

I stop swimming and turn around just in time to see the prehistoric head of a huge Hammerhead shark ready to attack me with all his primitive fury. I am kind of surprised that it is a hammerhead, because they are not generally known to surface attack. Maybe this guy never got the official shark-attack rule book.

Actually no wild animals are predictable, especially sharks. But you know that, don't you?

Hammerheads are grotesque-looking creatures with eyes that are spread widely apart on opposite ends of its sledgehammer-shaped cartilage skull. You've probably seen them before, but probably not in person. I make a very athletic move to my right, causing the monster to miss me by inches with his first bite. I plunge the Danger Dagger deep into his left eye and twist the blade, kick the creature with my heel in the side – they're not used to that kind of turtle – turn and start swimming like Michael Phelps going for another Olympic gold medal in the 400-meter relay. Eerily silent, the devil with jaws disappears into the abyss, but I know he'll be back, pissed off and hungry for whatever it is that just turned his left eye into raw meatloaf.

Only fifty feet from the beach now, and sure enough the bastard is zeroing in on me like a World War II torpedo. I stop and start treading water again, waiting for the inevitable. I don't have to wait for long. He is coming straight for me.

And yes, in case you're wondering, even I, Raven April, am petrified! Courage is not the absence of fear. People with *that* unfortunate affliction are simply called "fools." I can see his dorsal and tail fin, as God and Lydia, *literally*, as my witnesses, the blood glutton has to be at least ten or twelve feet long.

Shit! Why do I have to see that?

I decide to use the same maneuver I had just used, only in reverse. This time I move to my left and stab him deep and hard right on target, into his right eye with my trusty Danger Dagger. He is blinded. I kick him again, this time twice, extra hard and with both feet. He dives beneath the surface, again silently, as if this whole life-and-death ocean battle had never really happened. The sea is placid with hardly a ripple.

Did it *really* happen? Did it? I am pretty sure it did. You tell me. *Whew!* I think it did. Back to swimming like a man with a shark on his ass.

Ha! I think, *Lights out, big boy! Damn, that was close.*

Then suddenly, about a foot away from my rag-doll-on-valium body, the monster breaks through the surface and soars well over ten feet into the air, shaking his head wildly, thrashing, gushing blood from where his eyes once were, sending water high into the sky, probably visible a fuckin' mile up the beach in both directions (that's *all* I need). It was loud too, swooshing and splashing like an obese ten-year-old in a kiddie pool.

Gee, I gotta get out of here! And I swim, not looking back. Finally, as I reach the sandy bottom of my front yard, I look back as the sightless Hammerhead vanishes under the now-crimson surface. Never to be seen again. Other sharks are probably already feeding on him. Beer-man for lunch, Hammerhead for dessert. What a meal. Yummy. *I think I'm gonna be sick.*

I collapse on the beach, nearly unconscious... like when I brought Queenie home on that horrible day I lost my mind. I think I hear Lydia crying. I know I feel her wrap her arms around me and feel her kisses on my face. I can taste and smell her tears. I gasp a little.

"Help me inside the house, Mermaid?" She can't move me. I am much too heavy for her and dead-weight to boot. So, she runs in and brings out the *love blanket*.

"Baby," I say, in-between gulps of air, "I'm not in the mood." I laugh with the chest rattle of a near-dead man.

"No, no," she says, "this is where I have to take care of you for now, until you gain the strength to walk. Now, roll over onto the blanket. I'll help you."

"One, two, three – Roll."

Along with Lydia's push, I make it onto the *love blanket*. Little did I know at the time, but the sandpaper skin of the Hammerhead had rubbed the skin raw on some small areas of my body. No big deal, really. But, nurse Lydia is pouring fresh water all over me now, and it hurts like bloody hell. Then the peroxide! OUCH! So much for the *love blanket*. It's saturated with all kinds of nasty fluids. Gonna have to get her a new one.

Two hundred bucks for that thing, can you believe it?

The Next Morning

Lydia must have walked me into the main guest room sometime last night but I don't remember it – Art still has the master bedroom – and I must have slept like a baby. Every part of my body aches, including my roughed-up skin. I walk into Art's room, and Lydia is standing next to the bed talking to him while he sits up like an aristocrat, downing the breakfast of eggs, potatoes, bacon and beer that she, like a doting French maid, has prepared for him. Apparently, Art is coming along just fine, tough old soldier that he is.

"Yo, where's *my* breakfast?" I say, rubbing my eyes. "I can see who's getting all the attention around here!

114

Damn Art, I'm jealous. I might have to feed you to the bull sharks later today."

Art chuckles, chokes, and spits a mouthful of beer all over the place.

Classy guy, that Art, wouldn't you agree?

Lydia walks over to give me a big, pelvis-grinding hug and says my breakfast will be waiting in the main guest room under the sheets, if I am up to it.

Thank God she seems to be back to her old self today. Yesterday was another bitch of a day for her. Nearly a rape victim, stabbing a guy through the neck and then watching me tangle with a giant Hammerhead. She is one tough lady.

"I'll be right in, just let me talk to Art for a minute. Think I'll even have a beer with him. Okay, Mermaid?"

"Sure Raven. Love you"

"Love you too, Lydia."

"Should I be naked, or do you want to undress me with your teeth?"

"What, like a shark would do?"

"I'll be naked, you dickhead!" We have lots of fun with each other.

I grab a couple more beers for Art and me, and then sit down on the edge of his bed. Lydia and I really should have put him in the guestroom – what the hell were we thinking? But, I ain't got the heart to move him now.

Before I have time to say anything, Art wants to clink bottles and celebrate my victory over the Hammerhead. Apparently, Lydia had told him about the whole ordeal – including how *she* killed the beer-man.

Uh oh, and I thought she was better. But now I'm thinking her head is still got to be a little fucked up. It ain't every day you kill a man for the first time. And only time, I hope. Just remember though, the beer-man was *mine*.

Kill Number nine.

No bragging, just a fact. I don't know if it would do Lydia more harm than good to clear up the fact that she did *not* kill him – I did. So, I decide to let another sleeping dog lie for now, and keep a good, close eye on her. Queenie pops into my madman mind.

I look up and make a promise.

"Love you, Queenie," I say. *"I'll avenge you soon."*

I don't want this murder thing turning my sweet Lydia into a monster. It can also transform the vibrant Mermaid into mush. No good either. Just have to wait, observe and play it by ear. There's the devil you see and the devil you don't. I feel horribly responsible about how this could turn out for Lydia. A heavy weight, which is a very rare feeling for me, is hanging on my shoulders.

Uneasy is the head that wears the crown.

"So Art, how ya feelin,' buddy?"

"Shouldn't I be asking *you* that, Raven?"

"I'm fit as a blind man's fiddle, dude. Watch me kill the rest of this beer nonstop, the Breakfast of Champions. As a matter of fact, let's make a toast to all the pretty sharks in the sea. I never hold a grudge once I get even. Sharks, beer-men rapists, they're all the same. Once they are dead buddy, they are harmless."

Art raises his bottle to mine.

"Damn right they are, Raven," he says. "Here's to all those dead bastards in the world who deserve to rot in hell, down the hatch."

Damn, that beer tastes too good for being so early in the morning. I grab us each another one. This time I pull the chair from over by the window and place it next to the bed. I lean over a bit towards Art. He truly is a tough old boy. One of the best men I've ever known. No shit. He is healing fast, and I can tell how much he likes his new pad.

Kind of like Lydia and her pawn-shop wedding ring. It sure beats the hell out of a bus stop bench in the cancerous colon of Overtown. Lot of shit happens in the colon. Now, tell me I'm wrong.

You can't.

"Oh yeah, by the way Art...," I say, after a long pull on my Heineken. I must have put down almost half of it, because I want to go have my breakfast soon. I am really feeling famished – breakfast in bed, what a way to live. I look at Art and continue my thought.

"The Tedesco's are up in Twin Boys' Heaven. Your good pal Raven here took care of them for you. It was the least I could do for a war hero like you."

"Did you kill them quick, or make them *wish* they were dead, first?" Art asks hopefully.

"Both. It's a little complicated." I start laughing like a crazy man.

So does Art.

We both spit a mouthful of beer out, splashing each other.

"It was really, *really* funny up there with those two pussies. Kind of like a freak show. Wish you could've been there, Art. Oh yeah, man, I think 'T2' wished he was dead there for a while before I killed him. 'T1' was already history. I had to put him out of his misery right away. Dumb bastard couldn't keep his trap shut."

"How did you do it, Raven?" Art asks, still laughing.

"Made their hearts stop beating. How else can you do it?"

Slowly the laughter stops.

Art looks me dead in the eye and says, "God bless you, buddy."

We clink our bottles again.

I grab two more beers for Art before I head off to the guest room.

Lydia has the lights out, and the room-darkening curtains are drawn.

"Love Me Do" by the Beatles is playing on the stereo. She is naked. Need I say more? Don't think so.

During our hot quickie, which is very hot and not so quick, I am devising the next step of my plan to end the repulsive life of Sheriff Worthless as well as the cowardly B.V. West. Hey, I am still enjoying Lydia's affection. I'm a multi-tasker. What can I tell you? You should know me by now.

I need to contact Joe Lofton within the next few days. He doesn't know it yet, but he *may* play a huge role in the torture and murder of that empty shell of a man known as Sheriff Brian Vaughn West. I will do the killing – kind of, that is. My plan is a devious, heartless, still-developing one, and when it's over, I can only pray that the sheriff's dreadful demise will silence the lion and will set me free – as free as a *Raven in flight*.

A Confession

Look, I've got to try and get my shit together. *You see* what's happening here. And I know for a fact that something fuckin' crazy is going on in your life, too. So you can relate to my mounting dilemmas.

Hey, we're all in the same game, just at different levels, dealing with the same hell, only different devils.

And there is nothing more horrible – nothing more immortal – than the actions of a desperate man, especially a madman, such as I, Raven April. With that in mind, I must try and tie a ball and chain around the tenacious ankle-squeeze of desperation that I can feel creeping up around me like slithering snakes, as Sheriff Dead Ass gets closer to his day of judgment. Like jackals, trouble runs in packs. Hell Day approaches. I can feel it. Stick with me. I don't want to go this alone. The lion hasn't roared in the last few days, but I can hear and feel him stirring and purring.

Let's do this together. Okay?

"Thanks."

Your old buddy, Raven.

Four days later. Calling Joe Lofton

I take a few beers into my den. I close the door and take a couple of hits of some pretty good pot. I light a Newport and start thinking about how I'm gonna break the news to Joe Lofton that I am a murderer. Not just a killer, but a *serial* killer. Damn, all I can smell in here now is the new varnish on the floor. After Lydia and I finished the job of cleaning beer-man's piss and blood off the hardwood floor – actually I did most of the work – Lydia hired a crew of carpenters and painters to sand, and recoat it. They did a great job, and it looks beautiful, but man, I hope that smell goes away. The air filtration system helps a little, but *what the fuck?*

Back to Joe. Hey, I can just tell him the truth.

"Hi Joe," I can say, "this is Raven. Just thought I'd call and let you know that I'm a serial killer. Nine dead, and at least a few more to go. And guess what? You and a young stud named Placido, a Cuban buddy of mine, are gonna help me kill my final victim, my prize trophy. I'll let you hold his head up in victory. I'll even let you *cut* his head off! Then I'm going to mount it on the wall above my desk"

I'm laughing again. Sorry 'bout that. But I am just imagining the look on Joe's face if I actually said that to the friendly, happy, family man. But, I couldn't of course. Hell, he'd freak out. How about if he hanged himself in the basement with a note on his chest that reads: *"Raven April is a serial killer, I'm number 10?"*

I'd feel just terrible and probably wind up being executed. No, Joe will not know about Sheriff Bastard's murder. He will play a bit-part, but he won't know it until it's too late. Don't worry, he'll be paid well and hopefully will not get killed.

Placido, on the other hand will know about the Sheriff's awful fate beforehand. I think he'll be able to handle it, especially for a hundred grand. That will also make Mama Placido much more financially comfortable. Damn, I love that old woman. She is so real. Just looking into her eyes I can see the good, the bad and the beautiful of life. Mama Placido has seen it all. She has wisdom, but especially she has goodness in her soul. Like Queenie did. I won't even tell Placido about my first nine kills.

Remember, no one is to be trusted fully, because in a jam, they will always save their own ass before thinking twice about yours. Just like you and me. Admit it. I do. The only two people I completely trust on this planet are my daughter, Melody and my son, Dustin. Period! I will hold my cards close to my vest for now, as far as Joe and Placido go. But Placido *has* to know about Sheriff Burn-In-Hell, because I need Placido to get us the dogs.

More on that soon, my friends – yeah, it gets ugly.

I'm also gonna let Art in on the secret meetings we will be having here at the mansion. I'll have Joe fly into Ft. Lauderdale where Lydia will pick him up in *the* - I mean *her* - Beamer. I'll have to finally bring Placido over here. Actually, I'll bring him here a day or two before Joe arrives, so I can fill him in on the gory parts of our little adventure that I don't want Joe to know. Placido and I will have all our ducks in a row, so to speak.

He'll be shocked and amazed to realize that this is where Raven April, street roamer, drug and booze lover, lives. But he'll get used to it. He'll fit right in. Hell, he's as handsome as any movie star. Placido is tall and thin, with the coolest jet black hair, always combed straight back, somewhat resembling the Tedesco twins, with those sharp facial features of a young George Hamilton. He is also very polite and intelligent. Mama Placido did a good job of raising him especially considering their circumstances. I was even thinking about demanding him a role in the, *Standing on the Edge of Forever* movie.

Damn, I'm sorry, I almost forgot to mention that a major movie production company bought the rights to the book and is expecting to start casting characters in a month and would like to start shooting in four months. Good job Joe! I was asked to fly out to L.A. and help on the screenplay, but kindly declined. I told them that I would rather just look at it when it's done.

"If I don't like it, I'll edit it and get it back to you." Although they have final say in the matter, I'll interject a lot of input if I have to.

Yeah, good news, huh? Get the popcorn ready!

Anyway, I haven't seen Placido for a few days, so I'm gonna look him up tonight. It's Friday, so he'll probably be at Macabi's Cigar Bar around ten o'clock or so up on Las Olas in Ft. Lauderdale. There's a young Jewish barmaid who works there on Friday nights, and Placido is working on her. He usually has no trouble picking up beautiful women, but this little Jewish girl is playing it tough. Good thing Placido likes a challenge. If I know Placido, he'll get her in the end. No pun intended. *Really.*

As I see it, it will take a few days to devise and perfect my plan to kill Sheriff Shit Bag in clarity and pinpoint detail. I'll expect all four of us, Raven, (me) Joe, Placido and Art, maybe even Lydia, which would make five, expanding the circle and hopefully contributing in the thinking process that goes into something stupid like killing a sheriff. A heartless bully who controls the county in central Pennsylvania where I grew up, and where, thanks to him and a small band of coyotes, I lost my mind. I haven't decided on that yet.

What do you think? Should I include Lydia? Wow, you all say yes. Thanks for the help. We'll have to see. I'm thinking no – not a good idea.

This is where the men and the boys (and girls) usually sharply define and expose themselves as winners or losers. Most criminals, (which in our case happens to be murderers), don't plan well enough and leave some small detail to fate, which is only a 50-50 shot at best. Just like the Tedescos; they should have had a camera in that stairway. It's a perfect example of not covering every base. *Dumb asses.*

10

Macabi Cigar Bar, Ft. Lauderdale, Fla.

The cabbie drops me off across the street from Macabi's. I walk in around 10:30 pm, say hi to Pat, the owner, and he puts a Heineken on the bar for me. Pat's quite a guy; sixty years old, about 5'6" and thin with dark skin, but he's not a hundred-percent black. He has thick dark hair and wears glasses. Pat seems attractive to women in his own mysterious way. *Probably his money.* He's a classy, worldly guy. Smart too. Pat was born in Uganda, but has lived all over the world and speaks nine languages. While living in England during the early 70's he became good friends with Eric Clapton. Whenever "Eric" is in South Florida, he stops in to see Pat, but Eric doesn't drink anymore.

The place is full, and just as I have been expecting, Placido is at the very end of the bar having a close conversation with Julie, the Jewish barmaid. Julie is about 5'2", with long brown hair, an extremely exotic, beautiful face and has a build that would turn even Joe Lofton's head, sweet family man that he is.

Gee, I love that guy.

It's little wonder that Placido is so obsessed with her. Everybody is. Julie is why Friday nights are so big at Macabi's. I walk down and stand behind Placido for a minute or two before he realizes it. The stools are all taken, and the music is ear-deafening loud. "Maroon 5" is playing.

Placido finally sees me in the mirror that lines the back of the bar and turns around.

"Yo, Raven, my man. Hey, do you know Julie?"

"No," I say, "but I'd like to."

Placido introduces us. Even though I'd seen her a few times before, I'd never really spoken to her, other than to say, "I'll have another Heineken, please."

Picking up chicks in bars has never been part of my madman lifestyle. Well, maybe a little out in Boulder when "The Riders" were the hottest band in town.

"Nice to meet you, Julie," I say above the music. "Mind if I borrow Placido for a minute?"

"No, go ahead, I'm really busy and I don't want Pat to get pissed at me. Nice to meet you, Raven April. I really like your name." She smiles at Placido and walks down the bar a few feet to mix drinks, pour beers and light cigars.

"Yo, man, how ya makin' out with Julie? She *is* fuckin' hot!" I ask Placido after chugging half of my beer.

"Fuck Raven... you know me, she's in the bag. If she's even half as good as she looks, I might even keep her around a while."

I nod with a mouthful of beer. "Yeah, might not be a bad idea, she's one in a million, dude."

Julie returns, and I ask her to pick out a couple of mild Cuban cigars for Placido and me. Julie puts her elbows on the bar and her chin in her hands.

"What's your preference... Raven April." she asks with a smile.

Oh, damn, she likes me, *or at least my name.* I can tell that for sure, now.

"Surprise me." I say in a kind of cool way.

She scurries away in her tight short-shorts and comes back with two of Pat's specials. He only sells them to his "preferred" customers, of which I am one because I spend a lot of money there and tip so goddamned good.

"These are on Pat," Julie says, then clips the ends, sensuously places them between our lips and lights them.

Pays to be nice to people. And hell, it's a cigar bar, so what better thing to do than drink beer, smoke a sixty dollar cigar and plan a senseless murder? Nothing unusual about that, is there?

Macabi's is the best cigar bar in the world. No doubt about that. And to think that to some people it is quite unusual and childish for grown men and women to sit around, smoke cigars and imbibe while trying to talk louder than Mick Jagger can sing. Those "some" people live in a frighteningly small world. No fun, no adventure, no guts. The guy on the stool next to Placido accepts a twenty-dollar bill from me to move, so I can sit down next to my unwitting partner in a future horrible crime. *And I hope a successful one.*

"Thanks" I say, and the guy buys me a beer out of the twenty. The last two seats at the far end of the bar. *Perfect.* I take the stool next to Placido, set my briefcase down in front of my legs on top of my feet. I rarely let go of it. It's like my safety blanket.

"So, Placido, how would you like to make a hundred grand – cash, maybe more?"

He sets his beer down and looks at me with his big perfect, but disbelieving movie-star smile.

"Who the fuck wouldn't? Is this one of your jokes, Raven? You look serious."

I give him my poker face then reply.

"I am as serious as death. I've got a job I have to do, and I'm gonna need your help. It's not pretty, and it could be risky, but it pays well. I promise you on your mother's soul that I will do my best to try and keep you safe through this, shall we say, excursion into the realities of the macabre."

Placido gives me a perplexed look, as if to say:

"Like, what the fuck are you talking about, man?

"Look," I say. "I'm really gonna need you. Are you interested? Just say 'yes' or 'no.' If you are, we'll meet at my place tomorrow, and I'll lay it all out for you."

"Yes, Hell yes. I'm interested. Tell me more."

"Look," I say, "I'll be at your mom's house tomorrow in a cab at one o'clock sharp. Be ready. From there we'll go to my place, and I'll unfold all the details I have so far to you. The plan is still a work in progress and must be perfected. Pack enough clothes for about three days. I've got enough room for you. Is that cool?"

"Yeah man," Placido says, getting a little nervous, "that's cool."

"Don't say a fuckin' word about this to anybody. Not even your mom."

"Raven, the tone of your voice is scaring me, man."

"You should be scared. Not a word. Got it?"

"Got it. Not a word."

"You ever kill a man, Placido?"

"No, why?"

"*Could* you if you *had* to?"

"Maybe, if they were trying to kill me."

"How about if they weren't? Nevermind."

The lion was starting to roar. *Shit!*

"Finish your beer and come with me. Hurry. You'll be back before Pat closes. Julie will still be here. I've got to show you something. Just listen to my instructions and obey them to the "T," because I am going to *test* you tonight. That's all, okay?"

"Yeah, okay. I don't know what the fuck I'm gettin' myself into, but I trust you, Raven. Let's go."

I figure tonight is as good a time as any to show Placido who his friend Raven, really is. We empty our beers, I leave a $20 tip, and we shoulder our way out of the bar. We take a left outside, and start walking toward the beach.

The lion is a cacophony of ghouls, chanting and screaming inside of my head. It amazes me that Placido can't hear the roar and the deafening chorus pounding and screeching between my ears just a foot away. Lucky for him he is on the un-killable list.

Somebody must die though, and soon, at the hands of Raven April and my wicked slave master, the lion. Actually, if my idea pans out, *two* will die on the beach tonight. Placido will either fail or succeed in killing his first human being. I will be setting my tenth victim free.

Tonight I *must find out for sure* if I can trust him as a *helper* with my final and most elaborate execution coming up soon in Pennsylvania – Sheriff Evil. Tonight will be his Major League tryout. I need to see how he handles this. We walk in silence. He senses that I am up to something sinister, but he has no idea what it is. Placido is nervous. I sense that.

The lion is showing his teeth and tongue to me. Like before, we are becoming one again on this black night.

Tonight, I've decided to show Placido two ways of killing. The first will be how to sever a windpipe and instantly silence your prey, then slice through the carotid arteries for the kill. The second will be the three ice pick plunges deep into the top of the skull.

Confession: I really like that one. You could safely say that is the only thing Joey Stalin and I had in common. I laugh to myself, but only for a moment.

We are on our way to Bahia Mar Beach. When we reach The Habiscus Room, where I'd seen the pop-star, at the corner of Las Olas Boulevard and A1A, the palm-tree-lined, picture-perfect highway that follows the gorgeous coastline along South Florida, we cross A1A, and make a right. We walk along the dark beach.

We'll stop in The Habiscus Room on the way back, and then Placido will probably take a cab back to Macabi's to see, and hopefully, fuck Julie later. But then again, he may just puke his guts up and jump off the highest bridge in South Florida after what he's in for with me later on this lovely evening. Time will tell. There is a thin moon and millions of stars out over the Atlantic tonight. Beer-man is out there too, somewhere.

There will be a lot of people, *targets, I should say*, mostly homeless and fucked up on drugs, booze or both. Bahia Mar Beach is about a half-mile south of Las Olas and the cops kind of turn a blind eye and do not disturb the homeless who prefer the sound of the ocean to lull them off to slumber land and *sleep it off* on this particular "safe" stretch of beach. The other beaches are off limits to these types at night. Pristine beaches are what bring in the tourists from all over the world to Ft. Lauderdale, and most of them have money to burn. Ft. Lauderdale is considered "The Yacht Capitol" of the world, and her nickname is "The Venice of America" because of the myriad canals and so forth. Just thought you'd like to know these useless facts.

I am about to fall to my knees in pain. The unrelenting roar of the lion is thumping and throbbing through my body, nearly unbearable now. I want to scream, but Placido and I are still walking in dead silence. He knows something evil is about to happen, but he still isn't sure what it is. We are close to the more than two dozen bums sprawled out or curled up around palm trees on Bahia Mar beach. Two of them will die soon. Either that or my head will surely explode like a bomb and the shrapnel inside will kill everyone on the beach anyway.

I find us a clump of three palm trees where we wouldn't be noticed as I strip all of my clothes off and pile them against one of the trees.

"Raven, man" Placido whispers in amazement, "What the fuck you doing, going swimming or something?"

"No," I whisper back, "I'm gonna kill that dude over there." I point to a middle-aged guy who is out cold like a drugged gorilla – big dude, sitting against a palm tree. He is about thirty feet away. "And you, Placido, are gonna kill that motherfucker right there." I point the poor bastard out. He is face down, spread-eagle on a blanket. He is also about thirty feet away but closer to the highway. My guy is closer to the water.

"What? Kill the guy? Kill the guy for what?"

"For that hundred grand we talked about in Macabi's"

"I don't know if I can do it, Raven."

"Then fuck the money, and get the hell out of here."

"You still gonna kill that guy over there?"

"Hell yes. You in or out?"

"I'm in. Do I have to strip down, too?"

"Yeah, you do, just in case you get any blood on you. If you do, which you will, just casually walk down to the ocean and rinse it off. It's no big deal. A lot of the bums take their bath out there every night – or week – or month. There's no cops around now – get'em off."

Placido peels his clothes off, while I reach into my briefcase and grab good old Bucky. I was just gonna slice my guy's wind-pipe in half, sever his carotids and eat his left eye. A rather simple kill for me. I also grab the ice pick and hand that to Placido.

He takes it and looks at me, very jittery-like.

"What the hell am I supposed to do with this?"

We have a brief staring contest.

I am still looking him square in the eyes as I take the ice pick out of his slightly trembling hand, walk about five feet to pick up a coconut, and then I toss it to him.

He catches it.

We are still whispering.

"Lay it right there," I say, "next to my shirt."

He does as he's told.

I then put three quick, deep holes in the coconut and hand the ice pick back to Placido.

"Your turn."

Placido gets on his knees, lifts up his right hand, which now holds the ice pick and plunges the needle-sharp point three times into the coconut – all the way up to the handle.

Good! He is ready.

"Okay, that's what you are going to do to that guy's head over there. Three quick and hard jabs, with all your might to the top of his head. He's laying down right? So just casually walk over, kneel down next to the left side of his head, quietly, and bang, one-two-three! Oh yeah, keep this in mind; his skull will be a lot harder than that coconut. Straight and fuckin' hard is the key. Then, stand up and walk to the ocean. Clean the ice pick off, and any blood you might get on you. Got it?"

"Fuck Raven! Yeah, I've got it. I'll do it. I need the money. And I'm not even gonna ask you where you're gettin' it." He then says, "Man, this better be for real."

"You'll find out tomorrow afternoon," I tell him, "where this is all going. So, don't worry about it till then. Just worry about tonight. Learn to live in the *now*, Placido, my friend. Now follow me; I'm gonna show you another way to kill. Watch my every move and don't say a word or make any noise at all.

"Got it? Get it good. I'll be taking a swim as soon as he's dead, and goes night-night forever."

Not a bad place to die, really. Damn, the fuckin' lion wants blood and he wants it *soon*.

"Let's go." I can feel Placido behind me, his feet lightly squishing on the sand. We are only a foot away now from the poor, doomed sand flea of a human. He is sound asleep with his head resting against the other side of the tree. Perfect positioning. Really, he reminds me of a giant sand flea. You know how my mind works. I turn to Placido, who is scared shitless.

"Watch and be quiet. When I walk toward the ocean, you walk back to our trees."

"I think I've got it. Hey Raven, are you crazy? I mean, really? You can tell me."

I smile and whisper, "No buddy, the world is."

I reach around the tree with my left hand, gently pull number 10's double chin up a little then carve straight through his windpipe with the swift ease of a practiced killer, which I am.

The sand flea opens his eyes for a split second; though unable to make a sound, he says it all by that surprised last gaze before blackness gathers up his soul. Something like, *"What the hell's happening!"*

It's really pretty easy to cut the carotid arteries in half. He is dead rather quickly and, of course, silently. Tom Norris would have been proud. Gee, I would have loved to have been a Navy Seal. I salute them all. I'm very patriotic, you know. I've even been called a sweetheart, as you also know. I admit to being an enigma, a contradiction of myself. You've probably come to that conclusion on your own by now, *and you'd be correct.*

Placido watches in amazement, but what really blows his mind is when I bite, gnaw and suck the giant sand flea's eye out of its orbit in less than twenty seconds and proceed to swallow it whole, optic nerve and all. I tilt my head back just a bit like some folks do when slurping down a raw clam, while Placido gawks horrified at the messy little scene.

Have you noticed that I never chew? I know, bad manners. So shoot me. I am getting faster. Hey, practice makes perfect.

Kill Number ten.

I walk to the ocean, smoothly slide in and take a swim to remove any blood I might have on me. There is sure to be some.

Placido does as he was instructed, in horror, I'm sure, and walks back to our spot.

I meet him there after my short swim, dry off with towels I keep in my briefcase, get dressed and hand Placido the ice pick.

Placido seems frozen.

"Look motherfucker," I say, "go kill that bastard or the deal is off. I'll find somebody else."

The guy is still lying there spread-eagle like an already-dead man. Easy prey. Placido, standing there naked, surprises me and starts walking like a North-Korean-soldier-robot over toward the face-down, beach-bum loser he is supposed to brain-pierce.

I watch as closely as I can, while I finish putting my shorts, tank-top and sneakers back on, to see how Placido would, or could do this.

Okay, he's there now. He's slowly going to his knees next to the guy's head. Oh shit! He's just sitting there staring at the guy for maybe a minute, no fuckin' good.

Then like lightening, Bazingo! He slams the ice pick three times straight into the poor unsuspecting victim's gray matter.

I'm thinking, sorry buddy, but I had to test out my new partner. See you on the other side, *wherever that is*.

Placido was doing a good job so far, but instead of walking to the ocean as if nothing was amiss on Bum Beach, as he was *told*, he starts *running* toward *me*.

Dumb-ass move. That could draw attention to us, and to the bodies of the two fleeting spirits which we had just sent on to their final destinations. He makes it back to our little hideout behind the three palm trees in about fifteen seconds, but, like I said, never goes down to the ocean as instructed to wash his hands and the ice pick off. But with all Placido has been through tonight with his first kill, I decide not to admonish him for his rookie fuck-up just now. That will come later. The lion has gone back to sleep, and I feel like partying. Strangely though, I feel no remorse at all for the *sand flea* or the *beach-bum loser* Placido and I had just killed, and that bothers me a little. What am I turning into? A madman is one thing, a madman with no soul is quite another.

Placido gets dressed, and I give him a firm handshake.

"Not bad, but we have to straighten some things out first, like following my orders. You were supposed to walk down to the ocean to rinse off the ice pick and any blood you had on yourself. I'll overlook that for now since it was your first kill and *maybe* your last. Let's hope so, but don't count on that. Good job though, all things considered my friend. You're hired. And – you *could* be rich. Here's a little advance."

I reach down into my briefcase, and like an illusionist pulling a white rabbit out of a black hat by the ears, suddenly appears ten one-hundred dollar bills. I casually count them out, one by one in Placido's now somewhat steadier, outstretched left hand.

"I don't know," he says and smiles, "whether to kill you, kiss you or just say *thanks*."

I put my arm around his shoulder, and much like a Mafia don might do, speak softly into his ear.

"Say thanks. You'll live longer."

We started walking back to The Habiscus Club. Neither one of us have much to say. Earlier tonight was a game-changer. Our mutual silence says it all. When we get to the club, I buy us a couple of Heinekens, then walk out and flag down a cab. I need to get home and check on Lydia and Art. On the way, I have the cabbie drop Placido off at Macabi's Cigar Bar where his car, a five year old metallic blue Chevy Camaro, and Julie are waiting.

"See ya, Raven. Man, what a fuckin' night! Was I dreaming or having a nightmare or something?"

"No partner. It was real. Just be ready at one o'clock tomorrow when the cab pulls up at your Mom's place. And be ready for a few more surprises. Maybe I'll even tell you about that big lottery I hit up in Pennsylvania."

"You hit a lottery, a big one?"

I gaze out the window, pondering my fate for a moment.

"Yeah, a big one. Sleep tight man, with Julie, I hope."

We knuckle-knock as we often do, but this one felt different, I start laughing as the cab pulls away from the curb in front of Macabi's.

But the Haitian driver isn't in on the joke. He thinks I'm a nut case and glances around at my brief case which is sitting on my lap.

I say, "BOO!"

He flinches, and I start laughing again.

Yeah, he thinks I'm a nut case.

Who cares?

The Next Day, 1 pm

The cab pulls up in front of Mama Placido's at 1p.m. sharp. I have an interesting chat with the young looking Haitian cab driver (not the same one as last night) on the way over to pick up Placido. (I always strike up conversations with cabbies).

He is ranting about how this country is going to hell in a hand-cart, blah, blah, blah.

"Well," I say, "why don't you move back to Haiti?" He zips his head around like a rattlesnake and flashes the widest, brightest smile I think I've ever seen.

"Are you fucking kidding me, man?" he says, "I've got it made here!"

I conclude that he must be bipolar, and for a brief moment I think about holding my hands over his eyes until he crashes. Then he can check out our health-care system.

Yep, I'm laughing out-loud again. Now do you see why I don't like to do public appearances? I laugh at those, too.

Placido and Mama Placido share a rather nice, but kind'a small two-bedroom first-floor apartment in a mostly safe Cuban neighborhood, a few blocks removed from Miami's nasty Overtown section. Not far from where the Tedesco twins met their untimely fate.

Placido runs his web-design business out of his bedroom. He is a very efficient guy, much like Joe Lofton. That quality will come in handy I'm assuming, during our mission of unthinkable torture and death.

Sorry, rambling a little again.

Back to Placido's neighborhood. Everybody has a little yard and at least half the population there has chickens running around, so the people always have fresh eggs and high-grade chicken meat. And these free *little*

135

Havana-range chickens are fed without antibiotics and hormones which most store-bought chickens contain these days. Pretty smart, don't ya think?

The Cuban people are law-abiding, proud and dignified people. Sure, they have their punks, but don't we all? Here comes Placido, looks like he packed enough stuff for a couple of days. Good. I climb out the back door and give him a hug. He *forces* a smile. Uh oh.

"Hop in the back partner, I'm just gonna go say hi to your Mom. Be right back." I jog up to the front door just as Mama Placido is closing it.

She sees me coming and pulls the door back open.

"Hi Raven! Here, give me a hug! Mmmm, you're a good strong boy!"

Hell I'm almost fifty-four years old! What's this *boy* stuff?

"So, tell me, what are you and Placido up to for these next few days? He seemed a little upset last night, he came home early for a Friday night, and he's not much different this morning."

"Well, he's a little down about a girl. Didn't he mention Julie?"

"No, Raven, he didn't."

"Well, let's just keep it that way. He'll get over her. You know Placido."

"Did she break his heart?"

"Yeah, Mama, something like that."

She laughs.

"It's about time he got a taste of his own medicine," she says.

I laugh along, give Mama a peck on the cheek and leave a hundred-dollar bill on the kitchen counter behind the red, white and blue cookie jar. Mama Placido is very proud to be an American, hence the colors on her cookie jar. She'll find the money after I am gone.

"Oh yeah, Placido and I are just gonna hang out at my buddie's place on the beach for a few days and hopefully get some business done at the same time. I'll get your Placido home safe by Monday or Tuesday at the latest. He needs a break from *his* business. He works *too* hard sometimes. This'll do him good. Call Placido's cell if you need anything, okay, Mama? Just leave a message in case he's busy and can't talk."

"Alright, Raven. You boys have fun. Oh, and I won't mention anything about Julie. Why upset my baby, right?"

"Right."

I jump in the back seat of the cab with Placido, who is in a sullen mood – must be from last night. Killing a man for the first time does that. He'll shake it off once he feels comfortable at the house. Lydia already knows to tell him that I hit a huge lottery in Pennsylvania if the question over my wealth comes up, which I'm fairly sure it will. So, Lydia and I are on the same page there. Joe Lofton will be too if I decide to bring him in on this.

"Yo, Placido, man."

I punch him in the arm pretty hard.

He looks at me.

"Hey," I say, "put last night out of your mind, except for what you learned. The rest is garbage. What did you learn?"

I am deadly serious and not smiling. I am in charge, and Placido has to know that. Things will have to be done perfectly, if we are to torture and kill Sheriff Pond Scum and get the hell away with it.

"I learned how to kill," Placido says simply.

"What about it? Elaborate. This is serious shit and don't forget, serious money."

"I learned that I can do it, but I don't like it."

"Good. What else?"

"I don't want to go to jail, *or* to hell."

"Neither do I. I don't want to go to jail. But, hell? That's up to God."

Damn, I hope and *pray* the lion sleeps for a few days. If he roars over the weekend while Placido and Joe Lofton are there, I'll have to go out and make a kill, and that could fuck everything up.

Did I forget to mention that Lydia will be picking Joe up from the Ft. Lauderdale-Hollywood airport on Sunday afternoon? By then, I'll have had all of Saturday to explain my sadistic scheme to Placido and to fill him in on what Joe Lofton *cannot* and *must* not know.

As a matter of fact, I've been thinking and even dreaming, not lucid dreams though, dammit, of cutting Joe out of this mission of madness altogether. It's going to be very dangerous for my straight-and-narrow family man friend and *already* partner-in-crimes *of a different nature*. He's my money guy. Yeah, I might get him to cancel his flight. Just like writing a book or a song, cut the fat out. Less is more.

When Placido and I get to the mansion, I'm gonna take a long swim and make my final decision.

You know I make a lot of decisions while I'm swimming, but I'm already leaning toward eliminating Joe Lofton from all of this impending danger and death. He's much too valuable to me doing just what he's doing, which is making money for me and hiding most of it. Good old Joey Boy. You'd love him if you knew him as well as I do. Plus, I don't wanna get him killed for the sake of his wife, Eileen and kids. If you think I feel bad about killing Monster, just think how horrible my life would be, just knowing that I got a good guy like Joe Lofton killed.

Gee, ain't I a sweetheart, I've got a coffin-full of compassion, don't I? That's another fucked up joke.

Let's move on. Hope you laughed, though. I did. I'll bet Henny Youngman did too, up there in Heaven. To be honest, no, I really do not have compassion, empathy or sympathy when my lion, my *master*, roars. I've killed ten fuckin' people with at least two more to go. And I've orchestrated the killing of Number eleven.

I am a robot, obedient to the lion's demands, his hired gun. No, I am not a *sweetheart*... I'm a nightmare's nightmare, as Sheriff Shake Down and probably his ass-licking deputy, the one who dug up Queenie, will soon find out. And so will B.V. West, Mr. Big Shot. And so will you!

I must say – with a perverse amount of pride – that the *main event* I have created in my sometimes hideous brain for these bastards is beyond revenge, beyond murder, beyond torture and beyond your imagination. You'll see, in due time.

As you know, Joe Lofton keeps tabs on the doomed sheriff and deputy that Placido and I will soon appear to as grim reapers in the flesh. Nasty ones, too. Joe's latest report is that Sheriff Suck My Dick still runs the show from his little office on the outskirts of Granite, my hometown, and, as usual, has his shotgun lying across his desk. It seems that he and his deputy spend most of their days watching porn and game shows then sleeping the rest of the time. Good news; easy prey.

I gotta remember to get four sets of handcuffs for my brief case. That will be one of Placido's multiple duties. The cuffs are an integral part of my plan, and an important one. You're gonna love it!

You know we're still in the cab on the way to my place, right? Good. I am just thinking out loud. You can hear me, but Placido can't. We haven't uttered a word since I got in the back seat with him after visiting Mama Placido. That silence thing again.

Well, when we get to the mansion, that's all gonna change. Placido is gonna listen, and listen good. He is also going to have to interject some input, concerning and perfecting the unholy deed we must perform almost as a ritual in Pennsylvania. Input I may or may not use, but it never hurts to listen to other people's ideas and unique dimensions of thought. Gems are found there, as well as pyrite, *fools' gold.*

I've got to be careful here, no doubt about that. If I find out that I made a mistake in taking him on as a partner, I fear the lion will awake from his slumber and command me to take Placido off of the un-killable list.

I tap the cabbie on the shoulder.

"Right here's good."

I get him to let us off a couple of blocks from the beach and a block north of the house. So, we have about a three-block walk.

"Damn Raven, what are we doing here? We gonna kill a rich guy or somethin'?"

"No man, just heading to my place."

"How far away, I mean, you don't live around here do you?"

"Yeah, partner, I do. I'll explain later, we're almost there." I pause to light a Newport.

"Hey Placido, you ever play the lottery?"

11

Miami, Fl. Police Headquarters

Agent Rick Sansom is *more* than ready to fly home
and see his family in Virginia. Miami is nice, but there
isn't much time for fun in the sun when you are searching
for a killer who eats his victims' eyes out of their heads.
Only two more days to go – he is scheduled to fly home on
Monday.

Although this is Saturday, it's still a work day for
Rick, Miami Police Chief Mannie Bastardo and the entire
Zip-Team – the code name they gave themselves: *Sharp-
ass street cops and detectives trying to track down the
"Eye Eater Killer."* The Miami Herald created that
catchphrase to describe the brutal murderer after the
Tedesco massacre. Mannie Bastardo knew the story of the
murders wouldn't slip by the press for long. The Tedesco
killings are a big deal in Miami, and the poor guy at Ft.
Lauderdale Airport; you know, that clever fucker who
gouged out his own left eye and then hanged himself in the
shit stall? *That's a joke, folks. Are you laughing? I am.*
Well, that episode is now being linked to the Twins'
murders.

The Zip-Team is trying to put the pieces of the puzzle
together, a puzzle with no rhyme or reason – just a sick
killer with an odd calling card. Rick's cell phone, which
he keeps on the nightstand in his motel room, close to his
head, woke him at 5:41 a.m. on this already muggy, sultry
Saturday morning. No biggie. His wakeup call from the

motel desk is going to ring at six o'clock, anyway. It is chief Bastardo.

"Yeah Chief."

"Rick, how soon can you get down here? Looks like The eye-eater struck again last night."

"No shit?"

"Yeah, no shit. Up on Bahia Mar Beach in Ft. Lauderdale. We think he might have had a partner with him this time. I'll fill you in when you get here."

"Be there in about 45 minutes, Chief. Gonna take a quick shower and grab a cup of Joe. Sounds like this could be a long day." *And I hope it doesn't delay my trip back home on Monday.*

"Okay, Rick, See you in forty-five." Bastardo hangs up.

"Damn! I wanna go home." is all Rick can think now.

Rick walks into Bastardo's office exactly an hour after he had told the chief he would be there in forty-five minutes. Guess who is sitting next to the chief, going over the police report they had just received concerning the two murders on Bahia Mar beach? Yep, Frank Harding.

What the hell is he doing here? Rick thinks.

It is déjà vu all over again when Harding looks up at Rick, and then down at his Movado – late again. Harding and the chief both stand up without even speaking directly to Rick.

"Okay, let's go," Harding commands.

They ride the elevator in silence down to the garage floor and climb into a squad car. Chief Bastardo drives, sirens blaring. Rick sits in the back, just listening.

"We're going down to the crime scene. Ain't such a pretty sight from what I can gather. John Doe number one was pierced through the skull with what one of our CSI gals seems to think was an ice pick. The other guy was

142

nearly decapitated. I guess the eye-eater didn't have time to saw *completely* through John Doe number two's spinal cord and saw no need to. We know this one was done by the eye-eater himself, because, obviously, his left fuckin' eye is missing, and it wasn't cut out. She says it looks more like it was gnawed out or eaten out – similar to the Tedesco twins' affair. It also looks like John Doe number one was killed by someone other than the eye-eater, perhaps an accomplice. Maybe a coincidence, but I'm leaning toward accomplice. *He* still has his left eye. Chief, I've scheduled Rick down here for another week to work with you and the Zip-Team."

Harding turns around and looks at Rick.

"That Okay with you Rick?" he asks. He turns back around, glancing at his watch.

"Sure boss. Glad to."

Double Damn!

12

The Mansion

Placido and I enter through the garage door into the kitchen. I let him wander around in silence for a while, going from room to room. His mouth is gaping open like a poor kid in a candy store for the first time. When I bring him out of his stupor by handing him a cold Heineken, he smiles at me – a really big grin.

"Man," he says, you've for sure got some explaining to do, Raven. I mean, shit, this house, this whole thing – none of it makes sense. Dude, you gotta fill me in."

We clink bottles.

"Follow me Placido, I think Lydia and Art are out on the front patio."

Placido had never met either one of them, but knew all about Lydia – nothing about Art.

"Matter of fact, grab another beer out of *that* fridge over there."

I nod in its direction.

"That's the *beer* fridge. Beer only. I just hired a new supplier, *(inside joke)*. My last beer-man just retired. I'll get Lydia's wine. Hey Placido, don't freak out man, I'll explain this whole thing to you in a minute. It's no big deal, really."

We clink again.

Placido is still looking around like he's in a museum.

"Whatever you say, boss."

144

"Great, follow me. Time to see what Lydia and Art are up to."

"Who's Art?"

"Oh, Art is a friend of ours who lives here as part of our little family. Lydia wants to expand and get a cat though, but I'm thinking more along the lines of a small dog. I don't like members of the feline family. Do you?"

"Um, well, I guess you could say that I'm more of a dog person, myself."

I nod.

"Good, that's a very good thing to know, buddy. You'll find out why I say that later."

Placido gives me a questioning glance then extends his arm toward the front porch, feeling more comfortable now.

"Lead the way, Raven," he says.

We walk out through the open patio doors, and there Lydia and Art sit in their lounge chairs chatting away about how lovely the ocean looks today, how all the colors are mingling.

Ignorance is bliss.

Art already has a beer – I should have figured that; and Lydia is enjoying a Black & Mild along with what I'm guessing is her first zinfandel of the day.

Might as well join the party!

Actually this is a good way to start off our day, which for Placido and I will later turn to business, honesty, money and the discussion of death.

After all the small talk about "how nice it is to meet you" and all that nonsense is basically over, I bring out a joint and four roxie 30's. I had put them away (courtesy of the Tedescos) for this occasion. *See, I always plan ahead.*

I figure the roxies and booze will loosen us all up just enough to get the ball rolling. That's why I call this a weekend retreat in the first place. It's the perfect place to meticulously work out a plan with Placido as to how and when we are going to travel north to Pennsylvania, kill Sheriff Dog Food and get back to Miami safely.

Lydia, Art and Placido are all starting to get a little buzzed and talking more. I'm really just observing now and listening, but when the time is right, Placido and I will go into my den for his first briefing. Neither Lydia, nor Art can know anything about this. I've already made that decision. They'll be happily left alone on the patio to continue their party.

I've also been prudent enough to cut Joe Lofton out of the picture, so that leaves just Placido and me to accomplish this all-important assassination flawlessly. I think I'd rather be killed than caught. I'll fight to the death if need be, because this is it! *The final step in my lunatic journey to silence the roar of the mighty lion forever*, but for Mama Placido's sake, I'll do everything I can to protect her son from either of those two fates.

"Okay, guys." I lean over and give the lovely Lydia a kiss. "Time for Placido and me to go in and discuss our new business venture. We'll be out later."

"Wish us luck," Placido adds, then salutes Lydia and Art.

Art tips his ancient ball-cap, with the American flag on the front. Man, I think he sleeps in that thing. Other than that, he looks really good in opulence. Even with only one ear – gives him more character. Ah, the elegance of simplicity embodied in the form of Art.

Get it? *Art,* like in painting or sculpturing? *Henny gets it, I'm sure. Okay, joke time is over.*

I walk Placido into my den with a bucket of Heineken on ice. I mentioned earlier that the library and the den are the same room. This is where I'm writing my new book.

146

The one I must finish and publish before I even *start* on *Alien Island.* I think I told you about that one. Anyway, Placido takes a seat on one of the two leather loveseats which face each other. I sit across from him on the other and we place our beers on the cherry wood coffee table between us. I hand him this list:

Your Duties

NOTE: Do not speak until you finish reading this.

1. Buy new Chevy Suburban, loaded, with dark tinted glass all the way around. No back seats. Must be room for two large dog cages. I'll supply the cash.
2. Purchase two of the biggest, meanest, killer pit bulls possible. You will be driving them to Pennsylvania. And yes, I'll be with you. Make sure the dogs can be picked up the morning we leave. I *won't* be with you then, not until you get back here with the dogs. We will leave for Pa. when you arrive with the pits. Do NOT pull into the garage. Lydia must not see the dogs. Pull up out on the street.
3. As the day approaches toward our little trip up north, which I'm thinking will be this Wednesday, tell your mom that you are going with Raven to a business meeting in New York City and there is the distinct possibility of you making some 'real' money for a change. Excite her, make her happy. Do not worry her in any way. I already hinted to her that we might do some business, so, she won't be surprised or suspicious at all. If she asks

about the beach, just tell her that the meeting had to be moved to New York City.

4. We will be gone about seven days, give or take. But you never know. I will leave your mom plenty of cash to hold her over no matter how long it takes. Explain to her that there is to be no cell phone communication for the entire time we are gone, and that your phone will be turned off. Which it won't, just in case we absolutely need it. Otherwise, nothing.

5. Be prepared to kill if necessary; assume it will be. You'll be using a pistol with a silencer (very close range) or an ice pick. Or both.

6. Never *EVER* mention my name, except to your mom, of course. But ask *her* not to mention me. Tell her it's for secret business reasons or something like that. You'll figure it out.

7. Cop enough high grade crystal meth to keep us both awake for a few days. *Good* shit. You'll be driving straight through to Pa, and maybe even straight back to Miami. Get a few Klonopin too, for when we wanna crash, and a few roxies. No pot or booze.

8. Make sure your license, etc., is all up to date. Register and insure the suburban in your name. When your job is complete, it's yours. Little bonus.

9. Remember, not a word of this around Lydia or Art. Let me do the talking and follow my lead. If push comes to shove, just say, *"It's a business deal that Raven is getting me involved in, and I don't want to jinx it by talking about it."* And then change the subject.

10. Get four sets of handcuffs.

11. We'll talk about all of this when you are finished reading.

I light a cigarette and crack another beer while Placido is 'intently' reading his to-do list. I watch his body language. He is nervous. Wouldn't *you* be? If he wasn't, I'd be very worried about my choice of partners. After about ten minutes, Placido looks up, grabs his beer and lights a Newport.

"Can I talk now?" he asks.

"Talk."

"Okay Raven, now is the time to *really* fill me in on this. Fuck, I'm *still* in the dark."

"What would you like to know? Be specific."

"Well, for starters, what are we gonna be doing?"

"Killing a sheriff in central Pennsylvania."

Placido looks down, and then looks up.

"Okay, so I'm gonna be your driver, your accomplice and I'm gonna make a hundred grand. Am I on the right track?"

"So far, yes, you are."

Placido pauses, takes a deep breath and looks at me.

"I think I get it," he says, in such a serious, low tone I nearly start laughing, "but what are we going to do with two pit bulls? Raven, I don't even know precisely what we're supposed to do once we get to Pennsylvania besides kill a man."

I correct him.

"*Two* men."

"I'm in, okay?" Placido assures me. "And thanks for the Suburban, but I think now is the time for you to explain to me exactly what my job is in this whole thing. I understand the list and I can take care of all that stuff. But what I'd really like to know is why you need to murder a sheriff in Pennsylvania."

I ignore that last question. I'm good at ignoring things I do not want to reply to.

Placido presses me.

"I mean, what did he do? Did he throw you in jail or something?"

"More like in prison." I humor him by saying.

I place my beer down on the coffee table and put my hands in a steeple position in front of my face like I'm praying.

"This is a mission of revenge, Placido. I've waited forty-two years to kill the Sheriff of Granite County, Pennsylvania. I grew up in the town of Granite. That's where we're going. The sheriff's office is situated on the outskirts of my hometown. In short, we are driving to the sheriff's office and killing his deputy as quickly as possible. That's where you come in. I'll attend to the sheriff.

You'll have a 9mm Glock pistol with a silencer attached, and if I say the word "NOW" shoot the shit-bag in the chest four times at close range so you don't miss. If he's reluctant to die, ice-pick him. Believe it or not, even at close range pistols are difficult to aim…"

"Wait a minute, Raven, are you forgetting that I grew up near Overtown? Believe me, I can shoot a pistol. I'll make sure he's dead."

We clink bottles again, and each light a Newport.

"Sorry man," I say. "I should've known better; didn't mean to insult you. My bad!"

We laugh.

I had done a lot of shooting when I lived out in Colorado, so I feel good with a pistol, and I'm relieved to know that Placido does too. Comforting, because that is one thing which had concerned me about my new partner, and I don't have time to train him.

"What about the dogs and the cages? We're driving them all the way to Pennsy?"

"No, you are. I'm riding shotgun. I do not have a driver's license Placido. I thought you knew that."

"Yeah, but I thought it was because you were so goddamned poor that you couldn't afford a car. How did you get this fuckin' palace, anyway?"

I look into my buddies black eyes and sense a little fear there. He knew all along that he was going to say *yes* and be part of the operation, and so did I; yet now I can see he is shivering over it. But I think he'll be fine after he loosens up about his new hobby – killing. This is all virgin ground to Placido. He'll be just fine when it counts.

"Yo, Raven," Placido says, sounding a little insecure, "we gotta be honest about all of this, about *everything,* or we got nothing, man!"

He is almost right. But I skirt that *everything* crap by kinda walkin' around it.

"I agree wholeheartedly,"

"Hey look," I say, "just 'cause we're kind of business partners now doesn't mean we can't still be just plain old fun loving friends, too. Just like always. You can understand that, right? That's why I chose you and tested you last night on Bahia Mar Beach."

"And I passed the test?"

"Yep, you passed the test."

Placido closes his eyes and is quiet for a few seconds, then opens them. He glares – no, he stares at me, finally catching on that this is serious business times ten. Life-and-death situations always are.

He finally breaks his silence.

"Gee," he says, "if we fuck up, we're dead aren't we?"

"Yep," I reply in all honesty.

Placido questions me in the tone of a rookie Mafia hit-man about to follow his first murderous order.

So, naturally he's a bit nervous. He looks at the den door to make sure it's closed, I'm guessing. Then he looks back at me.

"Now what?" he blurts out. "Lay it out. Lay out every fuckin' detail of what I've gotta do for this hundred grand. You *sure* I'm not gonna get killed?"

I can't hide my frown.

"No," I admit, "but if you follow my instructions to a 'T,' maybe neither one of us will. The only dead men out of this little trip we're making with our doggies is gonna be Sheriff Brian Vaughn West and his deputy, who is not worthy of a name."

And although B.V. West will be named as author of my new book, his influence will be slain.

"Since I know you're going to ask this anyway," I add, "Yes, one of us will probably kill the deputy quickly. If it's me, I'll eat his left eyeball out of his demon skull. So, be prepared. That's why I wanted you to see me do that last night. Got it so far?"

"I've got it," Placido says solemnly. "I watched the news before the cabbie pulled up today. Raven, you are the Eye-Eater-Killer aren't you? You got the Tedescos and God only knows how many others. I hated the Tedescos; they banged a buddy of mine when they first moved in and started taking over the blocks. Knocked him out with a claw hammer and then poured hydrochloric acid down his throat and all over his face. He died the next day. Thanks, man."

I slap my knees, get up and grab us a couple more beers.

The mother fuckin' lion was beginning to stir, shit!
I hand Placido his beer.

152

"Let's finish these; then we'll head out to Overtown. I wanna walk around and clear my head."

I raise my bottle.

"Here's to you partner! Hey, I'd say we had a pretty good first meeting. We're on the same page."

"Here's to you too, Raven. But why do you wanna go to Overtown tonight?"

Because the lion is purring I've got to make a kill soon. Why else?

"I was gonna go to Macabi's and see if I can run into Julie."

I can't blame him.

"Okay, well drop me off in Overtown on your way to Macabi's, and say hi to Pat for me. I'll walk home later tonight. One of the guest rooms is ready for you. We'll have a lot more to talk about tomorrow, so even if you get lucky, do *not* bring Julie, or anyone else back here with you tonight. Try to be in bed asleep by 3 a.m. I want our minds sharp tomorrow. Sound fair enough?"

Oh good Christ, the lion is hungry for death. I can barely understand Placido's words, the roar is deafening, and the ghost children from my nightmare are bashing the inside of my skull with little ball-peen hammers. *We have to go now!* I can smell the nefarious lion's breath; it is hot with fury.

"Placido, let me grab my briefcase, and we'll get the hell out of here. Change of plans, fuck it, I'll go with you to Macabi's. I feel like a good cigar. Hurry up and finish that beer. Let's roll."

The lion doesn't even give me time to tell Lydia and Art that Placido and I are leaving. We walk a block and catch a cab.

"Macabi's," I instruct the driver, Las Olas in Ft. Lauderdale. Fast."

The Haitian driver just nods. He's the same one carrying on the love-hate relationship with the good old USofA. I still feel like covering his eyes with my hands. If I did, he'd probably sue the government for allowing a bastard such as me to roam the streets.

Placido can tell I am anxious, but he doesn't know what about. He still doesn't know about my lion, the lion that guarantees that I will kill tonight. Nor does he know how lucky he is that it is not him. Thank God for the un-killable list – short as it may be. My briefcase rides on my lap. I am going to kill tonight, I must. But who, where, *how?*

I'll devise a plan on the way to Macabi's. I'm thinking *brain scrambling.* Navy seals are experts at this. It's a quick, silent and virtually bloodless method if done correctly. To do so, you must walk up behind the victim in complete and utter silence. Reach around and grab their nose and mouth while inserting a very pointed and sharp double-edged knife into the little area where the brain stem ends and the spinal cord begins. Try to go in on a 45-degree angle at least a couple of inches and twist the blade.

If done correctly, your prey will fall limply and silently into your arms, releasing him or *her* into the mystical winds of heaven – or hell. You then just lay them down and move on. Oh, yeah, I've got the perfect knife.

Oh man this fuckin' lion is trying to kill me, trying to turn my head into an exploding hand grenade, with ghost-bangs, his white teeth, red tongue, burning breath and that ever-maddening roar. *BANG! BANG, BANG!*

A brief note:

I must tell you now that I wouldn't be travelling to Granite or anywhere else to kill even the disgusting sheriff if it wasn't for the roar of the lion.

Killing the sheriff is my only hope for freedom.

And I truly believe that the more he suffers both physically and mentally before death opens its merciful doors and ushers him inside to the lake of fire, the more satisfied the lion will be... prayerfully, forever.

And I will be free.

I look up.

"What do you think, Queenie girl?"

Free as a Raven in flight?

Raven April

13

Macabi's

When the cabbie finally pulls up in front of Macabi's, I get out first, walk in and order a double-shot of Jack Daniel's and a Heineken. I have to keep the lion at bay and time is running out.

"Fuck man," Placido says, coming in behind me. "You must be thirsty as hell, or you wanna get fucked up awful bad."

"You don't know how bad I wish they were the reasons," I reply. "Look, I'm gonna walk down Las Olas and look in some of the shops. There's Julie over there in the far corner. I'll be back."

"Yeah," he says, after spotting Julie and slapping me on the back. "See ya later, Raven."

I walk out on to Las Olas Boulevard, turn right, heading west toward the fancy shops and restaurant district. Before I get there though, I have to cross a little bridge that spans a narrow canal. Once I get to the other side of the bridge, instead of continuing straight into the sparkling lights of Las Olas, I make a sharp right and follow the shore of the canal until it is pitch black. I know that down there someplace is a little clearing where homeless alcoholics camp and even light small bonfires.

Hell, I even slept there once… funny story about that.

Just as long as these bums stay off of Las Olas, especially at night, the cops basically let them be. Sort of like, out of sight, out of mind. But *I* won't let them be. Not

156

tonight. I am looking for one on the outer perimeter of the group. I keep walking silently. I hear something... voices. I put down my briefcase and pull out my brain-scrambling knife – beautiful piece of craftsmanship, by the way. I creep up on the group of six like an Indian brave. No fire tonight. Good. But my "lion" eyes can see very clearly.

Did you know that lions have excellent nocturnal vision? They can virtually *see* at night.

Just another tid-bit of trivia you may have already picked up on.

And now as the lion roars, I have not taken on only his strength, but his vision and cunning as well. I spot my prey. He is off a little in the woods taking a piss. I had to make this quick, before he's done pissing. *Blood probably.* Hey, at least he can piss; think of poor beer-man.

I've made my way up to about two feet behind Mr. Piss Bucket. He doesn't suspect anything or hear even a twig snap under my feet. I take a soft, stealthy step forward, reach around with my left hand and powerfully grab his nose and mouth, while at the same time pulling his voiceless head toward me. Then, nearly simultaneously - with the nose and mouth clasped - I insert the knife perfectly on target between his brain stem and spine on a 45-degree angle. I twist the blade from side to side then noiselessly lay him on the ground. Dead.

Kill Number twelve – an even dozen.

The neck puncture is extremely clean, and I wait until his heart stops pumping before I bite, chew and suck the left eye-ball from his skull, the back of his head resting flat in the dirt. Just like taking a bite out of a Georgia peach. It smells and tastes like whiskey, though.

I start back toward the street and the lights. About 100 feet from Las Olas, I stop to clean up in the canal. I hurry, but do not *run* back to recover my briefcase from where

I'd hidden it after I pulled out the *brain-scrambling* knife. No. I walk at a good steady pace though, while enjoying a Newport. I do, however, want to get back up on to the crowded street sooner, rather than later in case any of his buddies find Piss Bucket dead by now. None of them see me, so I'll be safe on Las Olas, and they aren't allowed up there anyway. Another perfect kill? Let's hope so. I really am not very bloody. I need a little light from the street to refocus my eyes, for the lion is sleeping now and I have lost his power of strength and night vision, but not his cunning.

When I get back up on Las Olas, I turn left and casually stroll back to Macabi's where Placido is in a close conversation with Julie. I grab a beer, and walk down to tell Placido that I am heading back to the mansion.

"I'll see ya when you get there, Placido. Good night, Julie."

Good night, Raven April," Julie calls, as I turn to leave.

I walk outside and flag down a cab. As usual I get him to drop me off a couple blocks from home and give him a nice, fat tip.

I plan to have Placido stay at the mansion tonight, Sunday night and Monday night. Accomplishing his list of duties on Monday, we would finalize our hideous plan on Tuesday and be on the road by 6 a.m. Wednesday morning.

Sounds smooth enough, doesn't it?

Wednesday, 5:30 a.m.

Placido pulls his new Suburban up in front of the house.

I walk out and open the front passenger door to get a good look at the Killer-Pits. From the corner of my eye, I observe Placido, who is obviously pleased with himself, looking across at me from the driver's side.

"Damn," I say, "they're big. Glad they're in fuckin' cages." Upon closer inspection, I say, "Holy shit, Placido, are they dogs or just giant genetically mutated killing machines?"

He smiles proudly.

"Both," he says.

I reply with a handshake across the Suburban's center console.

"Good job, partner. They should do the trick."

"Aren't they just what you ordered, sir?" Placido asks. this time sounding like a soldier, a *private* speaking to a *Captain,*

I smile as I nod my approval.

"Damn right they are… perfect. But can you control them once we get there? Remember, we've got to get them into a small jail cell."

"No problem, I got some quick lessons yesterday and again this morning from the guy we, I mean *you*, bought them from. All I have to do is give them a command and they'll do anything I say. But you, Raven, have got to be careful around them. They will only *answer* to me. Remember they're trained killer-dogs with unbelievable friggin' strength. They weigh over a hundred pounds each."

"Okay," I say. "You are in complete control of the dogs. Just make sure they are hungry and pissed by the time we get to Pennsylvania. Do they like blood?"

"Hey buddy, they live for it."

"Good. Now, let's get the fuck out of here before Lydia wakes up and starts asking questions. I don't want her or Art to see these dogs. This is an innocent business trip as far as they are concerned. I'll call her in a few hours from your phone. Turn it off for now. Hop on I-95 and head north, we won't even need the GPS for a couple days."

I try to relax but the whole time my mind is consumed with what I'm thinking.

I hope the lion sleeps through this road trip and is ready to die forever after Sheriff Hell Bound is turned into mincemeat by my two new canine companions. Man, I hate to even look into their devilish eyes. They are the biggest, meanest looking dogs I've ever seen.

Placido sure followed that order to a "T." The pits are right behind us, their faces no more than a foot away from the back of our heads. I won't be turning around much on this journey, and I'm damn glad Placido is the one handling them. I ain't gettin' anywhere near those bastards once they're outside their cages.

14

Granite, Pennsylvania

Oh man, I'm just coming out of a lucid dream, a heavy one. Without going into a detailed and lengthy discussion of the dream's magical revelation, let's just say that B.V. West will definitely die along with the sheriff and the lion.

In my first book, *Standing on the Edge of Forever*, Mr. Asshole West made me use a lot of big, fancy words, which in my opinion were, and always are, unnecessary. My dream revealed to me that this is the root of my intense hate for him, not what I had thought it was, which was of all the fame and fortune the little lizard always gets.

My new book, the one I'm currently writing in the den is so fuckin' good that big, fancy words are not needed and probably would lessen the impact of the story anyway. You'll see. I can't wait for you to read it. I know I can't kill B.V. West with a knife or a bullet, so I must send him off to hell with power of mind. And I will.

The meth was blowing my brain cells into little bits of who knows what, so I took 4 mgs. of Klonopin a few hours ago and am just now coming to from a nightmare infested nap. I look over and Placido is still cruising along like a non-Haitian cabbie. As I'm trying to get my shit together by lighting a Newport and downing a half bottle of water, I see the sign welcoming us into Granite, Pa.

Turns out I didn't just "wake up." Placido had noticed a few minutes earlier on the GPS that we were getting close to my hometown and has been shaking me and yelling at me.

"Wake the fuck up!" he says, shaking me wildly.

He had driven straight through, around 1,200 miles.

"Good job dude, now find a dirt road. It ain't hard to do. This whole county was never anything *but* dirt roads and sure as hell doesn't appear to have changed much. Then get the meth out, I need a few lines to put my thought process back together. It's almost game-time. You okay, Placido?"

He laughs, but it isn't his usual *sane* laugh, which concerns me a little. Maybe the meth is interfering with his gray matter's ability to think straight by blowing holes in his cerebellum or something. Damn, I hope not. Not now.

"Fuck Raven," he says, "I have *never felt better* in my entire life!"

"Good, buddy, now hit that dirt road and pull over somewhere. I'm gonna do a few lines, then we'll carry out our plan and get the hell out of here, and thank God, *without* those fuckin' dogs. They're staying behind with the corpses. You sure you can handle those fuckers?"

"Bear shit in the woods? They follow commands. I know the commands. Even if *you* gave the same commands, they wouldn't listen to them. They'd just kill you. They are starving and pissed, just the way you said you wanted them, Raven. Can I shoot the deputy?"

"If he's there, yes; but, make sure he's *dead.* Dead! No witnesses. That means if anybody happens to wander into to that shit-house Sheriff's office, kill them, too - head shots, up close, if possible. That's why I only want you to use four bullets on the deputy. You may need the other ones. Your 9mm Glock holds thirteen bullets in the magazine and one in the chamber. Fourteen rounds should be enough. Let's hope you don't have to use them all. You'll also have your ice pick. I'll have my briefcase."

Those four lines of meth hit the *motherfuckin'* spot! I feel like a million bucks again, and I'm ready to get this mission accomplished. I just can't wait to see Sheriff Terror shake in his boots *(before I make him take them off, ha!)* and handcuff him naked to the inside of his own jail cell. Okay, enough of this bullshit with me thinking out-loud and all. I Promise. I'm really just waiting for Placido to finish up his lines of meth.

Are we crazy? Tell me now what you really think. I'm curious. I mean we are friends, aren't we? I'll even confess to you that I have this guilty feeling that I should be home in my den working on the new book. Hell, I've got a deadline, and I don't want to let Joe Lofton down. Oh well, I'll get back to work hard on it when we get back to Miami.

Gotta concentrate on the task at hand for now, seize the moment, slay the lion, the deputy, B.V. West and the sheriff. Not a bad day's work If I do say so myself. Placido's all done snorting his lines. Time to do this. I feel like a Comanche on horseback charging in against the U.S. Calvary. Yeah, maybe I am crazy, but who's to judge?

"Placido, reset the GPS from this spot to the sheriff's office. I want you to drive right up to the place. If it appears that the only ones there are Sheriff Shit and Deputy Doomed, then back this fucker right up to the front door. We'll know it's only them if just two cars are parked next to the building.

"Wait – if there's more, do it anyway! They die too. You do any strangers. I just want the sheriff. Remember, follow my orders, man. Trust me; and I'll get you out of this alive."

We reach over and hug like teammates before the Super Bowl, the dogs growling all the while.

Placido vigilantly resets the GPS. Then he puts the Suburban in drive. The moment I have been waiting for is about to arrive.

I'm gonna take you through this just as it happens, just as I promised you when I basically told you this wasn't really a book book, but a story I wanted you to hear. A story I needed to tell you.

I slapped Placido's cheek.

"Okay. Take off my brother-from-another-mother. Let's go make the kills of the century, and maybe the millennium."

We both start laughing, but not for long. The seriousness and sense of danger has returned – which is a good thing.

"Look Placido, I know you still don't have a clue about what I've got planned once we get inside the office; but like I said before, just follow my orders to the fuckin' "T" and things will be fine. The less you know the better. Hell, I can't even predict how this will all go down. Trust me and trust yourself. Be confident Placido, and always strike first."

He nods in silence, and I can tell he is getting a little shaky, even with the crystal meth – roxie combo swirling through his circulatory system. But I am, let's say, a little more experienced at this sort of thing.

This will be my biggest, and hopefully, last kill and *certainly* the most important. Oh shit, *just in time*. We are about five minutes away from the Granite, Pa. Chamber-of-Horrors-Jail, and the lion awakens from his merciful slumber. *Praise God!* Is this a good sign, or *what?* I feel that overwhelming need to kill again now, and I feel the strength of the lion overtake me physically.

Awesome!

See? Perfect timing! Raven April, killer, writer, sweetheart!

We go by the sheriff's office. Two patrol cars in the side driveway, which leaves the front door standing there like a vertical welcome mat. We stop about 100 feet away, not seeming or acting suspicious.

I reach into my briefcase and hand Placido the loaded Glock.

"Look," I say, "you are going to back up to the front door, not too close, make it look like a legal, nonaggressive thing. We'll both walk in casually with friendly smiles on our faces. You know that drill; right, Casanova?"

I am trying to bring a smile to his frightened-looking face.

I do.

"But," I say, "there's been a slight change of plans. I want you to go ahead and kill the deputy right away. I mean like – instantly. I'm not even gonna yell, 'NOW.' Just shoot him in the chest four times, and then ice-pick his head, but *only* if you *have* to. A total of four shots, and remember, no one will hear it.

And then you just stand and look out the window for anyone who might be coming up the lane. If they do, let them walk inside and shut the door. Then kill them with a head shot.

Placido, I want to warn you now. As soon as I walk in there, I am going to do something you might not want to see in the daylight. It will be worse than what you saw in the darkness on the beach. So, just look out the window if you need to. Otherwise, just do as I fuckin' say. Got it?"

Placido is listening intently.

"Yeah, I got it," he finally says. "Let's go do it!"

Placido does a perfect job of innocently backing the Suburban up squarely to the front door. We get out and walk in appearing (as I'd planned) as two hunters who had come in looking for information about hunting lodges or wanting to purchase a hunting license, Blah, blah, blah.

Neither the sheriff nor the Deputy appear at all alarmed. The sheriff has his huge feet up on his desk watching "The Price Is Right."

The building is a 24 x 24 feet-square, cinder-block-structure. I'm so impressed that I conclude the county must have hired Frank Lloyd Wright to design it.

The Deputy is sitting in another chair, his hands clasped behind his head, also watching the flat screen TV.

Placido immediately puts a bullet in the deputy's chest and another one through his forehead.

I'm thinking, *his forehead?*

He is obviously dead, but Placido (almost?) follows orders and puts another one in his head and chest. That's four. *Damn,* all four shots were supposed to be in the chest! But what the hell... the Barney Fife of Granite County just said bye-bye. Good riddance. What was his last name again?

Now, to more clearly illustrate the grisly scene.

Before Placido even fires his third shot, I am across the sheriff's desk. I bite, rip, tear, suck, and eat the sheriff's left eye.

He is screaming and fighting, searching for his shotgun, but he is no match for me and the lion who lives within me. His empty eye socket and surrounding orbital tissue is bleeding, but not as badly as you might imagine.

It is his screams which I am enjoying immensely. I strangle him into unconsciousness (like the beer-man) but not death. Then, rather easily with my temporary enormous physical power, drag his huge blubbery body into the solitary jail cell. Like I say, Granite is a small town. *I mean, one jail cell?* Once I get him in there, I yell for Placido.

"Placido, I need you now! First, go grab my briefcase out of the truck and get over here with the hand-cuffs before he comes to! *And hurry!"*

Placido is there in a heartbeat with the four sets of hand-cuffs and my briefcase.

My Cuban-American partner and I are working as fast as possible, both nearly in a fixated trance when we pull Sheriff Evil's right hand up to the highest point of the cell bars and cuff his wrist there. We do the same thing with his left wrist, which is not easy, even with my lion strength, because the fat fuck Sheriff weighs in at damn near 300 pounds. The next two cuffings are easy. We put his feet in a spread eagle and cuff his ankles that way to the bottom of the steel cell bars. He doesn't have a chance. No escape!

What a fuckin' shame.

Get this. This is what happens in the frenzy of a death scene.

Placido goes to the medicine kit hanging on the wall next to the TV, grabs some shit out of it, and bandages up the sheriff's left eye hole before he regains consciousness.

I'm thinking to myself, *why is he doing that?*

He told me later it was because he couldn't stand to look at the eye-hole.

Me? I cut all his shit-stinking clothes off of him with good old Bucky, the buck knife.

167

When he comes to, he will be stripped naked, chained like an animal within his own little prison cell – and thanks to Dr. Placido, a patch over his left eye-hole.

I throw hot coffee from their Mr. Coffee machine on his face to wake him up. It helps a little, so I do it again. That one does it. Finally the scumbag is coming around; the patch slides off his eye-hole.

Sorry doc.

Placido is back at his window post. I'd need him soon.

Sheriff Cry Baby is conscious now, and I get face-to-face with him from the outside of the cell. He is more furious than a trapped badger and more scared than a child with a monster emerging from under his bed. He is raging, trying to shake himself loose like King Kong in chains thrashing his immense body back and forth. His wrists and ankles are bleeding.

I smile and reach into my briefcase, pulling out my sharp-ass filet knife.

His right eye opens wide. He starts begging and pleading.

"Remember me, sheriff?" I say, as I hold the knife to his nose.

"No, I swear I don't. Please…"

"Do you remember a hound dog named 'Queenie,' the one the coyotes killed?"

The sheriff's eye freezes on mine, and he tries to get down on his knees, but the handcuffs won't let him. He is starting to shiver now.

"Oh God no, I mean yes… are you Raven April? Please, it…"

Before he can squeak out another word I stab him in his belly, but not deep, not past the many inches of fat protecting his vital organs, but deep enough to get his undivided attention.

"In the flesh," I say, "Sheriff Brian Vaughn West."

Man, I'm having the time of my life, but I don't want to take a chance of fuckin' this up by dragging it out like an all-night cocaine party. I'm too smart for that. Hey, does that lend any credence to the fact that I'm not crazy? I don't know either.

"Bring in the dog crates," I yell over to Placido, "both of them; and make it quick. Tell them that Uncle Raven is about to serve them dinner."

I smile at the pathetic creature through the bars. He is beyond fear now, just like Queenie and I were on that fateful day in the Granite county woods over forty years ago.

Hearing all that about the dogs and so forth, the sheriff rages even more frantically, pulling and shaking again and again against the impossible restraints holding him inside his soon-to-be tomb. He struggles even more wildly than before, the cuffs clanking wildly against the iron cell bars. He is screeching, no *squealing* like a pig for pity.

"No fuckin' way," I say.

At that point I slowly walk into the cell, stand behind him and start slicing his back horizontally with the razor sharp filet knife, drawing blood which is dripping on the jail cell floor.

He starts banging his head against the bars.

I speak to him from behind in my Vincent Price voice.

I start by informing him of certain information.

"The dogs are starving," I say. "Did you know that pit bulls are three times stronger than a full grown coyote? Especially, when they are trained killer dogs; and they lose their minds in fury at the smell of blood, something like bull sharks do. Did you know that? You soon will."

I make a quick maniacal move and put a deep slice down the back of his scrotum – in honor of my friend and yours, Art. Remember, I'm standing behind him at the moment.

He screams.

Placido, although not easy for one man, has maneuvered the dog cages near the door to the cell now; so when he opens the doors to the cages the dogs will have nowhere to go but inside the cell … for supper.

Also for my man Art, and just for the hell of it, I slice the sheriff's right ear off and throw it to one of the still-caged dogs, who swallows it whole before I climb over the cages and out of the jail cell. I then give Placido the go-ahead to let the dogs into the cell with Sheriff Scared to Death.

Hell, wouldn't you be scared?

As a matter of fact, he is so petrified, he falls totally silent for a moment, and it kind of gives me the creeps. He is also stiff with fear. Even through the fat you can see that every muscle in his partially blood-drenched body is tight and rigid.

You gotta remember that Placido and I are high as hell on not only crystal meth, but also adrenaline. This whole thing seems surreal even to me.

As he said he would, Placido handles the dogs, and he does it well. They are both inside the jail cell with the sheriff now. Placido closes the cell door, and I do the honors of locking it.

Yippee! Soon the fun *really* begins.

However, the first thing the 100-pound-plus pit bulls do is start fighting each other! Ripping the fuck out of themselves. Placido delivers a one-word command.

"KILL!" and like robots or Stepford-Wives dogs, they both lurch for the Sheriff, like bullets from a Glock.

The first dog tears a chunk out of his ass and takes only a few seconds to chew it up and eat it. The second rips off his bleeding scrotum along with his teeny-weenie, swallowing the sheriff's whole package easily in one gulp.

That one was also for you, Art.

Hey, you find humor when and where you can. If not, you'd go mad. The starving dogs are ripping the screaming sheriff into pieces, and he is bleeding out faster than I anticipated, especially from between his legs. He will be dead soon, and I want to be there at that moment, so maybe the fast-bleed is a blessing in disguise because it will get Placido and me out of Granite and on our way back to Miami sooner, and prayerfully, safer.

The whimpering, breathless sheriff is only a minute or two, or maybe three, from waking up in hell; so I whip my dick out and piss on him, not getting too close to the cell.

Hell, I ain't stupid.

"Hey sheriff," I say. "This is for Queenie."

Placido is starting to go nutso on me. He has just been part of a nightmare scenario that not even a horror writer could concoct. Except that this is *real*. We have to get the hell out of here, and soon.

"Placido," I say, "calm down. He's dead. Go start the Suburban."

His eyes are fixed on the carnage in the cell. He stands there, silent for a second.

"Okay, man," he says, "good idea. Raven, I *gotta* get out'a here. I'm fuckin' losin' it, man!"

"It's normal," I say. Take a couple Klonnies and roxies right fuckin' *now*, to level you out, buddy. Give me one of each, too."

I was as close to the cell bars as I dare be when Sheriff-Now-In-Hell drew his last breath, hanging limp, as the crazed pits seem determined to eat every last morsel of his flesh and internal organs. His rib cage is already exposed and his entrails are dangling to the floor.

Damn, those dogs know how to follow a command! They'll probably even chew on his bones.

I start laughing to myself wishing I could see the look on the face of the poor fucker that walks in here next. My guess is that they'll puke up their guts while choking on a scream. If I had time, I'd set up a hidden camera.

The lion was suddenly quiet.

Could it possibly be that I am now free...forever? That was, after all, my plan.

I pull a copy of *Standing on the Edge of Forever* from my briefcase (planned ahead again), and set it on fire as a symbolic killing of B.V. West. You must have realized by now that my pen name, B.V. West, was taken from Sheriff Brian Vaughn West's name. They both have the same initials. This happened because on the last day or two before *Standing On the Edge Of Forever* was to be printed, the publisher came up with the bright idea of not using my real name, but a pen name. So, in my excitement of being a published author, I blurted out the name, B.V. West.

Well they loved it.

Recall now, that the memory and hatred for Sheriff Brian Vaughn West was torturing me every moment of my life for what seemed like eternity. Therefore, it wasn't surprising that "B.V. West" was the first name that came to my mind when the publisher hit me with the pen-name idea. I sure as hell couldn't use Brian Vaughn West *verbatim*, but see what I mean? His name was always in some corner of my brain and right on the tip of my tongue. In case you've been wondering, that is the short version of how I became B.V. West, and the reason I pray he died along with The Sheriff.

I let the book burn in the middle of the tiled floor so the fire wouldn't spread and burn down this magnificent scene I have been dreaming of for such a long time. Now the uniformed devil is dead.

Kill Number 13.

Delicious, unlucky number 13.

I'm not superstitious, but I can't help but take a fair amount of pleasure in the fact that the sheriff's death holds an unlucky number. I take one last satisfied look at the unholy crime scene, walk out the door and then hop into the Suburban with Placido. We can still hear the dogs which will no doubt have to be shot inside the cell when the Calvary arrives. I reach over and give Placido a fatherly hug.

"Good job partner, now let's get the hell down the road. We'll celebrate the success of our *business* trip with Lydia and Art when we get back to the mansion."

"Sounds good, Raven. Ready?"

We take off, kickin' up dust.

Hey, I just had a thought cross my mind that I'd like to share with you, if that's all right. Let's ponder good and evil for a moment.

It is said that the one that thrives is the one we feed. Well, I feed both. So what happens to me?

Even though my evil sprang from the incident with Queenie (delayed post traumatic stress disorder), and that my hatred for the sheriff was manifested into the roar of a lion, I still have a hard time understanding it all.

Though it may well be true that the thirteen murders I have committed were not my fault, per se, I still feel somewhat responsible for them and slightly remorseful. So much for the elegance of simplicity. Think about that, will you? Thanks.

173

Miami, we're on our way! That's simple enough, elegant, too. I laugh to myself again as Placido heads down the gravel road and out to our first main highway home. Try and picture this:

The radio is blasting out the song, "Get What You Give," by The New Radicals.

Placido is calming down a little with those two Klonopins and roxies seeping into his bloodstream and I am laughing hysterically.

If this whole story seems to border on fantasy, it's because it does. For me though, it is breaking free from a decades-old memory that has haunted and taunted every moment of my life, consciously as well as subconsciously.

I say a silent prayer of thanks that all four are dead and will forever swim in hell's lake of fire – the sheriff, the deputy, the lion and B.V. West, mister big-word big-shot.

Although his name will be on the cover of the new book I've been working on in the den, the words will all be mine, this time. *"Fuck You, B.V. West!"* I yell above the music and start laughing again.

So does Placido.

The mission isn't over until we pull safely into the garage, but things are looking good so far, clear sailing.

Damn, I need a good swim in the ocean. A session on the "love blanket" also sounds pretty damn tempting about now. Plus, I need a beer! I reach in my pocket and pull out a 30 mg. roxie for Placido and myself. I know we both can use another one.

15

The Mansion

The garage doors open, and Placido pulls the Suburban inside. The doors shut. It is 11 a.m., and we both look and feel like hell.

Placido has earned his hundred grand and new Suburban. I just hope all the killing doesn't ruin his life. Hell, he might even end up with what the headshrinker in L.A. said I had: *delayed post traumatic stress disorder*.

Well, I sure as hell hope mine is over. If so, it's been a strange, bloody and exhausting cure.

Placido and I each take yet another roxie and head to the beer fridge. *Motherfucker,* that beer tastes good! We high-five and walk out onto the patio, where sure enough, there is Queen Lydia and King Art lounging, drinking zinfandel and Heineken, smoking Black & Milds and Newports.

"Wow," I say, "must be nice."

Lydia and Art turn simultaneously, a bit startled to see Placido and me standing behind them.

Lydia jumps up, runs over and gives me a big bear hug and a wet, juicy kiss.

Damn she's a good kisser. She steps back and looks both of us over from head to toe.

"Raven," she says, "you look like hell! And Placido, you look even worse."

Art just sits there and tips his old hat.

"Welcome home, boys." he says. "How'd that business meeting go?"

The roxies and the beer are starting to kick in, and Placido and I are feeling better, more relaxed. I feel like I am actually floating... high on *life* for the first time since Queenie died, because the lion has been silent since the moment Sheriff Dog Dinner met Satan face-to-face.

"It went great Art, but it's not a done deal yet, so I'm still a little leery of talking about it for fear that it might jinx the thing. Right, Placido?"

I kiss Lydia again and ask her to go inside and get that *ass-kick* blunt I had stashed away in the guest room sock drawer, which is now *our* room thanks to King Art and the fact that I really am a sweetheart.

And you damn well know it, don't you?

When Lydia comes out with the blunt, I hand her and Art a roxie. I figure shit, we really deserve a good fuckin' private party right here on "paradise patio." I even go into the den and grab one of my cameras.

I think I might have mentioned this before, right now I'm not sure, but I've loved taking pictures ever since I was a little kid. I got away from it for years, and then when I hit it big with *Standing On the Edge Of Forever*, I started buying cameras but really seldom if ever use them. I do, however, take a series of sunrise shots from the patio that come out pretty good. At least Lydia says they are "Wonderful, Raven, just gorgeous."

I take a few shots of Lydia, Art and Placido. I even set up my tripod so I can mount the camera and get a couple pictures of all four of us together. In my mind I call us the *Fucked-Up Foursome* and start laughing like hell. I can't stop.

The other three look at me kind'a weird for a second or two, but they had all seen me do this before and just figure, "Hey, that's Raven. He lives in two worlds, his own world and the real world."

Art goes inside and gets us more beer and wine. When he comes back, I stand up and blurt out, "A toast to the Fucked-Up Foursome! A bigger day than even *I* could have imagined. Cheers!"

We all clink glasses and take a swig.

Remember now, the other three know nothing about the lion, only you and I do. Oh yeah, and that headshrinker in L.A., Dr. Rothstein? I probably should have killed him. An oversight like that can cost me everything. Hope it doesn't bite me in the ass. What I'm trying to convey to you here is that today is the biggest day of my life, except for watching the birth of my children and my wedding day, way back when.

The lion has been silent. I really think I'm finally free from living under the brutal command of his tormenting roars, red tongue and white sparkling teeth. I have killed him. The great beast died along with Sheriff Chew Bone, the deputy and yes, B.V. West. So, am I borderline giddy this afternoon?

Fuck yeah, wouldn't you be?

I've been thinking again about telling Art and Placido, because I know they are both curious, but afraid to ask, how I make enough money to live here and maintain this little piece of heaven. This would be a good test for Lydia, too.

By the way, I'm really gettin' more than a little blasted on the booze, roxies and weed, but here goes.

"Lydia, my lovely little Mermaid, did you ever happen to let Art in on how I picked the numbers for the mega-millions lottery I hit in Pennsylvania?"

Lydia, who herself is getting wasted, is a little taken aback, but says perfectly, "No, I thought you did."

Placido pipes up before the statement ever gets into Art's brain.

"Fuck, is that *really* how you got so rich, hitting a lottery? Man, I thought you were blowing smoke up my ass that night on the beach. Congratulations Raven!"

He slaps his hand on the glass table we are all now sitting around.

"Damn it, I should have guessed something like that, but it was none of my business, so I didn't push you for an explanation. *Motherfucker*, way to go man!"

Placido, who is sitting across from me, stands up and so do I. We high-five, I finish my beer and decide to go for a short swim. The water is warm, calm and a crystal clear blue-green as it usually is. But before I can, Art puts his arm around me.

"Raven," Art says (*I could swear with tears in his eyes),* "when you hit that lottery, I guess I did too. I love you like a brother, and I can never thank you enough for all you've done for me. You too, Miss Lydia."

Art touches the brim of his hat, and again we toast, this time to me. Good old Art, and to think I almost killed him on at least three occasions that I can remember. Glad I didn't.

"My pleasure, Art," I say. Then, I stand up.

"Adios Amigos, I'm going for a swim."

Only those who dive headfirst flourish in the sea... I don't know where that phrase came from, but I like it. Maybe I'll find a place for it in the new book. Which reminds me, I've *got* to get back to work on that tomorrow. Gonna try to get into the den early and knock some pages out.

After all, I *am* on a deadline that Joe Lofton has negotiated with the publisher, and I don't wanna let Joe down. Besides, it's a great book, if I do say so myself.

Lydia still doesn't even know about it. I'll surprise her with the first copy off the presses. She'll appreciate that.

I'm still watching her for signs of a mental breakdown or anything else weird that might expose its self as a result of her believing she killed the beer-man. So far, so good. She seems fine. There's been no mention of him in the papers, so I can only assume the bull sharks did a good job of cleaning their plates, so to speak. In other words, there is nothing left of him.

Oh wait, yes there is... because *matter can be neither created nor destroyed.* Therefore the beer-man is now bull shark shit. Yep, I'm gettin' a *good* laugh out of that one! I hit the water head-first.

As you know, I do a lot of thinking when I'm one-with-the-water. Either while swimming in the ocean or during a lucid dream is when I, Raven April, *free man at last,* make my best plans for the future, both short-term and long. Today is no exception. In fact, this could very well prove to be the greatest epiphany that I, Raven April, photographer and animal lover has ever had!

Lydia and I are – I've just decided at roughly 100 yards offshore – going to Africa. *Hot damn!* A photographic safari to Kenya or Zimbabwe just to get away, relax with Lydia in a new environment for a couple of weeks and take pictures of the wild animals.

I'd already done a little research on these kinds of safaris on my own for the new book I'm working on, but not much. Going on safari might help kick-start my getaway from the slaughter and slavery that had dominated my psyche and actions for so long, before I silenced the roar of the lion in the Granite County Jail up in Pennsylvania. What do *you* think?

Is the safari a great idea or fuckin' what? I turn for the shore, and on the way back in, I am as excited as a

179

starving pit bull in a jail cell full of fresh meat. Damn, I almost *drown* laughing at that one.

Shifting my thoughts to more practical things, I plan on giving Placido the one thousand one-hundred-dollar bills he earned for a job well done, and sending him home to Mama's with his new Suburban. One permanent house guest is enough.

Yeah, it looks like Art is ours for keeps. However, he *will* be moving into the second floor guest room. I want my bedroom back; I mean, how the hell can we put him back out on the streets? Besides, he'll be a good house-sitter when we are on safari with our cameras, and Lydia fuckin' adores him. So there ya go.

Oh yeah, I almost forgot to tell you that even though Placido had left no doubt that the deputy was dead from the four perfectly-placed bullets, he also slammed the ice pick into the top of his skull just for good measure. I had caught this out of the corner of my eye when it happened during the horror-movie mayhem whirling like a tornado inside the sheriff's office of death and retribution, that fateful day in Granite. To be honest, I think he ice-picked him because he *liked* doing it. That unsettles me, I must admit.

Oh well. Gonna talk the photographic safari thing over with Lydia and see what she thinks of the idea. We'll pick a date, and I'll have Joe Lofton take care of all the arrangements, protecting my identity as usual. Joe knows that that stipulation always goes without saying. I'm heading back to shore now. I really needed that swim. It not only helped me make my decision about the photographic safari but it rejuvenated me, even though in reality I know I need sleep.

So does Placido.

Back On The Patio

"Well Raven," Art says, "how was your swim? Run into any Hammerheads?"

I light a Newport and crack another Heineken.

Art does the same.

"No Hammerheads, but I got a great idea for a vacation with Lydia."

Lydia is sitting in a lounge chair. That gets her attention.

"Ooooh, tell me, tell me!"

I walk around the table and stand behind her, crisscross my arms around her, give her a kiss on the top of her head and whisper in her ear.

"I love you."

Remember, I am still on cloud nine because the sheriff and lion are dead, not to mention B.V. West, and because I am feelin' high as hell from the roxies, booze and blunt. Hell, it's a party!

So I asked Lydia to sit back down, close her eyes and use her imagination, because…

"It's not a normal vacation."

She makes a funny face, like she's thinking, *what does this idiot have in mind this time? This madman that I love so much.*

Art and Placido are also still at the table gettin' hammered. I decide not to send Placido home tonight. He's too fucked up to drive. I'll give him the smaller guest room on the north side of the house.

So Lydia and Art, like in stereo, exclaim, "Well tell us about the vacation!"

Placido just sits there listening, probably too exhausted to talk.

I say in an almost mysterious whisper, just to fuck with them, that we are going to Transylvania to spend a week inside Dracula's Castle.

"Won't that be great? Lydia, you'll love it." Lydia just sits there speechless, lights a Black & Mild and drinks a full glass of wine down in one long gulp.

"Damn Raven," Art says, "I know you're a little off the wall, and I like that aspect of you, buddy. But why would you wanna go there when you can go anywhere in the world?"

I can't help it. I bust out laughing, spraying a mouth full of beer out on Placido.

I've got to stop that.

He just dries his face off with a napkin and resumes his zombie-like demeanor.

Damn, I love that kid. *Mama* Placido, too. I keep my promise to her and bring him home safe, which makes me extremely happy. I gotta call her later and let her know her little boy and *killer* is alright. I'm still laughing like a circus clown drunk on Vodka.

The other three are staring at me, thinking; *there he goes again, into his own little one man world.*

"Gotcha!" I say, when I finally stop laughing.

"Yeah, well paybacks are *hell*," Lydia says – and I can tell she is a little pissed, which is unusual for her, "so watch yourself. That freaks me out. You know I can't even watch a scary *movie*. Why in the fuck did you *do* that? You're such a fuckin' asshole sometimes! How come I love you?"

"That's why," Art looks at Lydia and says, and tips his hat my way.

I'm so happy that Art finally has a place to call home. *Damn,* the sweetheart side of me is showing itself again.

There is a moment of quiet as they all are looking at me to come clean about the vacation I'd planned while swimming. They know by now that the Dracula thing was bullshit, just one of my little jokes.

"Okay," I say, this is my *real* idea for our vacation, Lydia, my Lovely Mermaid."

Yuck, was that me? Too mushy!

"How would you like to go on a photographic Safari to Africa?"

Silence.

16

Police Head Quarters, Miami Florida

Chief Mannie Bastardo answers the phone while trying to enjoy his second cup of coffee. He knows who is calling.

"Morning, Frank. Tell me something good for a change. Have you guys in Quantico come up with anything at *all* on the Eye-Killer, because we sure haven't."

"Morning to you too, Mannie. Well, yes and no. You'll be getting this report emailed to you in about an hour, but I want to tell you personally that we think the Eye-Killer has struck again in a little back woods town in central Pennsylvania, place called Granite."

"Damn, Frank, the pieces of this puzzle are all over the place. This guy is smart. He's also insane and extremely fuckin' dangerous. Your guy Rick Sansom is a sharp cookie. Thanks for letting me use him down here.

"Hey Frank, look, Rick is really missing his family. I'm not telling you how to handle your job, but why don't you let him go home for a couple days and then send him to Granite? By then I'll have a couple of my guys from the Zip-Team up there, the same guys Rick has been working with. One way or another the Eye-Killer is gonna slip up. Maybe he did up there in Granite, and the local authorities missed something.

"I'd really like Rick and my Zip-Team boys up there to see what they can turn up. I also want them to talk to the coroner and go through all of the forensics."

"Mannie," Frank Harding chimes in, "there wasn't much left of the victim, and we think the Eye-Eater had an accomplice up there, because the second victim did *not* have his left eye eaten out. I know this is getting' more unbelievable by the minute, but wait till you see the *pictures*. They'll be attached to your email. They ain't pretty… get a chum bucket ready. As far as Rick Sansom goes, you're absolutely right, Mannie. Fly him home today. I'll have a car waiting to drive him home directly from the airport. From what I'm getting, he's gonna need a couple days rest before he gets to Granite, PA… Doesn't sound like a very nice place to visit right at the moment."

"Nope. Talk to you soon, Frank."

Mannie is holding a piece of paper and says, "Oh shit, get this, it just came in: *A human skull has been found washed up on Jensen Beach just north of Miami and Ft. Lauderdale. At first sight by the crime scene forensic team they speculated by observing the exposed orbital bone that the left eye may have been bitten out by human teeth and may be the work of The Eye-Eater Killer. More will be known after further study. No other body parts were found.*"

"This ain't gettin' any easier Mannie."

Mannie lets out a deep sigh.

"Nope."

He hangs up without saying goodbye.

17

Back at the Patio

"Okay, will you listen to me for a few minutes about the safari? Lydia, I can tell that you're not enthused yet - just hear me out?"

Art laughs, and slaps his hat on the table.

Lydia remains expressionless and un-amused.

Art clams up.

I crack a beer, light a Newport, stand up and continue my pitch, because between you and me, I *am* fuckin' going on this safari, and I know I can talk The Mermaid into it.

"*Listen*, Lydia, we will be experiencing one of the greatest wonders of nature on the entire planet. It's called 'The Great Migration.' It's when hundreds of thousands of Wildebeest make their massive migration across the Grumeti River into Kenya until they find better grazing grounds.

It's perfectly harmless, and only a few people in the world get this opportunity. You, my dear are one of those lucky few. Life is so damn short, let's make the best of it. You know I've been itching like a mangy pit bull to get back into photography. We won't be roughing it. Believe me you'll have the time of your life. Hell, we'll be staying in a state park. It's called, 'Masai Marsa,' top-of-the-line. They'll treat you like a queen, guaranteed! Like I said, I've already looked into it a little bit, but we'll get Joe to set it up for us. Art can stay 'home' and keep an eye on the house. Right, Art?"

"Anything you say, buddy. Goddamn, Lydia, this sounds like a once-in-a-lifetime chance to me. I'd sure as hell go if I was you. Raven, will you grab me the roach from that blunt? It's in the ashtray. Hell, this *is* a party ain't it?"

I grab the roach for Art, light it, and take the first hit before I hand it over to Art. Placido is asleep with his head on the table. Poor kid's been through some shit over the last few days. I'm gonna carry him into his room before he falls out of the fuckin' chair. I sling him over my back like a sack of potatoes as gently as I can. He never opens his eyes.

"I'll be right back. I'm tucking Placido in for the night and calling his mama. Be right out."

After I lay him on the bed I punch in Mama Placido's phone number.

She answers.

"Hello, Raven. Oh my God, I've been so worried, praying all the time! How is my baby?" Her voice is bordering on hysteria. I smile to myself.

"Placido is just fine," I say, eyeing him passed out on the bed, plastered out of his young mind. "Our business trip took a lot out of us, but I think you'll be happy with the results. Placido will tell you all about it when he gets home tomorrow. He's asleep now, probably dreaming about his own bed. How are you, Mama?"

"I'm a lot better *now*. Thank you Raven for taking care of my Placido."

"My pleasure, he's a fine young fella." *And a damn good ice-pick man.* "I think I'm gonna hit the rack, too. Placido will be home safe and sound tomorrow. Sleep tight, Mama."

"You're such a good boy, Raven. Good night."

Good boy? I'm not good, and I damn sure ain't no boy.

Before I go back out to the patio, I want to share a poem with you which I wrote while Placido and I were "tweaking" real heavy on our trip back from Granite. Here it is, this is just for us, okay? It's short, so don't panic. I know poetry usually sucks, but indulge me.

"The Death of B.V. West"

Before the lights go out
I need to hold you
One more time
Though you are the creature
Who has trampled me down
As knee-high meadow grass
Dies beneath the hooves of a
Thousand Spanish horses
I now must lift
The coffin lid
So you can crawl back in
Beside me.

I know it's weird. But when you're speedin' like hell on high-grade crystal meth and you've just slaughtered a couple of shit-bags, you never know what might come out of a writer's brain, especially mine. I've accepted the fact that I still have to use B.V. West as a pen name for my new book I'm working on, (it's in the *friggin'* contract) but since the demise of Sheriff Dog Shit, it doesn't bother me anymore. *Yippee!* There *is a God!*

Anyway, thanks for reading my little drug-induced poem. I'm heading back out on the deck now to see if Lydia wants to go to Kenya yet. I'm not going to show the poem to her or anyone else. As promised, it's just between you and me.

I'm on the patio now.

"Well," I announce like an all-knowing college professor, "Placido's asleep and his mama is happy as hell." I clear my throat, light a Newport and continue. "The Great Migration usually takes place in September, and Kenya is one of the most beautiful and romantic places in the known universe at that time of year."

I look deep into Lydia's eyes. As you can tell, I am not pulling out any stops.

"Baby, you deserve this, you really do. Like I say, one of the chosen few. I'll be there to protect you, just in case you're worried about wild animals, but we'll be traveling around with expert guides in brand new state-of-the-art Jeeps and excellent, safe sleeping conditions. I even bought us each new cameras. Hold on, I'll go get yours. It's in the den."

I come out and present the camera to her as if it is The Hope Diamond.

Presentation is everything.

"It's an extremely high-end Canon EOS 5D Mark 3 with 23 Megapixels," I explain, *whatever that means.* "It's the kind of camera they use for National Geographic magazine.

"All yours, Lydia, and with your artistic nature, you might even capture an award-winning shot. Who knows?"

After she takes her skeptical eyes off of mine, she picks the camera up off of the table and looks through the viewfinder.

I can see the edges of her smile on either side of the camera body, and I know she's hooked.

Kenya, here we come!

"Lydia, my dear,"(Art always calls Lydia "my dear" when he gets drunk.) "may I see that when you're done? I'll be careful with it. That fuckin' thing looks like a work of art."

Art turns in his chair and peeks up at me.

"Looks expensive as all hell too. How much did that set you back, Raven?"

"Too much, but what the fuck, this is the trip of a lifetime. Well, Mermaid, yes or no, are we going to Kenya? I'll sit near the window of the planes so you don't fall out."

I flash her the smile she can never resist.

"It's a long flight with a couple of layovers, but we'll be flying first-class again, helluva lot more tolerable. You'll be able to get a lot of reading and sleeping in during the flights."

Lydia suddenly throws her arms up in the air like an overly dramatic actress on, wine, weed, roxies and booze *(gee, wonder why?)*

"*YES! Yes!" she* fairly yells. "Who in their right mind wouldn't want to go see the Great *Fuckin'* Wildebeest Migration halfway across the world camping in the jungle?"

She is being sarcastic, *no shit, right?*

But, the answer is still "yes."

Raven April always gets what he wants, but you already know that.

Lydia rolls her eyes back into her pretty little head, and takes another long drink out of her wine glass.

Art and I wink at each other. Then we light another Newport and clink our bottles of Heineken for about the tenth time so far today.

To success!

Hell, it is a party ain't it?

I gesture toward her camera.

"Lydia, get the feel of your new toy. It's incredibly easy to operate, perfectly balanced and ready to go, so have some fun and start shooting away. Be right back, I'm gonna grab you the manual and then call Joe Lofton. Too bad he's not here to celebrate."

I bring the instruction manual out, kiss Lydia and then go into the den to call Joe. I'll have him set the trip up for the second week of September, about two weeks away. Man, I'm really gettin' excited about this trip.

Joe Lofton and me on the phone

I get Joe on his cell, using a new Track Phone I had Lydia pick me up in Walgreen's, so Joe has no idea who it is calling him.

"Joe Lofton," he answers.

"Listen *Motherfucker*," I say in a disguised voice, "you are now a walking corpse, because I'm going to cut your head off."

I am trying so hard to suppress my hysteric laughing, but I pull it off.

"Who is this please?" he asks, in a voice that barely disguises his fear.

"This is William Lester Johnson," I answer. "My wife Emma and I met you in Boulder, Colorado a few months back. And she just told me you raped her. You're almost dead. Do you pray, dead man?"

191

"You no-good fuckin' asshole!" Joe says, after a few seconds of stunned silence. "Is this you, Raven, with another one of your sick, sadistic jokes?

"Motherfucker, I almost had a heart attack. You suck *big* time! I'm fuckin' still shaking."

Me, I'm laughing out loud now, and Joe can hear me.

"I'm sorry man, you know I'm a sick fucker. The aliases Lydia and I used in Boulder I knew would tip you off. Hell, I didn't want you to drop over dead. Am I forgiven?"

Silence on Joe's end.

"Look buddy, I've got an assignment for you. I'll give you a five grand bonus to take care of it for me. Can we talk?"

"No, not right now, call me on my office phone in an hour. This sounds weird, even for you. Just a gut feeling I have."

"Okay, Joe thanks. I'll call you in an hour from the phone in the den. Still working on the book."

Joe seems a little calmer now.

"Hey, speaking of the den," he says, "how far along are you on the new book? Have you titled it yet?"

"Oh man, I've been hitting it hard lately. I've got four more chapters for you. I'll send them to you as soon as we hang up. You're really gonna freak, Joe. We've got another bestseller here. I plan on having the completed manuscript in your hands by Christmas, that way Mildred can start editing on New Year's Day if she's not too hung over."

Joe and I both chuckle at that a little, as Mildred Wolfe has a reputation for enjoying a cocktail or two. Or three. She is also a genius. Mildred Wolfe is the most sought-after book editor in the literary world.

She only works with the big boys. Now *I'm* a big boy, plus, Mildred and I get along great. She's a tough old broad with a lot of class, money and talent. She is an undisputed editing icon. Some people in the business, especially her competitors, actually refer to her as *Mildred the Wolf,* because of her seemingly animalistic instincts for sniffing out a rough manuscript with a unique story and polishing it into a brilliant diamond. She has been working her magic for more than a decade.

"I spoke with Mildred about three weeks ago," Joe says. "She's excited about your new book and wants to know the title."

"She'll know when I know, Joe. I've already got the ending outlined in my brain. The story just has to catch up to it. That's what I'm working on now. Hey man, sorry about the sadistic joke earlier, but if we can't have fun, what can we have?"

"One hour," Joe replies simply,

One Hour Later In the Den

Joe picks right up. I get straight to the point.

"Joe, I need you to set up a trip for Lydia and me to Kenya. We wanna go on a photographic safari and follow the famous, yearly wildebeest migration, in as much comfort as possible, I should add. Spare no expense. Thanks."

Joe stops me cold.

"Whoa, whoa, slow the fuck down and explain this to me so that I can grasp what you need me to do. You're talking too fast again, which you have a habit of doing sometimes whether you know it or not. Now, you want to go *where*?"

I pause and say, "Kenya, to experience and photograph what is called the Great Migration."

"I'm familiar with it," Joe breaks in.

I shoot back, almost ignoring Joe's comment.

"Yeah good, well the wildebeest migration is one of the most breath-taking spectacles on Earth. And as I may or may not have ever mentioned, I have a love of photography that stretches back to my childhood. This is a dream come true for me, Joe, or any other photographer for that matter. I'm also gonna do some work on the new and still "untitled" book while I'm there, if I have time.

"Back to the trip: I've done enough research on this little African excursion to know that I'd like to start following the migration from the Serengeti National Park in Tanzania, across the Grumeti River and into the Masai Marsa National Park in Kenya, where we'll probably spend the last couple of days before we board for home. Book the trip for two weeks from now, and I think we'll make it a 10-day adventure. I don't know if Lydia will be able to take much more than ten days. Is this all cool? You haven't said a word, Joey my man."

"Yeah, Raven, it's all cool. I'm just making a few notes here, go ahead."

Whew, I thought he is still pissed about my little sick, sadistic telephone joke.

"That's about it for now, just go ahead and use the aliases from Boulder. Lydia and I will be Mr. and Mrs. William Lester Johnson and Emma Johnson again. Hell, she's still got that fuckin' pawn shop wedding ring on."

Joe starts laughing, which sounds more like a snicker.

"Raven, she isn't ever going to take that ring off, and it would break your heart if she did."

"Maybe you're right, Joe."

Joe let about five seconds pass before responding.

"Look," he then says, "it's gonna take me a few days to put this thing together; what with fake passports and everything, I can't be too careful. This is very dangerous shit these days. You'll probably be landing at Wilson International Airport in Nairobi, and that could be tricky if everything isn't perfect. You'll be hearing from me in a few days. And hey, Raven, thanks for the bonus. We need a new roof."

"Later, Joe. Give my best to Eileen and the kids."

When I come back out to the patio about two hours later, Lydia and Art are standing knee-deep in the surf, each with a drink in their hand. I take a picture of them from the patio with Lydia's new camera. I feel like taking a swim, but instead throw three steaks on the grill and make a huge salad. We haven't eaten all day. I crack a beer, come out to flip the steaks and then go back inside to get the salad, olive oil, red-wine vinegar, sea salt and black pepper. Oh yeah, plates, drinks and silver-wear, too.

Damn right I'm a sweetheart!

I can't get my mind off of the safari. I've never been so pumped up about anything before in my life. It's like I'm being pulled to Africa by a pair of huge hands without a face. This *thing* has its strong, but, I don't know, *comforting* fingers not only wrapped around my child-like fascination of the trip, but around my physical heart as well. I can feel its knuckles rubbing against the inside of my rib cage. My sternum tickles from the inside out.

Strange-ass feeling to describe if you want the truth, which you know you always get from me. Even though the truth really sucks sometimes, it is something that must always be in the forefront of our consciousness and intimate relationship.

Did I just say that?

Guess so. Well, it's true and you know it. Okay, listen to this shit that just pops into my mind... *Many a good man has fallen on his sword in the defense of his own truths*...Wow, I like that!

Mind if I pat myself on the back? Just kidding, I'm not an asshole like a lot of people in my position would be. Hey, maybe that's why they're not *in* my position. Ever think of that? Enough of the esoteric cloud I'm floating on.

Back to reality – I'm turning the grill off. I'm also about to silently enter the water and swim up behind Lydia and Art; then I'm going to viciously grab their legs so that they scream like hell because the first thing they'll both think of is, "Shark!"

Funny – right?

Hell, this'll be about the third or fourth trick I've played today, too fucked up right now to be *exactly* sure how many. But damn, this is a banner day! I live for dumb-ass stuff like this. My victims don't seem to relish it, though. Remember when I exposed myself as B.V. West in Boulder? Damn-near killed my Mermaid.

Okay, here I go, are you with me?

At the moment, I'm slithering into the ocean like a reptile. The two unsuspecting drunk and high victims are still standing there in knee-deep water pondering the no doubt, blurry horizon. That would be Lydia and Art. As if you didn't know, right? Then again you *never* know about me, do you? I might kill them both for real, right fuckin' now. I don't need the Danger Dagger to snap their necks and feed them to the sharks. I could just rip their guts out with my bare hands. But they are both on the un-killable list. Remember?

I could always swim down the beach and kill a couple of strangers. Would you like that? I very well might do just that, because as you may or may not know, lion or no lion, I am still, and will forever be, a madman.

That deal was sealed the day Queenie and I fought the four *coyotes from hell*, the day I plunged my Buck knife through her brain with all the power of God and Satan combined into one nameless, indescribable moment in time. It was the end of one world and the beginning of another. It was the merging of two universes into one, the one that devoured most of Queenie's body and all of Raven April's spirit and innocence.

Never let an animal suffer.

"I didn't Queenie. I did the best I could do."

Tell me you can't see the tears on this page?

Thank you. It pays to be polite. *Please* and *thank you* and all that bullshit.

Lately, I'm thinking you may have noticed that the vile and insanely ghoulish side of me is peacefully resting. Don't be fooled. It merely may be waiting to be reborn in the most cruel and sinister of ways - as I privately suspect.

Do you?

Well? Some of you do, I'm sure.

I'll bet my next kill on it *if there is one*, or a hundred, or even a thousand more. I have another confession to make. This probably exemplifies the meaning of the phrase *"there's always a price"* better than anything I can think of right now, and I want to share it with you, my friends. It goes like this – I'll be brief, promise.

"Well, you all know how fuckin' happy I was when I eventually made my final kill? I mean, I was finally free from the roar of the lion at that very moment the dogs punctured the last breath of life out of Sheriff Shake Down's not-worthy-to-breath lungs. The dogs really did appreciate a good meal. Hell, the poor babies were famished!

197

I know, because Placido and I starved them from Florida to Pennsylvania.

I didn't tell you this before because I thought you may perceive it as cruelty to animals, *(don't tell PETA)* but we put slices of pepperoni on the floor of the Suburban next to their cages just beyond their reach. It was driving them wild. Being as high as we were on the speed, Placido and I laughed like crazy men in an asylum, louder than Led Zepplin blasting on the radio.

Sorry, enough of my ramblings, the point I'm trying to make here is that I *miss* the roar of the lion. Not so much the maddening roar and accompanying compulsion to kill and eat my male victims' left eyeball – no, not that part.

However, I must admit that those were glorious moments of total power in my Jeckyll-and-Hyde world. Ripping out eyes and slicing windpipes are awesome as well in the proper circumstance. But what I miss most is the incredible physical strength, night vision, courage and cunning that I possess whenever the lion roars inside my rupturing skull.

Now the curse that I carry is a nauseous yearning in the pit of my stomach at all times. It feels similar to what a broken-hearted lover endures when the one they cherish walks away and fades out of sight only to reappear in the arms of another. That constant, sickening desire to hear and to *become one with* the lion is the price I pay for the days and nights I became an extension of the heartless beast. Still, I fear his re-emergence. I am forever doomed to be a slave to the lion, whether he returns to me or not. That is the price I pay. It may not sound so terrible, but believe me, it is an all-consuming burden eating me away from the inside out… relentlessly.

Forget everything I just said. Please? I was just rambling again. Thanks again.

Now it's time to focus on our trip to Kenya. Joe emails me our itineraries. Damn, over twenty fuckin' hours in the air! Hell, I might finish writing my new book on the airplanes, while Lydia reads and sleeps.

Thank God for first-class. It says here that we leave Ft. Lauderdale and fly to JFK. That flight will take a little over two-and-a-half hours. Then the biggie – fifteen hours in the air from JFK to Johannesburg, South Africa. That's a lot of ocean to cover. We'll be in an Airbus 320, which is a damn good plane with a sound safety record. Big motherfucker, I can tell you that. Once we get to Johannesburg, we board a Boeing 737. That should get us to Wilson International Airport in Nairobi, Kenya in about four hours.

18

Landing in Kenya

Now the fun begins. Joe spares no expense, as I had requested. Lydia is ecstatic. It is beautiful weather with nice people and we are finally on the ground after twenty-one hours in air-born captivity. First-class or not, that's a long haul.

I did get a few pages written in the new book at 36,000 feet. In Nairobi, we rent a new black Ford Fusion Hybrid and Lydia drives us the two miles it takes to reach our hotel. The Savora Panafric is a four-star hotel. There are no *five*-star hotels in Nairobi, or Joe would have booked it for us. Our suite at the Savora though is gorgeous, water pressure is great and the bed is not too firm and not too soft.

Perfecto!

Lydia goes in the bathroom to take a shower and I follow. We make love in the oversized bath tub while the hot shower pelts us like soft darts from sex-heaven. My mind goes wild and our love-making is explosive. Talk about a hot quickie. Yeah, it was hot alright, but once again it wasn't a quickie. Lydia screamed several times. I couldn't stop looking at her closed eyes and climaxing facial expressions. What an awesome sight. Her hips arching and biting her bottom lip, her hands rubbing her nipples. I was pounding away and thinking how nice it was to be rich and how ironic it is that I met Lydia because she thought I was poor.

Thanks for that night on the computer, Placido. It's really paying off, buddy.

But you know me. Even in mid-ejaculation, I am thinking about the streets of Nairobi after dark and where I can find a knife. A big one, strong and with a long, sharp, double-edged blade. I'll also need a leather one piece belt-sheath. That's when the knife sheath is actually part of the belt. Like the holsters they used for their pistols back in the cowboy days. I'll hit the streets soon and find what I need.

Man, I love fucking Lydia.

Forgive me for thinking out loud but I just had to say that. It's still sinking in that I'm here in the heart of Nairobi, Kenya. Who the hell would have thought that fate would bring me here? What a world. What a crazy unpredictable world. After Lydia and I recover from our bath-tub extravaganza, we stretch out on the king-size bed naked for about a half-hour. Lydia falls asleep, so I put a light blanket on her and pull one of my old tricks. I write her a note telling her I am going out for some beer, wine, Black & Milds and cigarettes.

"We'll go down to the restaurant later.

Love, Raven."

I get dressed and leave the note in the bathroom. I have about $10,000 American dollars on me, but no weapon yet. You know how much I like to carry a weapon, especially a knife. And no, the lion isn't roaring. It's just me, the madman.

Our suite is on the eighth floor, so the elevator shoots me down to the lobby in about ten seconds. I exit the elevator, walk through the lobby and hit the streets. It feels good. I can't lie to you. I *am* looking for a knife, but I am also searching for danger. Don't ask me why, but like Dr. Rothstein, the headshrinker out in L.A. told me, it all has to do with that day in the woods with Queenie, and our death battle with the coyotes. The day I lost my mind, remember?

Victor's Bar

I stand out in front of the hotel, smoking a Newport, trying to figure out in which direction I should start walking. The section of the city to my left is all lit up and it looks like there is a lot going on. I head down there to a street full of bars, restaurants, stores of all kind and people just milling around in groups talking and laughing. The stores are all lit up, and the ornate street lights are on. They are cool as hell. Each glass globe is formed into a different size and shape. I'm assuming they were all hand-blown.

That's almost a lost art, but I know they still blow glass by hand in southern New Jersey back in the states. I am drawn to a little bar with dim lighting. I look inside. There are six Kenyans and two white guys sitting at the bar watching TV. They all have a drink in front of them and seem to be having a good time. I walk in and sit down in the last seat at the far end of the bar, back against the wall. The Kenyan bartender speaks perfect English. I'm gonna get some information out of him, I can just feel it. He comes over to me and says,

"What can I get you, sir?"

I reply as I offer my hand to him.

He shakes it.

"Call me Fish. I'll take a double shot of vodka and a bottle of beer. The strongest you've got."

"Call me Victor," he says, "I take it you're an American?"

"Yep, born and raised in Pennsylvania. By the way, I love your country so far. I just got here today, and I'm trying to gather up a few supplies for my trip to Serengeti National Park tomorrow. I just don't know where to look."

"What are you looking for?" Victor, in a deep, velvet voice asks. "Maybe I can point you in the right direction. As you can see, there are a lot of shops. You can get anything you want. Pot too, just in case you're interested. I sell pot here."

"Victor, you must be reading my mind." I hand him a hundred-dollar bill. "How much pot will that get me? I assume it's high-grade. Am I right?"

He pulls what looks like a hand-rolled stogie out of the top pocket of his red silk shirt. It is about the size of a cigarette, dark brown in color. Victor lights it up, takes a hit, and hands it to me.

I take a big hit; *oh shit*, it nearly knocks me on my ass.

I hand it back to Victor and he takes another hit.

After I exhale, and I can fuckin' see again, I look him in the eye.

"Damn Victor, this is good shit! I'll take some." I say.

Lydia will be pleasantly surprised. I take a long swig out of my beer.

"Victor my friend," I say nonchalantly, "do you know any knife-makers or a place where I can get a good knife? I might need it while I'm on safari. I didn't get a chance to tell you that I'm here to follow The Great Migration of the wildebeest did I?"

"No, Fish, you did not," Victor answers.

"Well that's why I'm here. I came to take pictures of them."

Victor smiles.

"Oh yes," he says. "I have met many Americans in Nairobi who come to witness The Great Migration. It is a spectacle beyond words. Now, about the knife you seek."

Victor takes another hit of the blunt, and passes it to me.

I take another big hit. I swear it's the best pot I've ever smoked. I look down the bar and realize that every guy in there is smoking the same shit. I'm wondering why there aren't any women in here when I see one of the Kenyans and one of the white guys kissing each other.

Fuck, I think I'm in a gay bar!

But for some reason, I stay.

"On the other side of the street," Victor continues, "two blocks east of here, there is a small dark shop with a large "X" carved into the door. It is owned by a strange but wise man named 'Fahari.' He lives a hermit's life and most people in Nairobi believe he has magical powers. They believe that he was raised in the jungle and disfigured by an encounter with a rogue lion. But they are wrong. I think I should warn you – he looks like a serpent cast up from hell.

"Knock twice on the door, five times. Wait ten seconds and do it again. That knock will tell Fahari that you are safe to talk to. He not only makes knives, daggers and the like, but he is also a collector, and seller of instruments for killing. You will find what you want there.

"Let me warn you that Fahari is also a user of his arsenal of death and has killed many people. Treat him with respect, and when he allows you, always look him in the eye. He only has one. His right eye was ripped out by a lion. His soul is disfigured too. He is a man torn between God and Lucifer.

"When he comes to the other side of the door marked "X," he will knock six times. When the six knocks end, tell him that Victor sent you. He will then open the door and allow you inside.

"Fish, he is very dangerous. Be on guard. Do your business and leave as quickly as possible."

The adventure sounds tempting, even though I must confess to you that I have this guilty feeling that I should be home in my den working on my new book. Hell, I've got a deadline! But I couldn't pass up this escapade.

Damn, I feel a little scared. I like it, though. It's exciting and I can hardly wait to meet this strange man named "Fahari."

"I'll have another double vodka," I say, "and one more beer. Victor, I truly thank you for pointing me to Fahari."

Victor sets up my drinks, and hands me the blunt.

"Fahari," he says, "is the only person who possesses the weapon you are looking for. The other traders sell junk made of weak metal and dull blades. Fahari forges the strongest knifes and swords made from the highest grade of solid steel, with thin, sturdy razor sharp blades. I have a feeling that Fahari has what you are seeking. He will have no care for your American money. Fahari doesn't believe in money."

I'm thinking, *damn, this guy Fahari is strange.*

I finish my drinks, and Victor hands me what looks like about an ounce of pot. A great deal for a hundred bucks, in my estimation, especially considering how fuckin' potent it is. This should last Lydia and me for the whole ten days we're in Africa. I shove it in my pocket and ask him if Fahari smokes weed.

"Yes," Victor says, "he smokes from a giant water pipe in the middle of his main room where all the knives, daggers and swords are displayed. Fahari has no electricity, but many candles. He makes them himself. Fahari is not like the rest. He lives in a world which exists in a different dimension than most of us.

"He is a killer, Fish. The authorities leave him alone because he casts spells on those who challenge his secret powers. The police are spiritually superstitious, and fear Fahari. Until he dies, he will be who he is, and do what he does, unchallenged by anyone."

As I am ready to leave, I hand Victor another hundred-dollar bill.

"Thank you, Victor," I say. "I'm not afraid of Fahari. I just want to do business with him. I'll be back to let you know how it goes and show you my knife."

Victor nods ominously, and I walk out on to the street again. I am on my way to Fahari's little shop of horrors. Truth be known, he *does* scare me a little.

To be perfectly honest with you, my friends. I just Loooooooovvvveeeeee, being scared. Don't you – sometimes?

The Wizard's Lair

I walk across the street and up the two blocks to Fahari's place. It's hard to see the "X" on the old, thick wooden door at first; but even in the dark, it is visible – barely, down here on the dark end of the street. I trace the carving with my hands. This place is eerie. There are no windows on the front of the little wooden house-cave, so I can't peek inside. I take a chance and walk around the side of the place. There is a window with a thin curtain hanging limply and slightly swaying. I can see flickers of light inside. There is a multitude of colors which had to be coming from Fahari's candle world. I can't wait to get inside. My adrenaline is pumping. This is my kind'a place.

I stealthily walk back to the front door and do the secret knock-knock thing, and he responds with six knocks. My heart almost jumps out of my chest when the mysterious Fahari opens the door to his hovel and beckons me inside.

I nod respectfully as I stoop, stepping through the doll-house-sized door. Once I make my way in, I realize that the ceiling is much higher than I had expected. Fahari, a very small, thin man draped in what looks like a woolen black cape, keeps his head down as he closes and bolts the door behind me. He reminds me of a miniature Hunchback of Notre Dame.

There must have been a hundred candles burning in the next room. But there are none in this first room, which I've already privately nick-named the 'room-cave.' Nuts, right? It is like I've stepped into another world, a world of magic. A strange place unlike any I could have ever imagined. I am in the presence of a powerful man, a man of mystic abilities. Is he a god or a demon? I'm not sure.

"Fahari" is a Swahili name which means "splendor" and "magnificence." Fahari *feels* evil to me at first, a diminutive demon from another time and place. Yet an aura of goodness can also be felt in his presence.

The giant water pipe which Victor had mentioned stands about four feet tall in the middle of this room-cave. There are two tubes stemming out of the top of the pipe's basketball-sized reservoir.

God only knows what he had in the bowl… Man, I'd love to find out and party with this guy. What a trip that would be.

My instincts tell me I'm going to. Hold tight, we'll both find out soon.

As my eyes adjust to the candlelight, I can see the hundreds of knives, hatchets, daggers, swords, slings, machetes, you name it. Everything you could or couldn't imagine for slaughter are there, mounted on all four walls of this indescribably grotesque-yet-breathtaking little room.

Edgar Allen Poe couldn't have dreamed this up. As I have said before, and this little journey into the unknown proves it; truth really *is* stranger than fiction.

I am mesmerized by how the multi-colored candles sparkle like prisms of diamonds on the polished gold-and-silver killing tools hanging on the walls. It is an awesome sight. A giant wild boar's head with huge tusks and teeth bared hangs above the stone fireplace. The walls are made of what looks like petrified wood. It seems as if Fahari and his forbidden dwelling *do* exist in a dimension of their own – in another time and place.

The room-cave is consumed by candlelight rainbows constantly dancing merrily like ballerinas upon the glistening metal weapons. Inside this fantasyland, all I had ever known or believed in no longer exists.

How do I get myself into this shit? Just lucky, I guess. Hey, you're not laughing and neither am I. This is too much, really.

From the ceiling in the room-cave hangs a coffin which extends down from the invisible rafters above to about eight feet from the floor. I can easily reach up and touch it. A voice in my head tells me not to. I listen to it. I can tell it is made not out of pine, but another wood, probably from timber that grows here in Africa. I suddenly get a shiver and wonder if Fahari has made the casket for me. After all, Victor did stress the fact that Fahari is a killer.

I've been here for almost an hour, and not a word has been spoken. I haven't even seen the Wizard's face yet. If you don't mind, I'm gonna be referring to this guy as the "Wizard" from now on, because that's what he reminds me of. Not that I've ever met a wizard. It just *fits* for Fahari. Wish you were here to be a part of this. I really do. It's way beyond creepy.

The ceiling is dark, and I can't see anything but endless black above the *suspended-in-mid-air* sarcophagus. Fahari, still with his head covered by the cape, walks over to the giant bong and adds more of whatever was already in the bowl. It doesn't look like any weed I'd ever smoked before. It is gray in color with the consistency of pipe tobacco. It smells strong and deadly. *I want some!*

Fahari finally speaks, and it startles me a bit. His voice is very high-pitched. He sounds like a munchkin from "The Wizard of Oz" when he talks.

"We will now meet God and Satan, together as one, our spirits convening within the most rare of all smoke. It is then I will judge you friend or foe. You will either reach the ultimate in knowledge tonight, or die tonight."

Now that really eases my mind.

I quiver. The weird little wizard hands me one of the two inhale tubes. I noticed his hands are blue, his skin dry and cracked down to the bone. He puts the other tube between his nearly-invisible lips. I stick mine in my mouth. I'm always ready for an adventure. Fahari strikes a long wooden match across the ancient wooden floor and lights the bowl. We each take our first hit together.

Hell, the chamber at the bottom of the bong is two feet around. The glass reservoir is wrapped halfway up in rope. Ten people could smoke out of this pipe with no problem. The chamber quickly fills with a green-tinted smoke. It is so big that it makes me wonder why he only has two inhale tubes.

Not a lot of company I suppose.

I take a big hit, just like Fahari does. I don't feel anything but lightheaded for a few seconds and then, *Whamo!*

I am suddenly floating in the cosmos, far away from reality. From the rafters I can see the countless candles in the next room and they are suddenly burning like bonfires. Then they morph into fluorescent dragonflies. *Huge* dragonfiles. And they are swarming by the dozens in the room-cave. I actually duck a couple of times and then talk myself into realizing they aren't real.

Or are they?

Fahari takes another big hit off the bong.

Damn he has big lungs for an 80-pound man.

My physical body takes another hit from the tube; remember, my spirit is floating among the rafters.

Oh shit, Fahari has shuffled to the corner of the cave-room nearest the fireplace. Wonder what he's up to? I'm still high as hell. I struggle like crazy to get my spirit back into my physical body, and finally succeed. I'm back.

Fahari is pulling on two ropes, which seem to be slowly lowering the coffin to the floor using some sort of pulley system. It creaks as it lowers.

What's this all about?

The dragonflies have flown back into the hypnotizing candle flames.

Why aren't there any candles in the cave-room? I wonder.

I keep opening and closing my eyes but nothing changes. The closed casket finally settles gently on the floor next to the bong. This whole scenario has just made an abrupt turn down the trail of genuine fear.

Yes, *fear*.

Even I, Raven April, admit to fear. Without it, I would have been dead a dozen times. Fear is necessary for survival. I was afraid of the coyotes, and I'm afraid right now. I'm finding this hard to believe; yet here I am. Is it me or is it the concoction Fahari put in the bong?

Not sure, but I know one thing, I've got to get to the point here soon. Motherfucker, *I need a knife*; no, a dagger. Lydia's waiting for me. I gotta speed this along no matter how much I'm diggin' the hell out of it, which I am, fear and all.

I speak in the steadiest voice I can muster.

"Fahari, I came here to purchase a dagger. I'm going into the jungle tomorrow, and I need something for protection, something lethal. I need a dagger with at least a 12-inch double-edged blade, razor-sharp, and capable of piercing the heart of any creature on Earth. I'll also need a one-piece leather belt sheath. I have enough money to buy anything you've got."

Oh that's right, Fahari doesn't believe in money.

"Look up, Fahari… let me see your face."

He doesn't.

Yes, Fahari is a killer. But so am I, and I am starting to get pissed off.

Fahari finally speaks again.

"Who or what are you going to kill, Raven? You've already killed so many."

How does he know my name? I let him talk.

He still hasn't shown his face.

"You and I have a lot In common, Raven."

That shrill, child's voice is killing me. He reminds me of a little alien, hunched over, and draped all in black. The child-like voice continues.

"You know God, and you know Lucifer. You are a man of great bravery. You tempt fate at every opportunity. You are a fool trapped between Heaven and Hell, just as I am. I will choose the dagger you need. If you were David, you could have stabbed the giant Goliath through the heart with the weapon I am about to offer you."

Fahari walks, head bowed, into a third room, beyond the candle room. He disappears beyond the candles into blackness. I am anxious to see what he will have when he returns. I also *have* to see his face. If I have to, I'm gonna grab the little wizard bastard and pull the hood off his head and get a closeup look at this living, breathing enigma. I'm also gonna find out how he knows my name.

That's really got me pissed… and worried. I might have to kill the wizard and lay him in his coffin next to the bong. If I do, it'll have to look like a suicide or natural death because Victor knows I'm here. I would be the first suspect.

My mind is racing, but I already think I've have a plan, and it *doesn't* include killing him. The risk is far too great. Hopefully we can just get on with the deal, and I'll leave, never knowing how he came to know my name. Hell, maybe I let it slip when I was blown away from that first hit off the bong.

Yeah, that's probably the smartest and most prudent thing to do. Just do the deal and leave. *But you know me.*

That way of thinking could change in a heartbeat. I can hear his feet shuffling, as he appears like an apparition in the second room among the candles. He is holding what is obviously a dagger or knife of some sort. When he makes it back into the room-cave he hands me the dagger which was inside the one-piece leather belt sheath.

Good man! He remembered the sheath.

"This is for you, Raven April."

Damn! I hate hearing him say my name.

He draws the dagger out of the sheath, as I hold it.

"This is the finest killing dagger in all the world. My masterpiece, Raven. It is now yours. I am too old to use it, and I do not need it any longer. You see, I have learned to live with the roar of the lion, too."

He sees the shocked look on my face, but continues. "Yes, I *know* your lion and the power he will forever have over you, because that very same lion has battered the inside of my skull also, and for many years. There is only one way to end this hellish nightmare we share, and I am too frail and old to carry it out."

Fahari slowly pulls away the hood which covered his face.

I almost pass out. I need a drink.

Fahari's face was but a maze of pink scars crisscrossing across his black skin, a genuine Saturday-matinee-monster, to put it mildly. Fahari's countenance makes Freddy Kruger look like one handsome devil. The wizard has only one eye, as Victor had told me. The eyelid is long gone, lost in battle. He is unable to close it.

That's gotta suck. How can he sleep?

The wizard puts the hood back over his face.

I am grateful for that.

Fahari speaks in that shivering high-pitched squeal – like long craggy fingernails on a blackboard.

"Raven, the only way our curse of the lion can be lifted is if one of us kills a full-grown male, man-eating lion with this dagger. It has been ordained. You must be the one. As the scars on my face may tell you, I have tried, and failed several times. Incredibly, by the grace of God I am still alive. He has kept me alive for a reason. You will understand why soon.

"Raven, there is so much more to the universe than most mortals can even imagine. But *we*, you and I, were chosen by God to do battle in His name. God and Satan have done this many times before, in many different ways, since the beginning of time. Each choosing a warrior to kill or be killed in their names. The winner can boast that it is he who mankind – flesh and soul – chooses to follow. If you kill the lion, God wins. If you do not, Satan will be the victor, and you will die in the lion's jaws before your journey to hell."

I listen in rapt silence, wishing what I'm hearing is just the after-effects of the bong's contents, but knowing full-well it's not.

If the wizard notices my shocked expression, he is ignoring it.

"You see, Raven," he continues, "this is the last battle, the climactic fight between good and evil for perhaps another thousand years. It will finally take place, Raven. You and the lion are the ultimate warriors in the entire universe at this time. Heaven and Earth are depending on you to conquer the Devil by killing the lion. It's been quite a struggle, hasn't it Raven? Something only you and I can ever know. I've killed over twenty human beings because of the 'curse' of the lion. I believe you have killed thirteen, haven't you Raven?"

I am in some sort of nameless shock.

"Yeah," I reply, trance-like, "something like that... maybe more, maybe less, I'm not sure right now. Hey look..."

"You are being tested," Fahari says. Did you know all thirteen of your victims were destined to die soon anyway? That's why God chose them as part of his test for you."

I am trying to absorb the wizard's words.

"Listen, Fahari, do you have any liquor? I need a couple of drinks to let this all settle in. What you just told me is off the wall. You know that, right?"

"I know it seems too fantastic to be true," Fahari says, but it *is* true; you and I are living that undeniable truth 24-hours a day, and perhaps forever. If anyone should know this as gospel, it is you Raven April."

Fahari pauses. He takes a deep, dramatic breath that seems to rattle in his throat and chest cavity.

"I was the Raven in the tree the day before you were born. The bird your mother saw. I was ordered there by God, and your mother knew it. As you must know from your Bible readings, God sent ravens to feed the prophet Elijah. Yes, I have known you since before you were conceived.

Raven, I am 130 years old. Soon I will die. I was chosen by God to fight this historic battle many times, many years ago, to prove what man 'in the flesh' will do for God.

I failed.

But, so did the lion.

You, Raven April, must not fail. Killing the lion in face-to-face combat will save us both from the fires of hell, proving what a mere human will do in the name of God Almighty. Jesus died a horrible death on the cross for us. Now you must slay a lion for His Father and all mankind. I have been told this by God himself, and you Raven, have been chosen. God directed your footsteps here tonight. He and Satan are using you just as they used Job in the Bible, this time manifesting their jealous

215

struggle into this battle – your battle. Will you do it Raven?

I out-right *scream* to Fahari.

"Get me a fuckin' drink! Just shut the hell up, and get me the strongest bottle of whiskey or whatever the hell it is you might have in this funhouse. This is freakin' me out right now. Get me that drink, Fahari."

The wizard shuffles back through the candlelight in room number two, and back to room number three again.

It is so fuckin' spooky when he does that!

He is back there for at least five minutes, and I'm wondering what the hell he is brewing up. Somehow I know this isn't a shot-and-a-beer joint, and nothing at all like The Hibiscus Club on Las Olas Boulevard. Oh man, now *this* decision.

If this is all real, that is. I think it is, and I'm seldom wrong. Damn it!

So, should I go after the man-eating lion or not? Do I have a choice? If it means that I'll be free from the lion once and forever, plus get a ticket to Heaven, which I've been worried about, how can I say no?

I walk over to the bong and using my lighter, take another hit of the enigmatic gray weed still left in the bowl.

Damn, here we go again.

This time I'm actually floating up near where the coffin had been hovering earlier. I am in the middle of an astral projection. That's when your spirit leaves your physical body and seems to float, and in some cases soar to other planets, solar systems and even new universes.

For now, I'm just floating around the room-cave again and enjoying the hell out of it. I can look down and see myself next to the bong. I'm laughing at a Henny Youngman joke I just remembered. Drifting over toward the room with all the candles, I see the wizard is making his way back to the room-cave. I better get back into my body.

Okay, I'm back into my skin just in time for cocktails. I'm getting pretty good at this, don't you agree?

Fahari hands me a large wooden bowl, tapered in one area to make it easier to drink out of. I take it.

"Thank you Fahari. May I ask what this is?"

"No Raven, just drink it, and your nerves will be calm. All anxieties will evaporate. Peace will come upon your troubled soul."

Before I drink the syrupy liquid in the bowl, I look at Fahari's scarred face. My eyes lock with his one eye. There is an obvious ambiance of holiness and mutual respect as I tell him my answer.

"Fahari, I will kill the lion."

Fahari nods silently.

"I will slam the dagger's blade deep into the man-eater's heart. I am taking on this most important mission for myself, for you and for God Almighty. But you must lead me to the lion. I'm not familiar with Africa."

I drink the entire bowl of what I can only describe as the best damn adult beverage I have ever had. It has an orange-like flavor, but within a few seconds I know it has something else. A sensation of complete happiness and well-being comes over me in a way I have never experienced before. I am quietly euphoric as Fahari, who, even with all his ugly deformities, looks beautiful.

He drinks a bowl of the elixir from the section of his lips that still exist. I can see now that he'd been torn from limb to limb in his fierce battles with man-eating lions in his attempts to end the curse. But more importantly, to help God defeat Satan. The future of the world depends on

217

it. If as it is said, God chooses his preachers, then he damn-well chooses his warriors too.

But why me, for Chrissake?

After about ten minutes of silence, he speaks.

"Bless you, Raven," Fahari squeaks out. "There is a rogue male lion that has been killing children while they play on the outskirts of a town called Busia. Satan has chosen this lion for the contest just as God has chosen you.

"Busia lies 270 miles to the west of where we are currently sitting, on the border of Uganda. You must travel there alone, or with a trusted ally, and execute this lion with the dagger.

"He will attack first. When he leaves his back feet and lunges for your throat, aim the dagger at his testicles. Doing that will give you a better chance to get the blade up under the sternum and into his heart. Once it's there, don't forget to twist the blade as many times as you can without dropping the dagger.

"Remember, aim for the testicles. It is the same tactic used for knife-fighting grizzly bears in America. If you aim for the heart you will miss it. You must aim your strongest thrust at the testicles if you are going to find the heart. If you miss the heart, go for his eyes or neck arteries. The blade is sharp and will slice through the lion's skin and muscle if you use all your strength, and the knowledge of what you are fighting for. That knowledge will be your edge in this battle of the ages."

We are both as high as two junkies on skid row, but this is different. We are fucked up but keenly lucid. I will never even *try* to explain this experience to anyone for the rest of my life… if I live to tell about it. First I must fight the lion face-to-face, and kill him.

Sound like fun? Well, stick around and find out. So much for the Great Migration I suppose. Lydia isn't really into it anyway. I'm afraid she might even be *less* into what's coming in place of the Great *fuckin'* Migration, as she described it on the patio that day.

Right now, although, my number one priority, as it should be, is to kill the lion. But damn fuckin' soon, I've got to haul my ass the hell out of here and get back to Lydia with her wine and cigars. Not to mention this ounce of pot I got from Victor at the bar. I look at my watch. I've been gone almost four hours. Lydia is gonna be pissed and worried. Its times like this I wish I carried a cell phone.

Fahari shocks the shit out of me when he speaks again.

"I know you must leave soon," he says, "to prepare for your journey and death-battle. But I have one final request before you leave."

I'm thinking, shit, what is he about to lay on me now?

He leans over close to my face, and asks me to smoke another bowl of the magic weed from the gargantuan bong next to the casket.

Get the picture yet? Don't forget the knives on the wall, the wild boar's head, the 100 multi-colored candles burning in room number two and the grotesque little creature that lives here.

I'm telling you, this is beyond surreal.

Fahari takes a huge hit on his tube, but I take a very small one. I do *not* want to astral project. I want to hear what this fuckin' request is all about. I also want to leave, and soon. I have decided to share at least some of this little adventure I'm having here tonight with Lydia, and take her along with me to Busia for the battle.

I hope and pray she can handle all of this. But I, Raven April, have no choice. This battle is of Biblical proportions. I understand that now, and goodness must prevail over evil. Why God has placed this burden upon me, I have no idea. There have been but a few of us mere mortals chosen for such an epic task throughout history. Am I afraid? Hell yes, but I've already got a plan for the Devil's man-eater.

Are you surprised? I thought not.

I've just got to conjure up my old nemesis, the lion. Yes, the vile voice which has tormented and roared inside my head and Fahari's for so long, torturing our very existence here on Earth. I must welcome him back, beg him back if need be, for with the lion's roar comes my inhuman strength, night vision, cunning and courage. It is the only way I can kill the man-eater and bring glory and victory to God.

Christ, I'm beginning to sound like a damn evangelist.

I don't even go to church, but in truth, I have always been a strong believer. Thanks, Mom and Dad. Have I told you that my brother is a Baptist Preacher? Well, he is. He's gonna love this story if I live to tell him about it.

This will be a Clash-of-The-Titans-type of battle. Good versus evil. The world is literally on my shoulders now, but I am comfortable with it. If only I can will back the lion's roar. Fahari breaks my train of thought when he speaks again.

"Go back and show Victor the dagger. He will arrange your trip to Busia. He will also answer any questions you have and supply you with all your necessities."

Fahari then slowly walks over to the coffin on the other side of the bong and climbs inside. He lies down, closes his eyes and folds his decrepit hands across his stomach. In a suddenly-strong voice, he commands me:

"Stab me in the heart with the dagger and then close the coffin. Be sure that Victor sees and tastes my blood on the dagger. He will then be certain that you Raven, are the chosen one."

I am not surprised at his request. Hell, nothing surprises me anymore. I have grown to like Fahari in the little span of time we have spent together and know I will find it hard, but not impossible, to kill him. I walk over to the coffin and stand above him clutching the dagger.

"Must I, Fahari?" I whisper. "You are my friend, and I have grown fond of you."

He pulls back the hood so that his lidless eye stares deeply and darkly into mine.

"Yes, you must. It is time. This moment has been etched into the stone tablet of forever since the beginning by God himself. Now place the dagger just below my breast bone and quickly enter the blade slightly upward and twist. Go all the way in, up to the handle guard. I will die quickly. My spirit will then rest in the arms of nothingness until you slay the lion. Only then will I be swept into Heaven for all eternity. It is time, Raven. Thank you, and good-bye."

Jeez, I hate his voice.

Fahari pulls the hood back over his cyclops eye and gently refolds his hands. The time has come, and Lydia is waiting. I will do as Fahari has instructed. I fall to my knees *(oh Lord, memories of Queenie)* and place the tip of the dagger's blade an inch below the bottom of Fahari's sternum. One, two, three… Go! The blade slips easily into his heart.

Damn, that thing is sharp!

I twist once to the left and once to the right. His body stopped twitching and lay still in less than a minute. Fahari is dead, resting in the arms of nothingness. I then solemnly pull back his hood cover and easily suck out his protruding left eye.

I feel blessed and stronger as it slides over my tongue and down into my stomach. Thanks, Fahari. I close and latch the coffin lid. As I strap on the belt-sheath, and slide in the bloody dagger, I say a prayer for Fahari's soul, which is now in my hands. I then leave to see Victor.

Victor's Bar

I walk in and take my seat at the end of the bar against the wall. Within a minute, the tall, thin and blacker-than-black Victor walks over to me.

I'll tell you, he is a damn good bartender.

He sets me up with a beer as well as a shot of vodka.

"Are you the one?" he says quietly, yet deeply, without looking up.

I drink the shot of vodka, pull out a cigarette and ask Victor for a light. As he lights my cigarette with a dark blue Bic lighter, I place the dagger with its bloody blade on the bar in front of him. Nobody else seems to notice.

The lights are dim and of different, subtle colors. Kind of cool-looking and reminds me of the candle room at Fahari's. African music is playing in the background.

Victor picks up the dagger and licks the stained blade with his pink tongue. Some of the coagulated blood liquefied by Victor's saliva drips onto one of his fingers. He sucks it off like a child enjoying a Popsicle. He cleans the dagger with a fresh bar rag and hands it back to me.

"You," Victor says, "are the one. Come back tomorrow at noon. There will be an old, but strongly-built man here named Gahee. He will be sitting on the stool next to where you are sitting now. Gahee has white hair and clear eyes. His name means 'elderly one.' Raven, Gahee is fluent in forty of the sixty-three different languages spoken in Kenya. He will be your guide and lifeline on your journey to Busia – and your victorious passage *back,* we all pray."

I finish my beer, and set the empty bottle down.

"Noon tomorrow it is." I say.

I start to get off of my barstool when Victor grabs my right forearm and looks me deep in the eyes. One of those subtle bar-light colors glistens on a tear trickling down his cheek.

"Raven," he says, leaning close to me, "thank you for taking on this mission for God, and for killing Fahari. He is free now and soon will rise into heaven. Keep the dagger with you at all times. You must become one with the dagger.

"Raven, just as Fahari did, I *know* about the roar of the lion, and how you must allow it back inside your brain just one more time. It *will* happen, for when you face Satan's lion in Busia, your lion will awaken from his sleep. He will roar within you, and your skull will pound with torment. He will bare his teeth and be ready to fight with you, even in your suffering. You, Raven will *become* the lion. He will give you all of his power and strength… and you will be transformed into one of the mightiest warriors in history."

"I appreciate your faith in me, Victor, and especially in the return of my lion. Let's hope you're right. Because that's the only way I can win."

I walk out.

Fuck! Lydia is gonna be out of her mind. I've been gone almost six hours. I'm just gonna tell her the goddamn truth and take it from there.

I have to focus on my battle now, and lying to her will just bother my mind and distract me from my *Holy Mission.* When in doubt, tell the truth. The truth is always easier.

But you know that too, don't you? We should all practice it more.

Room 2156, Sarova Panafric Hotel

Lydia is sitting at the desk with her head in her hands when I walk in. When she sees me she jumps out of the chair and runs to me.

Shit! I'm thinking. *She's going to smack me in the face, just as she did in Boulder when I revealed I was B.V. West, her favorite writer.*

Instead she just stands there and looks at me for a few seconds before speaking.

"Raven," she says, "I should be so *fuckin'* pissed off at you, but I've been too *worried* to be mad. Where the hell have you been? Are you okay?

"I love you, Raven. Thank God you're here. I had such a bad feeling in the pit of my gut and heart about your safety, it scared me half to death. Thank God you're alive. Hold me. Just hold me."

Whew, I hold Lydia in my arms for a long time while she cries, still clinging to me. I am just thankful as hell that she isn't pissed off and didn't do something crazy like call the police to send them out looking for me. Or knee me in the balls.

Her hand accidently feels the dagger at my side. She breaks our embrace, and pulls the dagger out of its sheath.

"Where did you get this?" she asks. "It's beautiful! This should be hanging in a museum somewhere. Did you buy it? Christ, it must have cost a fortune! Or did you sell your soul for it?"

She smiles at that.

I don't.

She is closer to the truth than she knows. It is a magnificent piece, as spectacular-looking as it is deadly, to be sure. It is like no weapon I'd ever seen before. After the battle, I'm going to keep it and display it in a place of prominence at the mansion where it never will be used again.

Since I don't come back with any beer, wine or cigars for Lydia, I give her one of my Newports to hold her over.

Then I call the front desk and send out for the booze, Lydia's cigars and something to eat. I throw the bag of pot I got from Victor on the bed.

"Way to go Raven!" Lydia says. "I could use a buzz right about now."

We don't have anything to smoke it with, so I trek down the hall and buy a can of soda out of the machine. When I get back, I open the can, empty it down the bathroom sink and make a pipe out of it. I puncture little holes for a bowl with the tip of the magnificent dagger. Didn't Victor say for me to become one with the dagger? I'm sure he did.

Damn, I don't know what combination of metals Fahari used to make this masterpiece, but it certainly is strong and sharp. I'm thinking he used diamonds in the mixture somehow. I suppose I'll never really know unless I have a metallurgist look at it back in Miami. Hey, that's a good idea, don't you think? If... I mean *when* I return in victory, I think I'll do that. The wine, beer and Black & Milds show up, and I tip the guy fifty bucks. The food comes a few minutes later; two steak dinners with bread and salads.

I tell Lydia as I pour her a glass of wine that I have something serious to discuss with her and that our plans have changed. We both take a couple hits of Victor's super weed on the soda-can pipe. Lydia can't believe how strong the buzz is. I didn't warn her, I just let her think it was your run-of-the mill average or slightly-above-average weed.

Man, is she surprised!

I tell her the entire story of what has transpired in the six hours I was gone. She sits, listening, mesmerized.

Lydia finds it hard to believe that I am the warrior God had chosen to slay Lucifer's lion.

Hell, so *do I.*

But then she thinks about it some more.

"Well," she says, "you did win your fight with that Hammerhead shark. Raven, if this is all true – I mean about Victor, Fahari and the battle that God and Satan have chosen for you and this killer lion, then I'm going to be there with you. I'm going where you're going. Period."

What a woman!

"I have to meet a man named Gahee tomorrow at noon in Victor's bar," I say. "I'll know more after talking to him. He'll be our guide and confidant through all of this. Lydia, I'm thinking the battle will take place soon. We better start packing and be prepared to leave at a moment's notice."

Lydia slowly lights a cigar and starts crying again before she says anything.

"Raven, please win," she says solemnly. "Please kill the lion. I couldn't live without you. Besides, if you lose, it will mean a victory for Satan. You have to win for me and for God. To prove what a mortal human will do to show mankind's faith 'in the flesh' for Him. You can't lose. You can't die!"

I hold Lydia close as we sit on the bed.

"I'll win. I'll kill the goddamned lion. What the fuck, he deserves to die for killing those children anyway! Now let's eat a little dinner, even though I don't have much of an appetite. Then we have to get some sleep. Tomorrow might prove to be an even bigger day than today, if that's fuckin' possible. I keep thinking I'm gonna wake up, and this is all a dream or something. But it's not, is it?"

Lydia shakes her head.

"I love you, Lydia."

"I love you too, Raven. Raven can I ask you a question?"

"Sure Mermaid. Go ahead. Gee, I miss the 'love blanket.' "

I really did too, 'because this is startin' to suck!

Lydia doesn't seem to comprehend what I have just said, and presses her question.

"Why *you* Raven? And why have we both accepted this insane situation so... so *casually*, it's like divine intervention, we should be petrified, but we're really not. It's as if this is just another little something that you have to take care of? This is strange. *You* are strange. That's one of the reasons I love you so much. But I know in my heart that *this* is something you really have no control over. The battle, I mean. You were *chosen*. I still can't get my head around the fact that I love the man handpicked by God to battle Lucifer's lion. Raven, the sooner the better. Kill the fuckin' lion and then let's get the hell out of here. I miss the 'love blanket' too."

We make love again, almost both in tears. Lydia knows as well as I do that killing that lion won't be easy.

Hey, let's face it. I could lose.

At least *now* I know that all of the killings commanded of me by the roar of the lion were committed in preparation for this, the final battle that could affect mankind, both dead and alive for the next thousand years – maybe more. And yes, I'm still scared shitless, but I can't let Lydia, Victor, Gahee or the man-eating lion in Busia know that. That stays between you and me.

Noon, Victor's Bar

Gahee stands out like an albino at an NAACP meeting. His snow-white hair is sparkling in the subtle bar lights. Victor's saloon looks the same at high noon as it did at midnight; the dark purple curtains are pulled shut to keep the sun and the rest of the world outside. The muscular Gahee is perched one-stool-in from the back wall, leaving my stool against the wall at the very end of the bar open. Gahee is talking to Victor, who is washing glasses. Everything looks normal, but you and I know that this whole thing is a far cry from *normal*. As I walk closer to Gahee, he stands up and shakes my hand. For some reason I like him instantly.

"Thank you for killing Fahari," he says, looking me dead in the eyes. "He was my father. His life was long and hard, and he deserved the reward of death."

Gahee has a handsome, somewhat round face accentuated by perfect white teeth. Another Hollywood smile if I've ever seen one. His expressions are genuine. There is no bullshit about this powerful black man with the snow-white hair.

"Pleasure to meet you Gahee," I say. "When do we leave for Busia?"

Why beat around the bush?

"I'm ready for the lion."

He looks a little surprised at my eagerness. I keep talking.

"Tell me, Gahee, have you also been haunted by the roar of the lion, or is it just your father and me? I mean, we can't be the *only* ones, can we?"

Gahee looks at Victor, then back at me.

"Yes. You are." Gahee says. "If I had received the same curse, then I would have been next in line to fight the lion in Busia. Only you and my father have ever experienced the giant cat's merciless clamor. My father started hearing the lion's roar in his 40th year. For the last ninety years, he has been killing humans at the command of the lion's tantrums inside his weary brain.

"Three times he has fought the devil's selected lions. Three times there was no victor. He was torn to shreds and disfigured, yet he refused to die until you were ready for the passing of the dagger.

"So the battle of the millennium must be carried out by you, Raven April. You were chosen for this by God since before your birth. Just as Victor and I have been chosen to help you conquer Lucifer's lion and bring glory to God. As you now know, the only way to quiet the lion without going mad is by killing it.

"In those ninety years my father lived alone, and you are one of the few people who have ever been inside his blessed, curious home. Fahari was a shape-shifter. He could transform himself into any animal or bird. He *named* you Raven. Your mother was prophesized to see him in the tree the day before you were born."

"Yes," I interrupt him. "Fahari had mentioned that to me."

"*We* were chosen…" Gahee continues.

I interrupt again.

"Yes, tell me, *how* were you chosen, and by whom?"

"In dreams delivered by angels, Raven," Victor chimes in. "Fahari, Gahee and I were all given the

229

knowledge of our responsibilities in dreams. But they were more than dreams. They were commands sent from God, which were impossible to ignore – unthinkable not to carry out. We have been watching you since birth, Raven. Or should I say, *Fahari* has. Neither Gahee nor I are shape-shifters.

Fahari would give us reports on your progress each time he returned from visiting with you. Of course, you had no clue he was there. Remember cursing, and throwing a rock at the vulture, after your dog Queenie was killed?"

"Hell yes I do! Why?"

"Because that vulture above you in the tree was Fahari. You see, Raven, you were destined, divined to be here now. We were expecting you. But Fahari had to be sure that you were the one, and that you were worthy."

I pull out the splendid dagger and place it on the bar. We all gaze at it as if it is a holy object.

I guess it *is* in a sense, seeing how I would be battling Satan's man-eating surrogate with it soon. I have to feel totally confidant if I'm going to be victorious. I also have to pray like hell that my lion's roar that ruined my life for so many years returns... just one more time. Even though I temporarily silenced him the day Placido and I fed Sheriff Shit Bag to the dogs, I will need him again – and soon.

Suddenly, I need a drink. This whole thing is starting to chip away at me, but I have to remain calm and focus on my calling.

Victor reads my mind.

I drink the shot of vodka and quickly chase it with my beer. Then I light a cigarette.

"Thank you Victor," I say. "Okay, back to my original question. When do we leave for Busia?"

230

"Tomorrow morning at eight o'clock sharp I will pick you up at your hotel," Gahee says. "Look for a blue Jeep Cherokee. From there we'll drive to the airport. Then we'll board my bush plane, and I'll pilot us to a small hut about a mile outside the city of Busia. A villager named Jomo will be waiting for us. His hut is close to where the devil lion prowls and stalks – the man-eater you are about to do mortal combat with, the one who has killed many of the city's children."

I interrupt again.

"I'm taking my soul-mate with us. Her name is Lydia. I can't go to Busia without her. I gather strength of heart from her. She will be an asset."

Gahee smiles and says, "Everyone should have a soul-mate. The plane has four seats. Your Lydia may turn out to be a blessing."

"She already has, Gahee."

I get up to leave, shaking both Victor's and Gahee's hands.

"Eight o'clock sharp. Lydia and I will be out in front of the hotel."

Victor pours three shots of vodka. We toast to victory. I start to leave but I have one more question for Gahee.

"If you don't mind me asking, your father was a 130 years old. How old are you?"

He smiles with those Hollywood teeth.

"Raven," he says, "I am ninety years old. My eyesight is perfect, and I've flown that bush plane over a hundred-thousand miles, if that's what you're worried about."

Now he is laughing.

"Don't worry. I'll get you and your soul-mate safely to Busia. Let's just hope I'll be flying you back in one piece."

"Lydia," I inform Gahee, "doesn't like window seats."

He laughs, and drinks a shot of vodka.

"It's a four seater. Your soul-mate, Lydia has no choice. She can always keep her eyes closed. See you in the morning, Raven."

"You will," I say, confidently, and leave the darkened bar for the blinding sun of the outside world.

Lydia and I have to pack only what we need, and leave the rest of our stuff in the room for *when* we return. See? I'm getting more confident of victory all the time.

Say a prayer, will ya?

By the way, except for the white hair, Gahee only looks to be about forty years old.

I ask Victor how old he is.

"I stopped counting at 80," he says nonchalantly.

Must be the water.

19

Landing in Busia

Gahee's bush plane, a Piper Super Cub lands smoothly on its tundra tires, which are purposely oversized, but make for a somewhat velvety landing in the middle of nowhere or anywhere, I suppose. We taxi to a stop in the savannah grass about a quarter of a mile before the lushness of the jungle takes over and gobbles up everything, including the soothing, undulating grass. Needless to say, there is no "airstrip" in this desolate wonderland.

As I look toward the jungle with my binoculars, I'm thinking, *Is that where he is?*

Lydia is silently awestruck by the stark difference between Nairobi and wherever the hell we are now.

Gahee breaks the silence.

"Well my friends, what do you think of Africa from a bush plane?"

There wasn't much conversation during our flight because the engine was so loud it was hard to yell over. Also because the view from only a couple thousand feet is so breathtakingly beautiful – and you can't say much with the wind knocked out of you. Lydia looks so cute in her safari shorts that I feel like asking Gahee to turn his head while my soul-mate and I have a hot quickie. But instead I just think about the possibilities.

"Gahee," I say, "this place is incredible. It seems more like a paradise than a battleground."

"Perhaps it *will* be a paradise again after you have killed the lion," he replies cryptically. "The giant feline keeps the people here chained in fear. They cannot watch their children every moment of every day and night. It is so like Satan to choose the most evil of creatures to do his bidding for him, and so like God to choose a brave Christian such as you to defeat them."

I am humbled by that statement – but when all of a sudden did I become a "brave Christian?" What the fuck, I've killed, tortured, swindled the government *(thanks Joe)*, you name it – I've done it. But I must say that I always pray to God, especially in times of trouble.

In my heart, as I've said, I truly *believe* in the Father, The Son and The Holy Spirit. It's just that sometimes my actions and behaviors don't seem to reflect that, now do they? That could be the understatement of the year, I know.

Gahee brings his binoculars up to his eyes and points toward the jungle.

"Raven, do you see that small opening just to the left of the three eucalyptus trees?"

It just so happens that I know what a eucalyptus looks like.

Lydia and I both quickly focus in on the little opening in the middle of the jungle.

"I see it!" Lydia says.

"Yeah," I echo, "I see it too, Gahee. What's up with it? Is that where we're headed?"

He keeps the binoculars up.

"No, that is where Jomo will be coming from in his American pickup truck. He should be here soon. There will be two others with him with rifles. They will be keeping an eye on the plane while we are in the jungle.

"Lydia, don't be alarmed by them. They will remain silent and will not make eye contact with any of us. They speak only to Jomo. Jomo knows we are here to kill the rogue lion and that we have brought a great warrior by the name of Raven to rid the community of this child-killing lion. Now that my father Fahari is dead, only Victor and I know the significance of your upcoming death-fight. And now you and Lydia know."

"What else can you tell me about this demon-lion?" I ask Gahee.

"Tell me everything you know about him. His habits, his size…"

Gahee has a whiskey flask in the back pocket of his safari shorts.

Good man!

He looks out across the savannah, twists off the cap and takes a swig. He then hands it to me.

I take two swigs.

So does Lydia.

Gahee turns to Lydia and me. He becomes extremely serious in his demeanor. This is the real fuckin' deal.

Damn! Tell me how I got into this again?

"Raven," Gahee then says solemnly, "your adversary is a monster. He stands almost six feet at the shoulder. He hunts only at night. He has never been seen in the light of day. He has killed men and women as well as children, but the children are the focus of the hatred toward the beast.

This won't be easy my friend. He seems to have a sixth sense. He's been shot at many times by some of Busia's best marksmen. They all seem to think he can anticipate where the bullet is going and evade it. Some have even hinted that he may be a ghost lion, and their bullets go right through him."

235

"*Damn!*" I declare, and ask for another pull on that whiskey flask. Lydia puts her arms around me, and we kiss.

She whispers in my ear, and *I can hear the tears in her voice.*

"Raven, you can do it, you can - you *have* to. I don't know why God chose you for this, but I know I'm supposed to be here with you."

I squeeze her reassuringly then gently push away, holding her by the shoulders at arms' length, and *somehow* forcing a genuine-looking smile.

"Lydia." I say. I'll be fine. You *know* that. We've been through a lot together, and we've always come out on top... the beer-man, the shark, Art... hell, we can do anything! Of *course* I'll kill the lion. We're on the right side of God and goodness. I can't lose. Divine intervention, remember?" I take her face tenderly into my hands. My smile was real this time.

"So, cheer up my Mermaid. Look! Here comes the pickup."

We both swing our binoculars up toward the tongue-like trail that leads out from the mouth of the jungle. It looks like a big Ford F 350. The truck is black and looked shiny and new. Extended cab and bed, she is a good-looking vehicle. Four-wheel drive no doubt. A black man with what looked like an afro is driving and there are two other black men sitting in the bed of the truck, dressed in military garb. Their rifles are between their legs, and are pointed to the sky. The truck is almost upon us when Gahee speaks.

"Let me do the talking at first" he says. "It will be in Swahili. Jomo is a cautious man. He has named your clash with the lion 'The Holy Battle of the Millennium.' Jomo is

236

also a sad and bitter man. The lion killed his only son just five weeks ago.

The man-eater will not be hard to find. He knows you are coming. He is in search of you as much as you are in search of him. Raven, are you prepared? Tonight may be the night. Just let me talk to Jomo alone for a few moments and then we will all confer."

I salute Gahee, and click the heels of my hiking boots.

I'm acting like a snotty little kid again aren't I?

But hell, my adrenaline is suddenly rushing, and I am even feeling very cocky. Because *guess what, my friends?*

I can hear something stir inside of my grateful cranium. The lion, *my* lion is awakening. He is yawning, and I can see his red tongue and sharp white teeth. I can hear him too. What a twist of fate. The sound that I hated more than hatred itself, I now love. The roar of the lion had gone from slave master to savior.

God damn, this is what I've been waiting for. I hope the battle *is* tonight. You gotta strike while the iron is hot.

That's what my dad always used to say.

Finally I rise out of my euphoric trance.

"Got it," I say to Gahee. "You talk to Jomo privately for a while. Yes *sir!"*

If Gahee gets the sarcasm, he doesn't show it. I put my arm around Lydia and wait for Jomo to stop and get out of his truck.

After circling us a few times, he eventually pulls up and parks the truck about twenty feet away.

That is weird, I think.

The two soldier-types hop out of the back and begin assembling a green canvas tent. Their home for now, I suppose. Jomo, who looks like he is sitting in the cab praying, finally opens his door, in what seems like slow motion, and steps out of his Ford F 350. He walks a few

237

feet away in the knee-high savannah grass, talking with Gahee.

While they are speaking Swahili, I am French-kissing Lydia. As I said, I am on cloud nine because my lion is home. I hate him. I love him, *my beautiful servant, my dangerous master, and* tonight my life, as well as the direction of mankind will depend on him. Can't let God down, *that wouldn't be nice, now would it?*

Jomo is a short stocky man with a lot of black bushy hair. He walks with confidence and determination, albeit slowly.

Reading his body language, I like what I see, and what I feel, about the grieving father. I'm seldom wrong. You all know that. I have a gut feeling that it is a good thing Jomo is one of the only four still-breathing human beings who are part of this holy crusade, part of the *team* I am fighting for where many souls will spend eternity, Heaven or Hell. A heavy burden for a light hearted guy like me.

Damn, I'm scaring myself!

After about five minutes Gahee and Jomo walk over to Lydia and me. They look very serious. So much so that it is a little unsettling, and Lydia squeezes my arm a bit tighter.

I extend my hand to Jomo, but instead of shaking it, he takes a step forward and gives me a teary-eyed genuine hug. The man is sobbing. He steps back and looks up at me.

Jomo stands about 5' 6" or so and I can feel his stocky strength. He finally lets me out of his bear hug.

"Thank you Raven April," he says, with a grieving father's sincerity. "You are a true warrior, and I am confident that you will avenge my son's death, allowing him peace in heaven, he…"

Oh fuck! My lion is getting restless. His army of little death gremlins are starting to hammer at the inside of my head again. If he awakens and goes into a full roar, I'll *have* to kill Jomo, Gahee, Lydia or one of the soldiers. I've got to keep him and his army of diminutive demons at bay. Just until tonight. Tonight *is* the night. I can feel it.

Jomo is still rambling on.

"Raven April, the great conqueror sent by God. You have come to slay Lucifer's lion. I can feel your power. You will be victorious."

Jomo's beginning to sound like a witch doctor or a high Swahili priest.

Shut up for a minute, Jomo!

I am trying to stay cool, calm and collected, but minute by minute the cacophony in my brain is growing louder. My lion is now purring loudly. Soon he will roar! I am panicking...

"*Jomo*, I can't tell you why right now, there's no time; but *please* shackle me to the truck, and get me to a place where I can be securely locked in until nightfall."

Lydia freaks out, and screams.

"Raven, what's wrong? Why do you have to be locked up?" She hugs me, crying.

Damn, everybody seems to be crying around here, don't they?

"Jomo! Gahee!" I yell again. "Do as I say! Somehow you've got to secure me to the truck! Then I'll explain, but if you don't do it soon, somebody here will die by my hand."

Jomo understands this is urgent, and commands the two soldiers *in Swahili* to handcuff me to the bed of the pickup truck. I am in the truck before they are, and instruct them to cuff both my wrists and ankles, which they do with their military-issue hand-cuffs. I am on my back in a spread-eagle formation. The roar is growing louder and louder, and the scene is chaos.

Gahee, Jomo and Lydia are all leaning over the side panels of the truck bed staring at me, trying to keep me calm. Lydia is crying, of course.

I feel like Lon Chaney in "The Wolfman," or "Sheriff B.V.West" in his death-cell. Damn I hope a pack of Dingos aren't prowling around looking for an easy meal.

Gahee knows exactly what is going on. He has seen the effects of the lion's roar many times in his father, Fahari. He takes over the situation telling Jomo to get us to his hut, and to get there as quickly as possible.

Lydia is growing hysterical.

Gahee finally convinces her to get in the back seat of the extended cab.

Jomo is driving, Gahee is riding shot-gun, and I lay strapped like Frankenstein to the bed of the truck. I am going mad. I can see the sun dropping down, and I know I will demand to be set free from the handcuffs the moment the sun sets. I decide that there is no reason to try and move me inside Jomo's hut. That can be dangerous. I will track the lion, and he will track me; and by midnight the battle will be over.

I have a plan brewing as to how I am going to get the dagger's blade into the lion's heart, a strategy. You'll soon see what a clever attack plan it is I have devised. I'll give you a hint, though – I'm *not* going for his balls first, as Fahari has told me to do.

Hell, look what that brilliant idea got him.

The lion is starting to quiet down. Frustrated, no doubt that his killing machine, *me*, is restrained and momentarily unable to carry out another death wish.

Jomo has been driving for about forty-five minutes when the truck finally slows down, makes a little half-turn and stops.

Mind you, all I have been able to see are the tree tops and the sky. I have no idea where we are.

Lydia jumps out of the back seat, and runs the couple of steps to the truck bed. It feels like she is gawking at me, but I know she isn't. She feels helpless. She isn't crying, but she is bone trembling scared. Looking down at me from the side panel of the truck again, she begins to talk, quietly.

"Jomo and Gahee," she says, "explained everything to me. They told me all you have suffered because of the lion and his commanding roar and rule over you. They told me about Fahari and Victor, and the importance of the dagger.

"My Raven, my poor, poor Raven. This will all be over soon. You could have told me all of this. Why didn't you?"

The lion is quiet now.

"Because I didn't want to lose you, Lydia," I say. "Pure and simple – because I didn't want to lose you, my little Mermaid."

Jomo and Gahee make their way to the freak show (me) in the back of the truck.

"Raven, Gahee asked if we should move you inside and secure you there as planned."

"No! Leave me here until dusk. Then unlock one of the cuffs on my hands; give me the other three keys and barricade yourselves inside Jomo's hut. Do not let me in for any reason, and shoot me if you have to. I might go mad and attack any of you."

Gahee puts his head down, and then looks up and to the west.

"Soon, very soon it will be dark. Are you thirsty?"

241

"Hell yes, I'm thirsty! Pour some of that whiskey down my throat."

Gahee pulls out yet another flask. This one was bigger.

How many damn flasks does he have?

He reaches over and pulls my head up a little. I open wide, like at the dentist, and he pours about two shots of the fire water into my mouth. I swallow it all.

"Gahee, that tastes like another one. Two more shots down the hatch please."

No sooner said than done. He's almost as good a bartender as Victor. I laugh to myself. Nobody else is in the mood for humor.

Jomo leans over with his elbows on the truck body's side panel.

Lydia climbs inside to be near me, and give me a kiss. They are safe now that the lion is quiet.

He better damned well wake up again soon, though!

It is almost dark. I am ready for the fight, and anxiously awaiting nightfall.

I address them all.

"Okay, listen up.

"Jomo, there's been a slight change in plans. Take off all the cuffs now. It's safe, my lion is asleep. Plus I'll need directions as to where my competition has been hunting and killing lately."

Jomo does as I say, and I am finally set free from the bed of the pick-up. The ride had been bumpy, but I felt no pain. I am now ready to engage my enemy in battle.

I hop out of the truck. Lydia and I hold each other in silence for a couple of minutes. I can feel the chill of fear through her skin. I must confess that I am much too excited to be timid or afraid. Kind of like a Friday night high school football game.

Put me in coach, I'm ready to play!

Gahee and Jomo ask to hold the dagger. I hand it to them. They draw a circle in the sand, place the dagger inside the circle, and say a prayer that I assume is in Swahili.

Over eighty percent of Kenyans are Christians, but Swahili seems to play *some* kind of part in their religion.

I never ask about it, because, frankly I don't care.

When the prayer is over, I put my arm around Jomo.

He appreciates it, and feels comforted.

It makes me feel good. I think he is impressed with my size, physical condition *(can't beat ocean swimming to stay in tip-top shape),* and the confidence I am exuding. I am defiant and confident.

Man I am ready to roll!

I have my plan for Mr. Man Eater. You'll soon see, if *my* lion comes the fuck back to life in time that is. He damn well better get his ass back here inside my butchered brain. I *have* to believe he will as soon as I see the demon beast. I'd *much* rather have him come to life before that, though. Time will tell. It's all up to my good buddy God and me from here on out.

I'll have the advantage once my lion roars. For I have the powers of a lion *and* the mind of a man.

A madman, you say?

Yes, but the lion made me this way by way of God's will. I've accepted that role. Now here I am on the night of reckoning. I turn to Jomo.

"Okay, Jomo," I ask, "tell me, am I more likely to find him in the jungle or in the grass? I need to know where his very last kill was.

"We all know that the child killer is hunting me tonight, as I am hunting him. Where will he likely be,

Jomo? I want to get this over with as soon as possible. So point me in the right direction, my friend."

I still have my arm around him. I look into his eyes.

"Jomo, it will be dark in less than fifteen minutes. I'm gonna leave soon. Just show me where to go buddy. I'll avenge your son tonight. I promise."

Jomo is still *fuckin'* teary-eyed. *I'm gettin' sick of this crying bullshit!* He points to a small foot-trail into the jungle, which is hardly noticeable.

"Follow the trail until you come to a clearing of savannah grass with scattered small scrub growth," Jomo commands, in a military-type voice. "Move west along the edge of the jungle for less than a mile.

"There, Raven, was your enemy's last kill – not a child, but a man in his thirties, a sharpshooter. He was hunting the lion, as you are doing tonight. But the only weapon that can kill the beast is the dagger at your side, made by Fahari.

"Remember, your dagger is his masterpiece, the majestic culmination of his life's work. The blade is 14-inches-long, two inches longer than you originally requested. I'm sure you noticed that. The razor-sharp tip is as strong as the thickest part of the dagger's shaft. Both edges are sharper than a surgeon's scalpel and impossible to dull. Fahari took the secret of the dagger to his grave. There is no other like it in the history of mankind. You will make Fahari proud tonight."

I take my arm from Jomo's shoulder and in the middle of an adrenalin rush, rip off my shirt. I will need full freedom of movement. Shirtless is the only way to ensure that. I have my jungle shorts on, (no underwear) and my hiking boots – which I decide to remove at the last moment knowing barefoot will be better on this night of nights. Last but not least, I have the masterpiece dagger at my right side in its sheath.

I shake Gahee and Jomo's hand then walk to Lydia. We look into one another's eyes. No tears this time. No words, either.

Always listen to what's not said.

I kiss her, turn around and start down the foot-trail through the jungle, hoping my lion will roar before I get to the clearing. There is a three-quarter moon which helps me see enough to stay on the nearly-camouflaged path.

I am walking fast and my blood is running like hot steam through my veins. I decide that I will be the attacker, the aggressor, when the man-eater and I meet face-to-face. Just as I am thinking how nice a roxie 30 would be about now, *guess what happens my friends?* My fuckin' lion comes through for me – a*nd all of mankind I guess!*

Wow! I was starting to worry.

Roar my lion, Roar, Roar, ROAR!

He is awakening and the members of his little tribe of torturers are beating their furious-but-welcome fists inside my skull again.

Love those little guys – tonight I do, anyway.

My lion is starting to roar like hell, and the first thing I notice is that I can see perfectly, almost as clear as daylight. I can feel my strength triple, and then quadruple. I am holding the dagger in my hand when I reach the clearing. I look up at the moon. It's all very simple.

If I win, God wins.

If the lion wins, Satan wins.

The Battle

I move west along the edge of the jungle as instructed. Even though Jomo had said that Satan's man-eater had made his last kill nearly a mile from here, I am wary.

Dagger in hand, I am moving fast and low, like the half human, half animal that I have become... the *creature* I have evolved into tonight. My lion is going wild inside his cage of skull bone, as if he himself wants to erupt like a volcano through my frontal lobe, and fight the deadly devil cat himself.

Suddenly silence.

My lion goes deathly quiet.

Oh fuckin' no!

Not now, don't fail me now! I freeze, petrified waiting for his minions to rip at my gray matter, and for his explosive roar to return.

I realize that he might have silenced himself so that I could hear my enemy. I still have the incredible night-vision of the great cats of Africa, which is a good sign that my lion is doing what is best right now. I also continue to feel the massive strength I always possess when my lion is fully awake and in battle mode. That relaxes my fears a tad as I noiselessly listen and look around, studying my surroundings.

I see nothing and hear every sound imaginable coming out of the jungle behind me. But no roars shake the night either inside my head or out. Nearly ten minutes later –but what seems like an eternity – north across the field of savannah grass, about a quarter-mile-away, I see two huge eyes emerge from another chunk of dense jungle.

He roars, and my soul shakes. He has seen me too, and starts walking across the field. By the heights of his eyes he appears to be incredibly tall. Easily six-feet high at the shoulders, maybe more! He could no doubt look me in the eyes straight on.

And that's on all fours!

Shit!

From what little bit of research I was able to do on African lions *before this fun little trip*, I can see that this man-killer was on the big side, to be sure. The full-grown males usually weigh about 550 pounds, and are between six-and-eight-feet in body length. This guy is more than any of those stats. He is a giant among mere lions.

I don't move a muscle. I don't even blink my eyes. I just watch him as he continues on in a low growl, looking from side to side with his massive head and then refocusing on me.

My lion is now growling, and roaring louder than he has ever done in the past.

Alright!

He knows that this is the Battle of the Millennium. He is God's invisible lion, and I, the tool of his trade. I am ready, and so is he.

As I mentioned before, it's as if we become *one* in mind and spirit, when it is time to kill.

Get ready, because I'm about to put the plan I teased you about into action.

He is getting closer.

I step slowly out into the field, crouched and balanced, with my dagger held tight and ready just behind my right hip bone. Hopefully, the move I am about to make will blow the gargantuan feline's mind for just a split second; hopefully a bit longer. Just a few more steps toward each other and we will be face-to-face... almost, almost. Here goes!

NOW!

I make a quick body fake, as if I'm gonna attack him head-on, but instead I drop to the ground and roll at his feet as fast as I can.

He stamps his two front paws down on me, caught off guard and trying to stop me from rolling.

I knew he wouldn't expect this approach!

I can reach just far enough to plunge the dagger through his right femoral artery from the inside of his thigh.

Got it! All the way through! Damn, that dagger's sharp!

I might trade it in for my Danger Dagger. Blood is gushing from the artery like a fire hose. My body is covered in my rival's blood in less than ten seconds.

He bends almost in half. Amazingly flexible, trying to bite my neck now, but I've got my head squashed down tight on my left shoulder to protect my jugular vein.

As I try to twist enough to reach his *left* femoral artery I hear and feel the crunch of his giant jaws crushing my left shoulder. *Hey, look at the bright side, he could have chosen my head to crush.* He tries to rip my shoulder off, which could have been a disaster for me and probably death. He is also lacerating my body, especially my back with his sharp, determined front claws.

(A lion's claws move independently of each other, making their wicked swipes all the more deadly).

I know if I can just get to his left major leg artery he would start to weaken quickly from blood loss. I make a lunge for it.

Whamo!

All the way through and bleeding like hell. He is still mauling me and trying to rip my shoulder off. It's as if he is double jointed with his head between his own legs biting my shoulder. I have to get to my feet, so I stab him a few times in the belly *(couldn't reach the heart)* from my prone position, to piss him off enough to let go of my shoulder and hopefully give me a chance to get to my feet. He is weakening from the pint after pint of blood gushing from his upper thighs. The femoral arteries are huge and run from his hip to his knee.

His balls, that's it! He still won't let me up, and I am bleeding to death almost as fast as he is.

He hasn't gotten to any of my major arteries yet, but I am laid wide open in so many different places, including my chest and stomach that it is just a matter of time before I too bleed out. Somehow I arch my back and lunge toward his crotch area. With all the strength in my being, I make a desperate swipe with the dagger and suddenly he is bleeding even more, this time from where his balls had been.

Success!

That gets his attention and in his weakening condition loosens up just long enough for me to roll a few feet and pop up to my feet. He roars and jumps at me. But he is tiring from massive blood loss.

I take a step back. His face is so close to mine I can smell his foul breath, and fall in love with his eyes.

I *must* be bi-polar.

Gripping the dagger with both hands, from below I thrust Fahari's masterpiece up through the beast's mandible, through his tongue, up through his snout with the two extra inches Fahari added to the blade protruding and twinkling with blood in the three-quarter moon.

He is mauling my back again now but I can feel the life draining out of him. Yet at the same time, I can feel *myself* dying.

The battle of all battles is near its crucial, brutal end. I still gotta pull the dagger out of his face and put it through the giant's heart. The dagger must enter the heart or Lucifer's lion will never really die.

Fuck!

All of sudden the beast swipes me across the face with his right paw. I think he ripped out my left eye, *how befitting, fuck, must be Karma.* I am blinded by the blood – both his and mine. I am also very pissed! In one quick and flawless move, I yank the dagger from his snout and jam it straight through his thick-ass sternum directly into his heart. *Damn, I'm good!*

The demon lion lay dead, and I lay dying beside him. I hear a loud clap of thunder and see the sky light up like day. It thunders again.

I float in and out of consciousness – at one point looking down on the lion, and myself, from the tree tops. What was happening?

I have just enough strength to roll over and bite, chew and eventually suck the monster's left eye out of his head, and eat it with spiritual pleasure and a warriors' sense of pride. I muster every ounce of strength I have left to do this, because devouring the man-eaters left eye meant total victory to me, Raven April, writer, singer, serial killer, madman and don't forget, sweetheart.

Finally! Total victory over the Devil, himself.

God, did I please you, and does this mean I will make it to heaven? At last, will I exist in peace after all these years of suffering? Will I even live to enjoy it if I do?

It is still thundering. I am awake, but I can't move. I am just trying to focus on the moon through the blood on my face, and remain conscious. I can't see out of my left eye – yep, it's gone, and I'm too weak to feel for it, and too scared.

The dagger is still in the man-eater's heart.

Shit, I want that for my mantel.

Jomo's Hut

Jomo, Gahee and Lydia are sitting around the small table on Jomo's wooden platform which he calls a porch.

Wish the hell I was there.

Jomo and Gahee are drinking whiskey, and Lydia is drinking it too, but watered down with some kind of tea that Jomo makes.

At the first clap of thunder, the same one I had heard, I assume, Jomo jumps out from the table. Lydia stares up at him. Gahee puts his head down and prays in Swahili.

"The battle is over," Jomo declares. "Get in the truck, Gahee," interrupting his prayer. "Did you put the rifles and flashlights in the bed?"

Gahee looks up.

"Yes, Jomo, and the battle *is* over. The thunder is our sign. We must go now. Come Lydia, we must hurry to Raven."

"Well, if the battle is over, who won it?" Lydia, shaking, says to Gahee. "Is Raven still alive? Is he dead? Who won, damn it."

She is near hysteria.

"Lydia, we will not know who won until we see with our own eyes. Just pray for Ravens' triumph," Gahee says. "Jomo will travel along the edge of the jungle. Prepare yourself, Lydia. Now let's get in the truck. I have a feeling that the battlefield is close."

Jomo starts the truck's engine.

20

Miami Police Headquarters

Chief Mannie Bastardo's phone rings at about 9 a.m. It's Frank Harding from ViCAP, the division of the FBI hunting the Eye-Eater Killer.

"Morning, Frank. What's up buddy?"

Frank takes another sip of coffee.

"That's what I was gonna ask you," he replies. "Ya got anything new on the eye-eater?"

Mannie sighs, frustrated.

"Hell no. It's like he disappeared from the face of the Earth. I've still got a couple of guys from the Zip-Team on it. If they come up with anything, they're to report to your guy, Rick Sansom."

Frank leans back in his chair a little and scratches his head.

"Ya know Mannie, he could be dead or he could have left the area, or even the country for that matter."

"Yeah, I know. I've thought about that too." Frank says with a sigh, thinking, *I sure could use a beer.* He frowns. "Okay, Mannie. "Well, keep in touch. I have a feeling he'll strike again."

"Yeah, me too," Mannie says. "I'll keep you informed. Good talking to you Frank." He adds, "I could sure use a cold beer."

"Yeah, me too," Mannie, kind of amused by the coincidence, replies.

252

21

The Battle Field

Jomo, Gahee and Lydia pull up almost on top of the dead monster and me. The headlights and flashlights revealing a gruesome scene, I'm sure.

I am dying. I can feel it. Jomo jumps from the pickup and leans down next to me.

"We've got to get him to Nairobi!" Jomo shouts to Gahee and Lydia. "He is bleeding to death and his left eye is gone, ripped from his head."

Gahee has other plans, though.

"First, I must use the dagger to cut the lion's heart out. I will place it in my father's coffin. Only then can we bury Fahari.

"It is written."

Jomo is very uptight and anxious. He doesn't want me to die. He is in a hurry to get to get me on Gahee's bush plane, and fly me to the hospital in Nairobi.

"Okay, but hurry. The dagger is still in the beast's heart. Don't forget to bring the dagger with you. That must also go in Fahari's coffin."

Damn! I wanted that dagger.

"Hurry, Gahee!"

Lydia, God bless her is loyally standing at my feet with her face in her hands crying, staring down at my red, lacerated body and the carnage around her. The size of the lion, covered in blood as well, amazes her.

I remember thinking that I must be a pitiful sight laying there. Lydia and I are *both* pitiful sights on this preordained night, just in different ways – me torn apart on the outside; her, falling apart on the inside.

I try to say good-bye.

Then, blackness!

Epilogue

The Revelation

As darkness closes in around me, I smell the lion, the stench of battle and of death. The deep, painful sadness of Queenie's slaughter creeps into every capillary of my being. Will I see her soon? Someone is crying at my side.

"Lydia, are you there? Is that you?"

Did my words come out? I can feel the soft cloak of Heaven enfolding me now.

And so it is time for me to confess something to you, my readers, my friends.

In case you are curious and wondering about whatever became of the book I was writing in the den... you just read it.

Raven April

Other Books of Interest

Also written by Nelson Trout:

Blood On The Ceiling, Second Ed.   Amazon.com / Kindle

Selected Books from Fireside Publications
Available from:
http://kadinbooks.com
www.amazon.com / **Kindle**
BN.com / **Nook**

Silver Strands	Eileen Bennett
Amanda's Voice (Kindle or Nook only)	Eileen Bennett
The Furax Connection	Stephen L. Kanne
The Find	James J. Valko
Above Honor: Rachel's Story	Donald Himelstein
Beyond Forever	Taylor Shaye
The Cleansing	B.F. Eller
The Long Night Moon	Elizabeth Towles
The Cost of Justice	Mike Gedgoudas
18 Days in September	Allen N.Hunt, Ph.D
Independence Day Plague	Carla Lee Suson
The Serpent Sea	Linda Lehmann Masek
Texas Justice	Judith Groudine Finkel

www.ingramcontent.com/pod-product-compliance
Lightning Source LLC
Chambersburg PA
CBHW070814180626
46818CB00001B/254